The Merciless Dead

John Burke

© John Burke, 2008

John Burke has asserted his rights under the Copyright, Design and Patents Act, 1988, to be identified as the author of this work.

First published in 2008 by Robert Hale Limited.

This edition published in 2017 by Endeavour Press Ltd.

We do swear by the oak and ash and thorn that we do hate your whole accursed race and will hold at deadly feud against all your namekindreds maintainers and lickspittles so long as any of us yet has life.

— Blood feud vow

Table of Contents

1	7
2	13
3	22
4	29
5	36
6	44
7	52
8	62
9	72
10	82
11	91
12	100
13	108
14	121
15	129
16	143
17	151
18	164
19	172
20	185

1

Over the years Mr Angus Macdonald had invariably taken the same route home. From the kiltmaker's establishment in Leith where he worked in partnership with his brother he would walk at a steady pace, his head held high and imperious, down a brief stretch of cobbled street and along the newer road behind a high-rise block of flats. He could have taken a short cut through an archway leading to the lane beside a wine warehouse and the back door of a pub, but he would never have allowed himself to stray that close to such accursed premises. Mr Macdonald was a teetotaller, a man of austere tastes, and a pillar of the kirk. On Sundays he would sit in his pew giving thanks for God's mercies, meagre as they sometimes seemed, while meditating more approvingly on the well-merited torments of the damned — among whom, in the Lord's good time, would surely be numbered all his competitors.

Which made the evidence provided by one vague and possibly drunken witness all the more questionable.

Detective Chief Inspector Jack Rutherford sat in the interview room facing the only man who claimed to have seen anything unusual that Friday evening, and said: 'A woman? Are you positive, Mr Thomson?'

'Well, there was a bit of a spring haar drifting across the docks, but aye, there was this woman following him. Or that was the way it looked.'

'She was accosting him?'

'Well, I did think she was calling after him, but I couldnae hear what she was saying. And he was waving his arms, shooing her away. And he started running.'

'Fast?'

'Och, no, he wasnae that sort of man. A kind of stagger — all clumsy, stupid, not looking where he'd be heading.'

The idea of the puritanical Mr Macdonald running away from the advances of a prostitute was mildly amusing, but DCI Rutherford was more puzzled than amused. That part of Leith was quite a way from the usual red light cluster of streets.

'Did this woman keep going after him? Did she actually assault him?'

'I didnae see it all that clear. But when I read in the paper, I thought I'd better ... well ...'

'Very public-spirited of you, Mr Thomson.' Thomson was beginning to look as if he regretted his decision.

'It was the wife told me I'd better come forward. Very keen to be into things, my Jessie is.'

Rutherford suspected that Jessie would have given her husband no rest until he had agreed to come and do his bit, and report back any facts or guesses she could gossip about.

'If you didn't see all that clearly, I suppose you can't give any specific details about the woman?'

Thomson shook his head. 'Tall and wearing a sort of cloak, I think. Tall, anyway. Just about as tall as that poor old bugger.'

'You didn't see how he came to fall — or was pushed?'

'No. There was a sort of ... well, him and his arms whirling, him waving her away, like ... and it was all a lot of shadows.' He groped woozily down into his memory. 'Not him being pushed. Just the way she ...'

'Yes, Mr Thomson?'

'How she was looking at him. Nae just keeking, but ... staring, fixed on the back o' his heid, like she was wanting to bore into him. Into the back o' his neck.'

'You didn't approach them — to help him, or find out what the situation was?'

'That I did not. None o' my business, I was thinking. I went off to have a dram.'

'Your first of the evening?'

'I didnae say that.' Thomson was looking even more uncomfortable. 'I thought little more on it, until Jessie read this piece in the paper, and I told her what I'd seen, and she told me ...' He shrugged despondently.

The corpse had been found on the Saturday morning face down on a wide patch of waste ground which was waiting to be converted into a car park for the luxury flats being built into two derelict warehouses. There were some rusted scaffolding poles jumbled up with buckled, sharp-edged metal shelving ripped out of the buildings. Angus Macdonald's body had been impaled and torn by some of the sharper ends.

'He was a heavy man,' reported the police surgeon, 'and he must have come down very heavily on that pile of scrap.'

'Any indication of him being pushed?'

'Not that I found. Not impossible; but on the whole I'd say he simply tripped and fell. Though why he blundered off the pavement and across that waste patch, I'd not be wanting to guess.'

The next of kin was Mr Angus Macdonald's brother Ian. He was smaller than Angus, and, within the confines of their kiltmakers' premises, fussy and jerky in his movements rather than solemn. The premises were musty and unpretentious. For Rutherford's taste they were at least preferable to the Old Town tourist shops with their swaggering declarations of authenticity, their windows and shelves padded out with tartan, tins of shortbread, cairngorm brooches, and Argyle pattern pullovers.

He said: 'I see you're open for business as usual, Mr Macdonald, in spite of the family tragedy.'

'Angus would have wanted it that way.'

'I'm sure you're right. But you can spare me a few minutes?'

'There'll no' be many customers on a Monday. And most of *them* will be here for the gossip and little else.'

'Well, now. Can you think of any reason why someone should wish to attack your brother?'

'From what your officer told me Saturday, I understood he'd slipped and fallen.'

'Yes, that's how it appears. But could an assailant have stolen his keys and come back here to rob the place?'

'No sign of that. The place was as usual when I unlocked the door that morning and today.'

'Nobody would have had a grudge against him? No spurned woman friend, or anything of that kind? A witness thinks he saw a woman pursuing him and maybe causing him to break into a run.'

Ian Macdonald's red, freckled face puckered into a grimace of disbelief. 'Oor Angus, chased by a woman? Nay, never in a million years. Nor him chasing *her*, neither.'

His tone was not so much amused as derisive. Rutherford surmised that their partnership might have been one of ill-matched brothers who nevertheless believed that keeping the business in the family and spending as little as possible on assistants came before any mutual hostility.

'Mr Macdonald — Mr Angus, that is — wasn't married?'

'For a wee while. A woman from the kirk, o' coorse. She didnae fit in, least of all with Angus's ideas of running the firm. And running her life. She left.'

The Merciless Dead

'Recently?' Rutherford sniffed a possible motive for a vengeful woman wanting Angus out of the way.

'Seven or eight years ago now.'

'And your brother never remarried?'

'He was too stingy.' Ian Macdonald said it half admiringly rather than with contempt. 'And outside o' business, he was a wee bit glaikit. Put people off.' He waved vaguely towards the large pattern book open on the counter. 'Never did well with lady customers.'

'What do you mean by glaikit?'

'All muddled up in his mind. I think he was haunted by a silly thing from some years back. During one of His Lordship's parties.'

'Parties?' Rutherford's acquaintance with local puritanical sects had never taken in the idea of anything as frivolous as a party.

'When we were just wee lads. Before we came to Edinburgh. Oor grandfather was factor on Lord Inverstrachan's estate in Wester Ross. His Lordship used to give two parties a year in the old school-house — one for the tenants, and a week later one for the bairns.' Ian Macdonald allowed himself a thin smile. 'That was his good deed for the year, and he expected us to be thankful. We were all expected to come along and enjoy ourselves, and be grateful, and go awa' home when we were told.'

'And your brother did enjoy himself?' Rutherford prompted.

'Angus was ne'er one to enjoy himself. And just that once there was that wee incident. Haunted him ever since.'

Ian let out a long breath and began shaking his head pitifully. Rutherford waited. He knew when not to prod a witness too impatiently.

Slowly it came. 'Couldnae have anything to do with this. But that falling on those bits o' metal, and a few o' them going through him ... now, that's weird itself.' He paused, then went on: 'Such a silly thing. Knickers.'

'Knickers?'

'Wee Judy Muir's knickers. Och, he wasnae the only one.' He seemed to be staring back into his own past. 'She was a flighty lass, that Judy. Grew up too quickly. Not old enough for the grownups' party, but too old for the bairns'.'

He would have made a good witness in any court. The dry way he described the party summoned up a picture of a sober affair in the cramped schoolroom, with a bit of hymn-singing and a speech of thanks to the laird for his generosity, and only a few pink-iced buns to add colour. Most of the chairs which had been provided were wooden ones with hard seats. But there were a couple of blue cane chairs, and of course Judy Muir had commandeered one of those for herself.

'Even her name' — Ian pursed his lips as puritanically as his staider brother might have done — 'wasnae what ye'd call a respectable one, now. In our sort of community, that was no name to be calling your daughter. Not even the Old Testament name of Judith — and even if it had been, *she* was no' what ye'd call an admirable character.'

He told how he remembered Judy Muir's eyes. Sharp and observant, they had been. As she lolled back in the chair she knew young Angus was looking, and trying not to look, at her legs and up her knickers. Lots of the lads did.

'But with oor Angus, it was naughty. Couldn't keep his eyes away. He really did suffer, poor laddie. When they passed in the wynd by the old chapel, or in Sunday School itself, I'd catch him trying to make himself look at the preacher or the harmonium; only he'd be back at it again in no time, keeking back at her.'

And on that distant day at the party, Judy's chair gave way.

Ian Macdonald vividly recalled, as if it had been only yesterday, the sharp crackling sound. The sides of the chair seemed to fold in on the girl's thighs. She squealed. Her bottom sank through the splintering strands, and a long rent was torn down one side of her knickers. A few drops of blood spattered to the floor.

'I knew our Angus thought for months she must have been nigh on killed. Stabbed through and through by the sharp bits. I'm sure that's what it was. And it was partly his fault, for staring at her and thinking … well, the sort of things he did think. Long after we'd grown up and moved here and set up in business, he got a book from the library about martyrs and tortures, and he'd stare for ages at a picture of one of those coffin-like things wi' spikes that went from all sides into any poor sinner they'd packed into it. I'm of the opinion that looking at those spikes he saw that chair all over again. And for him to die that way …' Ian Macdonald let out another sigh. 'Haunted,' he repeated.

'Have you ever had any hint that, because of that sort of obsession, he might have resorted to … well, ladies of the town?'

'He could never have lowered himself that way. Never.'

You never knew, thought Rutherford. Pillars of kirk or chapel often had flaws in the masonry. It was an interesting speculation about a disturbed psychological case; but not, when you got down to it, much help in the present inquiry. Hardly a melodramatic suicide. Just a coincidence. Accidental death, no more.

But he remembered that shiver through the man Thomson's hands — more than the usual shiver of the typical local dipso — as he spoke of the woman's concentrated gaze: *staring, fixed on the back* o' *his heid, like she was wanting to bore into him.*

2

The two faces swam together, the contorted one in the painting blurred by real-life features edging closer through the glass. Then the viewer's reflection moved to one side, allowing the full horror of the picture to blaze out again. Red flame licking around the silently screaming face mingled with blood bursting from the scorched flesh. The artist had all too skilfully conveyed that the blood was beginning to sputter as it dripped into the fire, like a joint roasting on a spit. There was smoke, but not enough to hide the excruciating detail of the agony: eyes bubbling, skin peeling away from the jaw. The whole ravaged face was twisted into what looked like a last attempt to curse the onlookers.

Mrs Ross said: 'Incredibly lifelike, isn't it? You'd think the painter had actually been there when they were burning that wretched woman, whoever she was.'

'Supposed to be one of the Nor' Loch witches,' said Beth.

'A real authentic witch?' The tall, lean woman stooping to get another angle on the painting gave Beth a creepy feeling that she would really have liked to be there, and was trying somehow to project herself into the scene.

'They found a lot of charred remains when they were draining the North Loch to make way for the railway and Waverley station. It used to be a place for burning witches. Some had been strangled before being burnt. That was regarded as merciful.' Beth glanced at her watch. 'Mrs Ross, I think it's time we —'

'Do call me Morwenna.'

In her PR world, Beth Crichton was used to trotting out Christian names within a few minutes of an introduction. It was the accepted way of getting down to business on matey terms nowadays. But somehow with this woman it wouldn't come naturally.

Beth had taken even more care than usual over her makeup and what to wear. She was usually confident in calculating her own appearance for different occasions, different people. It was part of the job, and she was good at her job. Before setting out she had stared earnestly at herself in the dressing-table mirror, trying to assess herself as a stranger. Her sleek brown hair with its hints of bronze might almost have been designed as an accessory to her taupe linen suit and the high white neck of her blouse. Her hazel eyes, with pale green flecks, were unalterable, and on the whole she had learned to be content with them. She never reddened her mouth nowadays: with any heavy shade of lipstick it looked just too bright and cute a little bow. In her job she had found that men were somehow more drawn to, and at the same time more respectful towards, her natural colouring and the faint crinkle in the left-hand corner of her mouth which made her look knowledgeable and sceptical.

Yet no matter how carefully she worked at it, she couldn't ever quite relate that smooth, confident image to her real inner self. She was always afraid that somebody, sooner or later, was going to find her out.

And this time there were very special factors. As yet they didn't know just how influential this Morwenna Ross was going to be; but if the big boss had chosen to send her over at a time like this, with so much to be decided, then she must be a pretty powerful piece in the game. Unless, as someone in the office had speculated, it was merely to occupy her mind after her recent bereavement.

She was in her early thirties. Her hair was such a dusky black that when they walked out into the open air it seemed to soak up and stifle the sunlight. In the exhibition gallery, with her back to the window, she had presented a dark silhouette, but out here it was clear that her clothes were not those of a widow still in mourning. She had chosen a grey jacket and a deep purple blouse which she must have known would emphasize the flecks of mauve in her deep-set eyes. Daylight struck a bright spark from the amethyst brooch at her throat.

'That painting was of course quite the wrong period for us,' she said regretfully as they walked away, 'and of course it was only an imaginative work. What we want is original, authentic material.'

'That's going to be difficult. There wouldn't have been any painters or photographers around at the time of the Clearances.'

Morwenna Ross smiled a wintry smile. 'I'm aware of that. And even if they're as vivid as that re-creation of the witch burning, we don't want horror-film dramatizations of old women being pushed into their own fires.'

'If there really were any actual incidents quite like that.'

'Oh, there were. There were indeed!' It came out fiercely, emphasized by her crisp Canadian accent. 'There's plenty of evidence for that. Surely you've had somebody checking out all the records these last few months?'

'Oh, Luke's been beavering away like mad.'

'Luke?'

'Luke Drummond. Our archivist. He's been piling stuff up in every category he thinks you might need.'

'Great. Lead me to him.'

There was a brisk enough wind along Queen Street for the flag on the Ross Foundation building to flutter a salute over their heads as they climbed the three steps to the entrance.

Simon Ogilvie came fussing towards them from the main staircase. Beth suspected he might have been watching from the boardroom window on the first floor, ready to dash downstairs the moment they appeared. Slimy Simon had probably spent even more time than Beth staring into a mirror this morning, brushing his hair, splashing his most expensive cologne across his sandy freckles, rehearsing a few urbane lines then trying a different inflection, twisting his features into variations of the gravity becoming his status as European Regional Coordinator — yet never realizing, as his staff did, quite how shiftily it came across.

'Ah, dear lady. Everything going smoothly, I trust? Being well looked after?' His condescendingly comradely smile at Beth hid a threat of less comradely repercussions if their visitor made even the slightest complaint.

'Things are going just fine. Now, where's this man I just have to see, this … what did you say his name was, Beth?'

'Luke Drummond.'

'But of course,' said Ogilvie. 'Luke. Made great progress since he became one of our team. But first, I'm sure you need a cup of coffee while we discuss the timetable I've worked out for you. Naturally Luke's a part of it. Just one part.'

For a moment Beth thought the woman was going to override him; but there was a brief, sardonic twist to her pencil-thin lips, and she gave a nod which permitted him to lead her fussily away towards his office.

Beth made her own way to the library.

Luke was seated on the far side of his vast table behind his usual array of books and documents. He looked her up and down as she came in, and she knew from his appreciative grin that he was mentally undressing her. Not speculatively, as lots of men did, but reminiscently. The grin was just suggestive enough to be flattering, showing that he remembered what lay beneath the trimmings. Not so long ago he would have followed it up physically, later that same day or when current business had been wrapped up. That was all over now, but they still felt at ease in each other's company, enjoying the same commitment to whatever project was currently being worked on, and preserving their own standards against the niggling of Simon Ogilvie.

'All tarted up,' he said. 'And very nice too. Well, how did it go? What d'you make of her?'

'Pretty powerful stuff. But keeping it all under tight control for the moment. You know the sort of thing — very formal but friendly, but with a lot kept in reserve. No telling how intense things may get.'

'Intense?'

'There's a lot bottled up there. But right now I'd say she's committed to this venture one hundred per cent, and she's not going to be distracted. Maybe, having lost her husband, she's got to have something to take her mind off things. Though somehow she ... that is ...'

'Don't waffle, Beth. Not like you.'

'Well, she doesn't seem like a grieving widow. Though it's six months or more, isn't it? And maybe they weren't all that close. Or ... oh, whatever.'

Luke drew a sheet of paper from a small stack close to his left hand. He had always been proud of his ability to pluck a relevant document out of a pile or off a shelf. As archivist he was no dull pedant, but always quietly precise, loving to track things down and tidy up loose ends.

As a lover, he had been the same. He had once studied academically the positions in the Kama Sutra and then tried them out on Beth, starting dispassionately, like trying the temperature of the water with his toe, then opening up to the warm gentle affection intertwining with the text and climaxing with no further need of instruction.

Now he impassively read out the facts.

*

Morwenna Ross, née Chisholm, had been born in Toronto. Her father was a merchant banker involved in a number of business ventures with Ross Enterprises. At twenty-one she met and married Calum Ross, older son of James Fergus Ross (known, though never to his face, as Old Jamie). Obviously a dynastic marriage. Old man Ross was a shipping and transcontinental transport millionaire who had built up a web of interwoven production and distribution companies, based on the family's original logging and timber sales business in Nova Scotia. Like Carnegie, in later life he had begun to plough large proportions of his profits into charitable works and the endowment of museums via the Ross Foundation — especially, like Carnegie, with sentimental preferences towards his forebears' homeland although, unlike Carnegie, he himself had not been born in Scotland.

'I get the impression from our copies of internal memos,' said Luke, 'that when the historical documents started piling up in the Ross Library in Winnipeg, old Jamie found himself snowed under. Like so many tycoons, no matter what enlightened opinions he had from time to time, he probably couldn't give his undivided attention to anything other than the basic moneymaking. So he would have been pleased to find that his daughter-in-law could talk the language he wanted to hear, at the same time taking the more routine administration off his hands.'

'And her husband?'

Calum Ross, as they had cause to know as far away as the London and Edinburgh offices, had taken after his father in business ruthlessness. Single-mindedly devoted to their commercial operations, he regarded the ageing Jamie's belated charitable commitments as due to senile sentimentality. A few donations to good causes for tax and prestige reasons, sorted out by their accountant, all right; but not too lavish.

Jamie's younger son had been very much at odds with his brother. Born in Nova Scotia, David had studied in the US at MIT. His father meant this to fit him to contribute in some high profile way to the family's business development. Early on he showed what his brother Calum sneered at as 'arty-crafty bunk'. There were suggestions of a final falling-out when, soon after their mother's death, their father remarried. His new wife, Nadine, came from a background of old family money and status. Luke's collection of gossip column stories and fashion magazine features showed her as an expensively dressed yet flashy blonde with a fixed, petulant smile. Calum might have disapproved of a woman so obviously capable of making further inroads into the Ross family finances, but he wasn't going to risk any open breach with the old man, who still had his hands on the controls.

David Ross had different ideas. Even before his father's gaudily publicized wedding he threw up his planned career and was written out of Ross history. There were rumours of him ending up in some hippy crowd in Los Angeles. 'Probably going in for psychedelic painting after a few drug sessions, that kind of thing,' said Luke.

'Nobody ever bothered to follow up in detail?' asked Beth.

'We were given no instructions to maintain a file on him. Mr Ross isn't the sort to follow up on people he thinks have let him down.' Luke turned over three sheets of paper. 'And then old Jamie's second woman gets involved with another man and there's an acrimonious divorce.'

'But this David doesn't come back.' It wasn't a question. Beth knew that the name of David Ross had not featured in any of the Ross Foundation internal memoirs, annual reports, or news stories.

'Never heard of again. Or mentioned. Seems to have been written off by the rest of the family. And then Calum gets written off too. Leaving the old man without an heir to take over.'

Luke unfolded a photocopy of the front-page story of a Newfoundland newspaper. One of Calum's few indulgences had been his boat, kept moored in a creek in Cape Breton. He and his wife Morwenna had gone for a weekend's sailing and, reported the paper, had been caught in one of the fogs characteristic of those coastal waters. The whole community regarded it as a tragedy that such an accomplished yachtsman as young Mr Ross should somehow lose control and get thrown overboard. Morwenna managed to get the boat back to port but then collapsed, too hysterical to recall exactly what happened. It took a search party two hours to find Calum's corpse. There were theories about his having been hit by the boom and knocked over the side, but there was no mark of any severe bruise on him, and the shuddering Morwenna simply could not confirm or deny the idea.

Since the collapse of his second marriage, old Jamie Ross had come to rely on her more and more as a confidante, possibly to her husband's irritation.

'And,' concluded Luke, 'I think we can reasonably assume that for once Slimy Simon is right. It's to take her mind off the tragedy at Cape Breton that he's now sending her over here to hustle us along on his pet project.'

'And *she* is the potential inheritor of the whole works?'

'Could be. Interesting to know what's in her mind, deep down.'

The door opened. Ogilvie made a dramatic entrance, swerving round to hold the door open for Morwenna Ross.

'Thank you for the coffee.' She swept past him and held out a hand. 'You must be Luke. So now we can really get down to work.'

Ogilvie edged towards a chair at the end of the table, but she turned a dazzling yet fierce smile on him. 'I really mustn't take up any more of your time, Simon. I know you have a lot of commitments. We all keep up with your regular bulletins to head office back home.'

He backed awkwardly away, not happy but not willing to risk disobeying.

'Now,' said Mrs Ross. 'I won't bore you with details which you probably know better than I do. What I would like are details you know about and I don't. Where and how we collect the artefacts to authenticate the setting. Our manager back in Cape Breton has dug out a few souvenirs — a spinning wheel that one family managed to take with them, a loom, and a couple of peat irons. We've put out an appeal for souvenirs all over Nova Scotia and Newfoundland. And a few settlements in the United States, plus Australia and New Zealand. But we need a lot more. Above all' — her voice became surprisingly hushed and almost reverent — 'we do have to find the Ross Tapestry.'

There was a long silence. Morwenna looked from one to the other, waiting for some kind of response. Beth felt sorry for Luke. It was rare to see him fazed, but she sensed that he was struggling between a polite reply and blunt scepticism.

At last it came out. 'If it exists. If it *ever* existed.'

'Oh. It exists.' She was no longer quietly companionable. 'Every which way we look, there's mention of it. It's an essential part of the fabric of our plans. What we *don't* know is *where* it is. All the indications are that it was left behind, here in the Old Country.'

'Oh, but —'

'Before we go any further,' said Beth hurriedly, to stop Luke blundering into a confrontation so soon, 'I can confirm that we have you booked, Mrs Ross, for the local arts programme immediately after the television news tomorrow evening.'

'Yes, Mr Ogilvie did tell me he'd had that set up.'

Beth caught Luke's eye. Slimy Simon had set it up? They were both aware of a twitch of shrewd amusement from the woman sitting opposite.

'They'd like you in the studio tomorrow morning for a couple of hours,' Beth went on, 'to time the inserts of scenes from those location suggestions your office sent over. They've rustled up quite a few from an earlier documentary.'

'Didn't know you could get those folk organized so fast.' Luke's narrow, rather austere face offered Beth one of those comradely grins that were more flattering than any of the sweet-talk she often got from her pushier PR contacts.

She went on: 'It might be a good place, Mrs Ross, to appeal for contributions from the public. Some souvenirs must have been handed down through families who did contrive to stay on in the Old Country.'

Luke prodded forward a small cluster of booklets rather as if he were betting a pile of coins at a roulette table. 'There are some museum catalogues here, Mrs Ross, and —'

'If we're going to work together, I must insist that you *both* call me Morwenna. And if that's not correct form in the Old Country, too bad. Just for once let's enjoy a few anachronisms.'

'Morwenna.' Luke smiled his sunniest, most relaxed smile. Beth laughed inwardly at the suavity with which the name slid off his tongue. 'Catalogues,' he repeated, 'from a couple of public collections, and one from a tourist exhibition three years ago. I think we might get some items on extended loan. But when it comes to purchasing things, there might be difficulties.'

'There are no financial problems.'

'All the same, there'd be some longwinded negotiations, and I understand we don't have that much time.'

'Too right we don't. Mr Ross' — the way she intoned the name reverberated solemnly in Beth's head, just the way it did when Simon Ogilvie uttered it — 'wants to see the croft and contents restored before he ... before he's too old to appreciate it.'

Was the woman hoping, as they had half suspected, to inherit the whole business, and pandering to the old man's every whim so that she could stay in his good books right to the end?

Beth said: 'I think your appearance on telly tomorrow might bring in some valuable responses.'

'I guess so. But there's one hell of a risk there as well. We give an address where we can be contacted, and —'

'And,' Luke finished, 'every greedy chancer in Scotland turns out the attic and lumbers us with ... well, lumber.'

'We're going to need someone to sift through whatever comes in. And someone with specialized knowledge to go hunting on our behalf.'

Beth was aware of Luke trying not to bristle. 'With all the resources I have ... we have on the premises —'

'I always believe in getting the best specialist in whatever field we're working in. Save us a whole lot of time. And a lot of errors.'

To Beth, Luke's expression was so familiar, as if he were mentally standing in front of those rows of bookshelves and filing boxes or checking on his computer screen, identifying the most important reference and reaching out to pluck it from its place.

The shift hadn't escaped Morwenna. 'You know somebody?'

'Well ...'

'Come on, out with it. Something suspicious about the guy?'

'It's a woman,' said Luke.

'And nothing suspicious,' said Beth. She was still closely enough in touch with Luke to know who he had in mind. 'Just the opposite. But I've heard she's very busy at the moment, working on a book. Probably not in the market for outside work right now.'

'We make it worth her while, she can leave her book over till later. Who is this woman?'

'Lady Torrance of Black Knowe, in the Borders.'

Quick to pick up Beth's cue, Luke played his keyboard and summoned up a colour photograph of a tall, dark stone tower rising from a hill with a cluster of more modern houses in the vale below.

'Some kind of aristocrat with a hobby?' said Morwenna dubiously.

'Before she married Sir Nicholas' — Luke was happily summoning up every detail from triggered memory — 'she was a police detective. Specializing in art thefts and forgeries. She was the one who unearthed the truth behind those Sargent and Ramsay fakes in the Brigid Weir scam a few years back. I believe she still acts as part-time regional consultant to Scotland Yard's Arts and Antiques squad.'

'Get her.'

'We can't be sure she'd be interested,' ventured Beth.

'*Make* her interested. And make it clear that money's no object. We want the best, we pay for the best.' Morwenna's gaze was like the sudden glare of a torch stabbing at each of them in turn. 'When Mr Ross is well enough to fly in, everything has to be ready.'

3

The mail rarely reached Black Knowe before the middle of the morning, delivered by a postman who also brought the morning papers. Today there was a heavier package than usual. Mrs Robson stumped upstairs with it under her arm, dropping two letters on the landing and having to stoop and retrieve them.

'Sir Nicholas.' She panted with some exaggeration as she put the package and envelopes heavily on the coffee table. 'Your Ladyship.' Then, to show that she was really fond of them and didn't mind the effort, 'It's a fine morning, so it is.'

Nick pushed his coffee cup to one side and reached for the paper, nodding at the package. 'That one's for you, my love. Some blistering comments from your chums, I'd guess. And I'd also guess it'll be an excuse for you to shut yourself away for the rest of the day.'

Lesley had been eagerly awaiting the arrival of these proofs. Work on her book on art forgeries had taken the larger part of a year — not counting those past years of experience in the CID Special Operations Unit which had led up to the publisher's commission — and now there was just this last stage to get through. Nick was right. She intended to shut herself away and go through eagerly, if a bit apprehensively, the comments and criticisms she had asked for from old contacts in the Art and Antiques squad. It was good of them to spare their time, considering that they were being cut down in size in the latest of a misguided series of supposed economies. She was glad to be out of that rat race; but glad to know she still had friends there.

The screen at the side of her desk showed she had an email waiting. It could wait. With a lovely feeling of self-indulgence she opened the bulky package and stacked the proof sheets up in front of her.

Then the phone rang. She sat very still, silently pleading with Nick to stop reading the paper and pick up the extension beside his armchair. After a few rings he must have done just that.

Then the buzzer near her knee sounded.

'A Beth Crichton of the Ross Foundation ringing about an urgent email you haven't answered,' said Nick apologetically. 'Just can't bear to wait, can they? I've tried to tell her you're very busy, but she insists she's got a very important matter to discuss. She's sure you'll be interested. Shall I still tell her to push off?'

Lesley looked longingly at the top sheet on her desk, with a scribbled comment in familiar handwriting. It was bound to be more interesting than some stranger's impatient concerns. Yet she was unwilling to let Nick shoulder the task of finding a polite — or maybe not so polite — way of sending the caller on her way.

'I suppose I'd better take it. But darling, listen in, will you? Just in case I'm in danger of letting myself be dragged into making some silly mistake.'

'So I'll be the one to carry the can? Oh, very cunning.'

'Lady Torrance?' The young woman's voice on the line achieved just the right tinge of respect without sounding too gushing. 'This is Beth Crichton from the Ross Foundation. I don't know if you've read about the work we're undertaking to restore a Highland croft which used to be in the Ross family before they were driven out during the Clearances.'

'I seem to remember there was a feature about it in one of the Sunday supplements.'

'Yes, we've had quite gratifying coverage. And you'll recall that one of the important aspects is to assemble as many authentic artefacts of the time as possible, as well as any original paintings which are relevant to the theme.'

'Such as Nicol's *Lochaber No More*? And Wilkie's *Distraining for Rent*?'

'Lady Torrance, that's exactly the sort of know-how we need. Time's getting short, and we do have to get things moving. We'd be glad to offer you whatever retainer you think would be appropriate to act as our artistic adviser. Sorting out the genuine from the fake. We don't want anything *contrived*. The whole atmosphere's got to be evocative but real, not gimmicked up. I'm sure you know what I mean.'

'I know what you mean, all right.' Lesley eyed the proofs a few inches away. 'But I really don't think I've got the time right now. I'm sure you can find someone else with just the qualifications you need.'

'We're told you're the best in the field.'

'Flattering, but … oh, of course, I know who I'd recommend. My old colleague Dr Smutek. He has a gallery just off Thistle Street. Only a brisk short walk from your office.'

'Mrs Ross is set on talking to you personally.'

The Merciless Dead

'Mrs Ross?'

'Mr Ross's daughter-in-law. In this country to check on progress. She's appearing in the arts programme on local TV at ten-thirty this evening. Please, Lady Torrance. Could I ask you at least to watch it? I'm sure you'll find it interesting. And then if we could have a word afterwards ...'

The young woman sounded so genuine, eager yet not pushy, that Lesley couldn't quite bring herself to cut the call short and hang up. In the end she found herself promising to watch the programme; but promising nothing else.

Nick was waiting for her to emerge. 'You're weakening already,' he accused her.

'I'm vaguely curious, that's all. It won't hurt to watch for half an hour. I do know something about the Ross collections here and there.'

'Like so many tycoons, plastering his name all over the landscape in the hope of achieving immortality. And all of it a sitting target for all the forgers and con-men in the business. There's a subject for another book, my love.'

'As it happens, there's a reference in the present one to a very dubious Landseer in their Winnipeg gallery. Don't know if that's likely to endear me to them.' Lesley turned back towards the proofs still waiting in her study. 'All the same, I don't mind being a couch potato for a short time this evening.'

*

The first five minutes of the programme were devoted to a brief review of a new book about ghosts of old Edinburgh, with a shivery sound track provided by a group calling itself The Creeps, desperate to be featured in the Edinburgh Festival. Then Mrs Morwenna Ross was introduced, sitting on a couch with the usual presenter on a high stool opposite. The contrast between the two women could hardly have been greater. The interviewer's dress was adorned with multi-coloured chrysanthemums flowing down long, puffy sleeves, twitching continually as she leaned forward to ask questions or make statements, emphasizing every other word by waving her arms and making stabbing or vaguely circular movements with her hands which Lesley found hard to relate to what those words were saying. Her voice combined a pretended deference with easygoing chattiness, yet left an aftertaste of implicit condescension. Mrs Ross, in a charcoal grey two-piece, hardly moved, yet dominated the screen. She was dark, elegant, and apparently offhanded in her replies to the interviewer's volleys of questions. But when she was allowed to speak at length for herself, although it was at half the speed of the interviewer, every word and phrase sank in and went on echoing in the mind. A face and voice, thought Lesley, which *meant* something.

'The ancestors of James Fergus Ross were driven off their lands in Strath More by greedy lairds who wanted space for their sheep in preference to living space for their clansmen. Mr Ross's great-great-grandfather was only a lad when he and his parents were thrown bodily out of their croft and forced to watch it burn down.'

The silhouette of a ruined, roofless cottage appeared on the screen against a background of fiery sky. As Morwenna Ross told her story, other images were slotted into place, and the story itself moved far out across the world. Lesley found herself remembering bits and pieces from historical studies and magazine articles she had read: disjointed fragments which were now being smoothly joined up.

Great play had often been made in the Ross Foundation press releases, she recalled, of James Fergus Ross's humble origins. They made a good story at the first three or four tellings, after which editors and financial correspondents began to get a bit bored. But Morwenna Ross was quietly bringing it all back to life as if it were all new and vibrant.

The legend began in one of the bleak little clachans on the borders of Sutherland and Wester Ross. Caught up in the mass eviction of the crofters to make room for sheep runs, young Fergus Ross and his parents were thrown out of their home, and by burning it down it was made ruthlessly clear that there was no possibility of their ever returning. Protests were suppressed by factors and the police. Supposedly compassionate resettlement was offered in half-finished fishing villages which were utterly alien to the crofters. When his mother died of a broken heart and failing body within a few weeks of their eviction, the lad was taken by his father to brave the hideous Atlantic crossing on which so many sickened and died.

The sea passage and guarantee of employment had to be paid for by the father indenturing the two of them for ten years to a lumber company in Nova Scotia. Forests which for a couple of centuries had supplied masts for the sailing ships of Britain and America were proving even more prosperous as suppliers of pulp paper mills. Increased production of newspapers all over North America meant an increased greed for newsprint. Smaller mills amalgamated into large combines. There was a rich future for hard grafters.

Fergus's father, robbed of home and land and wife, did not have the willpower to live long in this new world. 'Left to his own devices,' Morwenna Ross intoned, 'his son slaved every hour that God or the devil made, growing to tough adulthood without ever having had a childhood. The day came when he had saved enough money to go into partnership with another immigrant and become a master instead of a slave.'

'And after another ten years,' murmured Nick, 'he fiddled his partner out and acquired an unassailable corner in newsprint mills.' As the woman on the screen talked of dogged determination and integrity, he tossed in some muttered accusations suggesting a background of financial chicanery and a ruthlessness towards competitors which echoed the behaviour of the Highland lairds towards his own forebears.

By the time James Fergus Ross was born in 1925, Ross Enterprises had become a conglomerate of companies astutely juggling seasonal losses from one arm against profits from another.

His father was killed in action with a Canadian division during the crossing of the Rhine in World War Two. By the end of the war young James was left with a stake in a construction company which had done tolerably well out of military contracts, and the longer term holdings in the timber and wood pulp business.

'Which,' observed Nick, 'in the absence of its managing director on military service, had been in danger of missing out on the fortunes to be made by paying appropriate backhanders during the recent conflict. But young Jamie soon caught up.'

His interruption was itself interrupted by the interviewer asking, with breathless earnestness and an accompaniment of outthrust fingertips, 'Hasn't it been suggested in certain parts of the media that Mr Ross's present restoration work in the Highlands is just another story of a tycoon persuaded late in life to seek — what shall we call it? — heavenly insurance by giving lavishly to charity?' She allowed herself a self-congratulatory little giggle. 'Balancing the costs, of course, against special tax breaks.'

'There'll always be people eager to bring down those who've been more successful than themselves. I've studied my father-in-law's work in depth, and I know what benefits it has brought to thousands of people worldwide.'

Colourful fragments of film offered glimpses of Ross Foundations in Canada, New Zealand, the United States, and here in the United Kingdom.

'Libraries and museums with a slant on pioneering history.' Morwenna's tone became almost an incantation. 'The contribution of Scots driven from their own lands to make a new life in the New World.'

A tracking shot flashed up on the screen of Gaelic signs on the causeway linking Nova Scotia and Cape Breton Island, then cut to a dazzling array of fiddlers, pipers and drummers at a music festival on Prince Edward Island. There was a display of kilt and plaid, and heraldic flags. Music of the pipes swelled up.

'The Mountain Games in North Carolina based on the Braemar Gathering,' explained Mrs Ross reverently. 'And every year the Fort Lauderdale Highland Pipe Band' — there was a brief blur as one scene was superimposed on the original — 'plays the Palm Beach Highland Fling. Many of those elements will be attending the great Gathering of the Clans in Edinburgh next year. We want to tie in the formal opening of our reconstructed site with the presence of these homecoming exiles. Invite them to contribute.'

'And in the longer term' — the camera swung towards the interviewer's face as if she had dragged it back impatiently — 'you envisage a sort of memorial park in memory of the supposed victims of the Clearances?'

'There's no 'supposed' about it. The true folk of the land were thrown out to make way for sheep walks. Thrown out without mercy. And the local minister would preach from his pulpit about the sin of resisting the lawful wishes of the landlords. Of course,' said Mrs Ross with relish, 'once he had done his bit for his patrons, he found he had no congregation left to preach to.'

The picture of a small hotel cowering under a windbreak of pines came on screen. 'The minister's abandoned manse was converted into a comfortable home for the factor who had driven the crofters away, and later into a hunting lodge for well-heeled visitors. And later, the hotel which still stands there today. It's part of Mr Ross's regeneration scheme that the hotel should become part of a fully equipped visitors' centre. And, of course, it's within walking distance of the real heart of the development.'

The ruined croft which had opened the programme was graphically transformed by a turf roof sliding into place. The collapsed stones of the doorway reassembled themselves, and on the sound track a fiddle began a slow, nostalgic tune.

'The home from which James Fergus Ross's forebears were brutally driven, but to which he is calling them back in spirit.'

The interviewer babbled some platitudes, the sound track mixed the plaintive melody with a swelling pipe march, and the picture faded through a superimposed photograph of James Fergus Ross staring into the distance.

'Looks rather like Dr Livingstone,' said Nick, 'but without the beard. And I don't suppose Livingstone would have gone much for the idea of financial leverage. Keeping profits on investments in his own hands while his lenders got only the agreed interest on their money.'

'But getting sentimental in old age,' mused Lesley. 'Conjuring up idealistic memories of the simple life of the crofter.'

'All neatly packaged. Only I'd not be too sure about it working out all that neatly. There could be some toes trodden on. I've met some of the present landowners during that conference a couple of years ago to discuss the new Crofters' Acts. They put on a big act of looking down on us Lowlanders, but they're keen enough to get us on their side every time there's a conflict with the legislators. Could be difficulties with some of them. Long ago gave up chucking crofters out to make room for sheep, and then got rid of the sheep to reserve the space for their stalking and shooting friends. Shouldn't imagine historic re-creations of their ancestors' wrongdoings will go down all that well.'

'Could be interesting, though.'

'You don't really fancy getting involved? Filling a gimmicked-up heap of stones with bogus bric-a-brac just to please an ageing entrepreneur going soppy round the edges? Not quite your scene.'

'The whole idea, the way I heard it, was for me to make sure there *isn't* anything bogus.' The phone rang.

'Beth Crichton here, Lady Torrance. What did you make of the programme?'

Close to Lesley's right cheek, Nick silently mouthed: 'Well, what *do* you make of it?'

4

Among others who had watched TV that evening was one Rab Thomson, who reluctantly showed up again at DCI Rutherford's office three days later, once again prodded by his wife. It was hardly the sort of programme Rutherford would have expected him to choose, and Thomson did seem a bit sheepish about it.

'Been away staying with oor daughter, or I'd have come in sooner. It was her wean's first birthday, so we had to … well, ye ken how it is.' It was only because he wanted to get away from the family and watch sports results on the telly that he had blundered across the arts feature.

'And that woman,' said Thomson. 'That one talking about the auld crofts and all that. I'd swear she was the one I saw behind that puir auld bugger.'

'You'd *swear* to it?'

Rutherford was not too surprised when Thomson immediately began to hedge, saying that well of course in that bad light no, he couldn't be all that sure, but all the same his wife had thought he really ought to come forward again, because he was as near sure as could be … only he wouldn't want to take his oath on it.

It was a familiar pattern. So many promising leads in so many cases had turned out to be false leads that Rutherford was protectively sceptical about this one, which didn't add much to Thomson's original vague statement: so vague, indeed, that you could hardly call it a statement. Yet there was something in the man's manner, confused as he might have been, that persuaded him there could be some truth behind those blurred memories.

'I'm grateful to you, Mr Thomson. When I've pursued the matter further, perhaps we can —'

'I'd no' be wanting to get anyone in trouble because of a wee mistake. I mean, ye'll no' be calling on me for one of those identity parades or whatever, wull ye?'

'That depends on developments. But we certainly wouldn't want to cause any more disturbance in your domestic situation than is strictly necessary. Thank you again, Mr Thomson. Believe me, we do appreciate how public-spirited you've been in this matter.'

That would give him something to boast about to his mates, if not to his wife.

When he had gone, Rutherford checked back on the television arts programme to find out who this mysterious female might be.

It didn't take long. A young woman PC in the Fettes Avenue road policing branch had been watching, and had no difficulty filling in the background details. A Morwenna Ross — yes, *those* Rosses — had been talking about a historic restoration scheme which the Foundation was backing in the Highlands.

'Mighty powerful lady,' she recalled. 'Bags of clout behind her, I'd say. She's the sort who'll probably be on Desert Island Discs in a week or two. All part of the PR.'

'Didn't know you could bribe your way onto that.'

'Not exactly, sir. But my guess is that if you happen to be in town and you happen to have enough influence to get to the front of the queue, you stand a good chance of being asked.'

'What sort of music d'you suppose she fancies?'

'Sinister stuff. *Danse Macabre ... Night on the Bare Mountain* ... that kind of thing.'

'Thanks, constable. I'll watch out for the incantations.'

He decided to go along to the Ross building and tackle this Mrs Ross head on. If the woman was out, then he would have to adjust his tactics. But making an appointment was rarely in Rutherford's procedures. He preferred to tackle things full tilt, catching people unawares. It had led him into trouble more than once, but he wasn't going to change his ways now.

He and his sergeant were kept waiting at the reception desk until a Simon Ogilvie appeared and made a big fuss about him showing up unannounced.

'We work to very tight schedules in this business, Chief Inspector. Each one of us depends on the smooth integration of our respective functions and the time available to our communal efforts. Unwarranted intrusions — quite unwarranted, I would say, in this instance — can cause serious disruptions.'

'I'll cause as little disruption as possible, sir. It's simply a matter of having a few words with Mrs Morwenna Ross to clear up a possibly foolish misconception.'

'If you're aware of its foolishness, then all the more reason not to come here without even the courtesy of a prior phone call.'

Rutherford had come across so many of this type before. The man's sallow complexion suggested that he spent very little of his life outside the office, and was determined that every aspect of existence should be caged within a recognisable social and business hierarchy. Determined to sound imperious, he became shrill and nasal, pinching his words into what he thought was an authentic Morningside voice.

'I am minded to have a word with your superior officer about this clumsy intrusion.' Meaning, thought Rutherford, that there might be a nudge and a snide remark at the next Lodge meeting. If he was on a high enough level. Or the golf club. No, Ogilvie didn't look healthy enough to be a golfer.

'Perhaps, sir, you'd be good enough to let Mrs Ross know that we'd like a word with her.'

'I think I may say that I am sufficiently in Mrs Ross's confidence for you to tell me what the matter is before I disturb her.'

Rutherford took a deep breath and was about to risk getting tougher and more bleakly official when two women came out of a side door and began crossing the foyer. The tall dark one fitted the description of the one he was looking for. The other ...

It came out before he could stop it. 'Lez! What the hell are you doing here?' Then, awkwardly: 'Oh, God. Sorry. What do I call you now — Your Ladyship?'

'Makes a change from 'You stupid bitch'.'

'I never —'

'Frequently.' She held out her hand, as warm as her smile. 'But it's good to see you again, Jock.'

Tit-for-tat. He was foolishly pleased that the one-time DI Lesley Gunn still remembered how DCI Jack Rutherford hated being called Jock.

'Oh, and this' — she turned towards her companion — 'is Mrs Ross. Mrs Morwenna Ross ... Detective Chief Inspector Rutherford.'

Rutherford said: 'It's Mrs Ross I've come to see. I've got a few questions to ask.'

Ogilvie was twittering, looking irritably from one face to another and then concentrating on the tall, imperturbable woman. 'I was trying to make this police officer understand that he has no right to burst in here and —'

'I can't imagine why the police should be interested in me. Pretty sure my papers are all in order, and I was checked for terrorist weapons at the airport. But I've no objection to answering this officer's questions.'

She was the kind, thought Rutherford, who would always be in charge of a situation. It would never occur to her to be apprehensive. Whatever came at her, she would somehow deflect it without any sign of effort. Admirable in a way; but right here and now he didn't like that arrogance, and wasn't sure how things would go if he was the one who had to throw his weight about.

'If you're really prepared to allow this officer some of your time,' bleated Ogilvie, 'I think I had better sit in on the interview. Just to safeguard Mrs Ross's interests,' he added defiantly.

'I guess I can get along well enough with Lady Torrance as a witness.' She smiled at Rutherford. 'I gather that in her past she had considerable legal experience. You'd have no objections to her being present?'

'None whatsoever.' Rutherford was more than happy to have his ex-DI around as back-up and reputable witness to the correctness of his procedure. The woman presumably thought Lesley would be on her side; but Rutherford hoped he knew Lesley better than that.

Ogilvie reluctantly fussed ahead of them to open the door of a small room to the side of the main reception office. Before leaving he gave a critical glance at the small table set exactly in the centre of the room, with four chairs set around it with mathematical precision, two facing the other two exactly, and four glasses and four bottles of mineral water between them as if permanently in place for any urgent conference which might arise at any hour of the day.

'This has the makings of a great movie,' said Morwenna Ross. 'Ruthless interrogation, and the accused finally beaks down and confesses all. Isn't that how it goes?'

To his irritation, it was she rather than Rutherford who immediately took charge of the seating arrangement, waving the two men towards the chairs facing the door, and Lesley to the chair facing the sergeant. Only when they were seated did she deign to sit down.

'The only trouble is,' she went on, 'that I've got no notion what I'm supposed to be confessing to.'

'Mrs Ross.' Rutherford came out with the sort of question he had asked, in so many words, on so many occasions. 'Can you tell me where you were around nine or ten o'clock last Friday evening?'

'That would be a week ago today?'

'It would.'

'Let me see, now. I had arrived only that morning. I suppose I could have been unpacking, and — no, wait a minute. Late evening? I reckon that would be about the time I went out for a stroll. To clear my head.'

'An evening stroll from your hotel? Where are you actually staying, Mrs Ross?'

'The Foundation funds a private hotel and residential club just behind Charlotte Square. I'm being accommodated in a suite there.'

'That would be the Drovers Court, sir,' the sergeant said quietly.

'A long walk to Leith,' Rutherford commented.

Morwenna Ross looked blandly innocent. 'Is that where I was?'

'I don't know, ma'am. *Was* it?'

'I know I must have walked some considerable distance. I always do walk for miles when I first get to a new place. Shake off the jet lag. Get the feel of the place. You with me? Soak up the atmosphere. But that hasn't become a crime in this country, has it?'

He wanted to wipe that lofty indifference off her face. He wanted her to show some sign of guilt, or at least some twitch of alarm. But even while he plunged into a recital of the bare facts of Angus Macdonald's death, she seemed just mildly interested rather than concerned either for herself or for the facts of that death.

'Now that you mention it, d'you know, I do recall seeing a rather tall, gangly sort of guy stumbling about near the water. Some sort of river, that would be?'

'The Water of Leith,' said the sergeant.

'But it was late evening, wasn't it, and there were quite a lot of men staggering about at that time.' She smiled a tolerant smile. 'I can't say I was greatly concerned.'

'And when he collapsed, you didn't think of going to his assistance?'

'I don't recall seeing him collapse.'

'We have a witness who says he saw you right behind the man before he went down. Staring at him as if to … well, the impression he got was that you wanted to injure Mr Macdonald in some way.'

He caught a sidelong glimpse of Lesley's left eyebrow going up warningly. The hell with it. He still wanted some reaction from this woman.

She said: 'And you imagine I'd try to strike a complete stranger dead by just staring at him?'

'I have to take into account the report of any witness nearby at the crucial time.'

'And your witness,' said Lesley, 'was in full possession of his faculties at the time?'

He glared at her. But he knew her well enough to know that she could guess the condition of the sort of witness he would get at that time of the evening in that neighbourhood. His only lead was a flimsy one at best. He had had to follow it up and meet this woman, but it was all too vague, too silly. Write it off, and accept the fact that the verdict was going to be accidental death.

'I'm sorry, Mrs Ross.' He was going to have to accept the rightness of that lofty expression of hers. 'It was a report I was in duty bound to follow up. I must apologize for having wasted your time.'

'And your own, Chief Inspector. But of course I quite appreciate the way your police over here have to work. Something else to add to my interesting experiences in this country.'

Their chairs scraped back. As they got to their feet, Lesley said: 'I'll show you out.' She ushered the two men to the door, giving a half-apologetic nod back towards Morwenna Ross.

On the steps outside, Rutherford grunted: 'All right, say it.'

'Say what?'

'Say my great big flat feet have made too much noise to too little purpose, as usual.'

'Wouldn't dream of it.' As the sergeant moved tactfully a few yards away, she added: 'They've promoted you, then? From the wilds of the Borders to the Big House itself.'

'Promotion? Aren't you going to ask why I haven't made Superintendent by now?'

'You know me. The soul of tact.'

'You'll need it, if you're working with that woman in there. And no, I'm not going to ask what you're doing in this place, because I've been told about her telly programme, and it's my bet you're bored with the life of the laird's lady and you're getting back into the fine arts and crafts racket. You and' — he repeated the words with a rasp in his throat — 'that woman. Just mind how you go, Lez.'

'You know something, Jock? I got a sort of feeling in there that she was rather taken by the idea that she could force someone to drop dead simply by staring at them and *willing* it.'

'Casting a spell on the poor sod?'

'Just so.'

'You know damn well we can't take fantasies like that into serious consideration.'

'All I'm saying,' said Lesley, 'is that she fancies the idea.'

'Then you'd better watch how you go,' said Rutherford. 'Wouldn't want her bringing a curse down on you.' He waved to his sergeant. 'All right, let's be off. Back to some sensible everyday work, like chasing drug dealers and the regular wife-beaters.'

5

Luke's prediction about results from the television programme soon proved all too justified. There was a flood of phone calls, emails, letters enclosing photographs, and invitations to visit out-of-the-way homesteads across Sutherland, Wester Ross, and the Hebrides. Croft museums in Angus and Caithness sent brochures and guides which they hoped might be of use. Before Lady Torrance was called on to pronounce final judgments, Beth had the task of sifting all incoming calls and material.

It could have been a thankless chore. There had been many Ross PR campaigns which had been just that. She had often been grateful for Luke's presence, when they could share sour jokes about prostituting their art, running flags up the flagpole to see who'd salute them, and devising precautions to ensure that the devious Ogilvie didn't load them with blame when a project went pear-shaped. But this present job was different.

Of course some submissions were try-ons. Others could be poignant. A very early photograph, lovingly preserved over several generations, showed an elderly woman in a dark dress, shawl and white mob cap sitting on a stool outside a stone cottage in New South Wales. The painstakingly neat handwriting of the accompanying letter said that this had come from the writer's 'Great-grandma MacKinnon', the last survivor there of the MacKinnons sent away from Skye with the assistance of the Skye Emigration Society. There was also a photocopy of a creased scrap of printed paper ordering the emigrants to 'convert into cash every article of property you possess to procure the means of carrying you to the Colonies'. They had been forced not merely to leave their homes but to sell off belongings to raise a few miserable pence towards their fare. What remained: a few souvenirs so pitiful that they were not worth taking along?

There were offers of authentic cooking pots, cherished paintings of family groups — unlikely, one might suppose, that crofters could ever have afforded to pay an artist for such a luxury — and any number of wooden boxes claiming to have been babies' crude cots. Photographs were submitted of slivers of old timber salvaged from burning roofs: as many, thought Beth, as the fragments of the True Cross worldwide. One more substantial piece of doorpost carried a deeply etched mark with fragments of white paint still clinging — the 'laird's mark' ordering the occupants to quit their home. A much-thumbed copy of MacLeod's *Gloomy Memories*, a contemporary account of evictions and burnings. Yellowing, crumpled letters from Canada, the United States, Australia and New Zealand, some optimistic about the future, some despondent. A few abusive modern letters asking '*What* Clearances?' from correspondents claiming that the tales of brutal evictions were a myth, and that those who sailed away for new worlds did so eagerly — a local equivalent, it could be, of the World War II Holocaust deniers.

To Beth it had become all too real and immediate. Over and done with two centuries ago, yet still alive and heart-breaking today. The landowners and clan chiefs to whom their tenants and clansmen had turned as father figures had set about turning out these supposed kinfolk to make way for sheep runs. There was no discussion, no sympathetic ear for representations from the cottars. Making money from sheep was more important than traditional loyalties. Families given abrupt notice to quit, and failing to do so, often because they could not believe what was threatened, were thrown out and their roofs torn down and set on fire to make sure they could not return. Beth sometimes felt, all too vividly, that she could smell the burning and see, as folk far across doomed Strath Fleet had once reported, 'the red glow in the sky'.

She was putting her heart into this job. It was a tale which must never be forgotten. Whatever misdeeds James Fergus Ross might have committed in the contemporary rat-race, at least he was committed now to establishing a lasting memorial to the brutal tragedies which had smitten his ancestors and their neighbours.

There was a lot of rubbish to be ploughed through, a lot of doubtful material to be evaluated, a barrage of time-wasting queries to be coped with; but she believed in what she was doing. It hadn't always been the case. But this time she was committed.

*

Beth's parents had brought her up in New Galloway. Her father worked for the Forestry Commission, and her two older brothers followed him into an energetic outdoor life in the Galloway Forest Park. Although they enjoyed their work, all three men felt that 'our wee Beth' was the special one of the family, destined for greater things: someone to look up to, and boast about, to say they had always known she was special, and then sit back and accept the tributes of neighbours and workmates. Far from the childhood of Luke Drummond, who had allowed some dismal remarks to seep out about his father, always yelling 'Got your head stuck in a bloody book again, fat lot of bloody good that'll do you,' she was encouraged to read, go in for literary competitions, and join the school debating society. She was a good debater, though sometimes half ashamed at her own glibness.

There was no doubt that a respectable office job could be found for Beth as a stepping stone to that golden career everyone predicted for her. Leaving Heriot Watt University she worked for a while in the local tourist board — 'Just finding her feet,' the family assured friends and neighbours — and then answered an advertisement for a Public Relations assistant with the Ross Foundation in Edinburgh. The name was famous. If you worked for Ross, it was something your folks could boast about.

For part of the time it was almost too easy. Within six months she was not merely an assistant, but Public Relations Officer. With that school tradition behind her, she was good at talking people into things. It was important to look sincere, which meant you had to be sincere. Talk yourself into believing that what you did was worth doing, at any rate during the time you were actually doing it. At the end, pride in having accomplished a task. But all too often there was the aftermath — like sheepishness after a rather unsatisfactory hour in bed with Luke. It might all seem so real and urgent to start with, but afterwards there could be a feeling of it being not quite such a good thing. An unpleasant taste lingered from knowing that she had had to persuade herself to persuade others to believe in something she didn't really believe.

Her family suffered few doubts on her behalf. They took pride in the fact that she now had a position working for one of Scotland's most successful organizations. 'A position': — the word hinted at so many grand skills. In only one way was she a slight disappointment. Her mother and father were waiting to hear of her marriage to someone important, someone capable of looking after her and fathering a grandchild or two for them. On visits to the capital they had met Luke a couple of times but, without saying any derogatory word, gave the impression of not thinking him worthy of their daughter. They would have disapproved even more if they had known that he and Beth frequently shared a bed when the mood took them.

Nor might they have regarded Luke more highly if they had known that he had in fact proposed marriage. Of course anyone would want to marry their daughter; but he was not the someone they would have hoped for. Luke had proposed twice, and twice Beth had refused him. The proposals had been too much of a formality — genuine yet without passion. Like so many things Luke did, the gesture was timed and tidily introduced into a sequence from which he ticked off commitments at the correct moments so that he could then go on to the next item on the list; rather as if there was a gap in one of his shelves which needed filling, or a recurrent blip in a computer file which called for a tidying-up of the template. Beth had turned him down because it was too predictable. She didn't make an issue of it; simply said that she didn't want to spoil things.

There were no mutual reproaches. Without any complicated discussion, they simply did not go to bed together any more. Beth wondered if she had perhaps, after all, spoilt something.

But in the office she still turned to him without hesitation when she needed help. Or even when she simply needed the relaxation of a brief gossip. Their partnership was just what it had always been. Whenever there were questions to be answered, he was always there, eager to help — much keener, she sometimes thought ruefully, than he had really been about the marriage idea.

Now, after so many run-of-the-mill campaigns, she found herself working on something in which she did believe. Perhaps, having so recently refused to commit herself to Luke, she needed some other commitment to occupy all her energies.

After two hours of sorting letters and emails into two piles classified as rejects and possibles, in mid-morning she went into the library with a query.

'Do you have any gen on a Randal Grant? A photographer?'

Predictably, Luke's head turned towards his shelves. He did not so much consult indexes or a specific filing system as play the conjuror, plucking out memories from behind file covers or leather bindings with a flourish of the hand.

'Glossy magazines,' he said. 'Interiors of stately homes, historic sites, that sort of thing. Did some striking work for *Paris Match* and others before coming to Edinburgh. Churns out some expensive picture postcards. And illustrations for coffee table books. Rather good quality stuff, though. Why? What's the interest?'

'He's been on the phone. Saw Morwenna's programme. Thinks he might have covered some subjects that would interest us. Family portraits, documents, and old drawings from those stately homes. And some less stately, he hinted.'

'Could be something relevant among all the posh stuff. Fixing for him to bring a selection round?'

'Says he's got too many things for him to lug a portfolio over here. Suggests someone goes to his studio and he'll give them a good look round.'

'What does her ladyship think? Or Morwenna?'

'They're out. Visiting a collector I sorted out from the pile. Lady Torrance had heard of him, and agreed he was worth a follow-up. Meanwhile I thought I might go to this bloke's place and have a preliminary recce.'

'Watch it, girl. I seem to remember he's done some sexy fashion shoots in his time. Probably try to lure you into posing in the nude.' Luke looked her up and down in what might have been regretful reminiscence; or merely a kind of amiable punctuation mark in the conversation. 'Not that I'd blame him.'

Beth decided she was entitled to a breath of fresh air. The walk across the gardens and down the hill would provide a welcome break from that suffocating accumulation of letters, emails and faxes.

*

Randal Grant's studio was at the top of three flights of stairs. When he opened the door he appeared all too convincingly the sort of young man Luke had conjectured. He was tall, broad-shouldered, dark-haired and with a ragged beard which did not conceal sensually smiling lips. Some might have called his grey-green chinos and stained blue corduroy shirt arty-crafty; but he was rather too hefty for anyone to risk doing so out loud. After they had shaken hands he let his fingers drift, apparently by chance, a few inches up her arm. Beth stiffened; yet the sensation wasn't entirely displeasing.

'Miss Crichton, right? Do come in to Chaos Towers.'

The interior was cluttered with bits and pieces of photographic equipment, lamps, and a miscellany of benches and tables, some with large prints spread out on them.

'My last girlfriend called it carnival night on a rubbish tip,' said Grant.

Last girlfriend ... intimating what?

Beth said: 'What have you got that might interest us?'

'Let me show you the general subjects first. The backdrops you may need, that sort of thing.' His hand was on her arm again, steering her round the hazards on the floor towards a display along one wall. 'You probably think you've seen these places often enough before. Always churning out pretty picture books of Bonnie Scotland for the tourist. And for boxes of shortbread. Keeps me in business.'

It was true, many of the scenes were overfamiliar. Eilean Donan, Urquhart Castle, sunset over Ben Loyal. Yet there was a freshness about them that set them apart, as if a painter rather than a photographer was bringing out hitherto unnoticed colours, shadows, depths. Beth could not repress a murmur of admiration, only to find that it provoked a disturbing reaction in the way he looked at her, as if he too had found something to appreciate.

There were also prints of works by the Faeds, Hornel, Ramsey and others. 'All authorized by the owners or the relevant public authorities,' he said in a mock solemn tone, as if to anticipate any query she might raise.

'Not really relevant to the period we're covering.'

'Something a bit less pretty-pretty, then?' His fingertips were very light on her arm as he steered her across the room again. 'You could build up a selection of the genre painters — Geikie, Allan, Wilkie and one or two you may not be familiar with. There's this sad one of a ship carrying folk away … and this is one that gave me some difficulty. Getting the right light to bring out the lettering without blurring it.'

The photograph showed a hazed church window with a wavering pattern of scratches. A few initials had been incised more deeply. Running unevenly across the glass were scrawled messages: *Glencalvie people was here … John Ross shepherd … Glencalvie is a wilderness blow ship them to the colony …*

'Scores of them, men, women, children,' said Randal Grant, 'driven from their homes and huddling in Croick churchyard, wondering where the hell to go next.'

As if to emphasize the unremitting darkness of the theme, he flipped over a number of photostats of illustrations from old newspapers such as the *Inverness Courier* and the *Military Register*. One etching seemed to scream off the page at Beth. It showed a young woman sprawled on the ground with a horseman leering down at her from above. Her shawl and a part of her woollen dress had been ripped aside, showing the dark, bruised imprint of a horseshoe above her left breast.

'Or something less grisly?' suggested Grant. 'Domestic stuff from the kitchens and firesides.'

He produced a sequence of pictures of a flat iron, a cruisie lamp, a pair of button boots, a cotton weaver's pirn, a crude carding comb, and a fragment of patchwork rug.

Beth ventured: 'And the Ross Tapestry. You wouldn't by any chance have come across that on one of your various assignments?'

'The Ross Tapestry. Mm.' She could not tell whether he was seriously considering it or mutely jeering at her. 'A lot of folk would like to have that in their collection. If it exists. If it ever did exist.'

Hadn't she heard those words before?

'You do know about it, though.'

'I've read about it, yes. Like a lot of things.'

Abruptly he was closing a folder of prints, tidily stacking up a few loose photographs, and letting one slip to the floor. It was a full-length study of a nude girl, lying relaxed on a plumped-up mound of violet velvet cushions.

'So that's the sort of magazine you contribute to?'

'When commissioned. No drapes or thongs or pouting lips. There's nothing pornographic about the naked body itself.'

'No.' She looked at the set of his shoulders and the hair as dark and sleek as sealskin down his forearms, and wondered … and forced herself to stop wondering. 'No, of course not. She's very beautiful.'

'Very.' He was smiling, not quite mocking, but …

What right had she to wonder whether that graceful figure was that of an old flame, or one still burning?

'A pity,' he went on airily, 'that when she's achieved the modelling status she's set on, and perfected the correct sullen pout, it'll take quite some genius of a ghost-writer to produce a readable autobiography without the word 'me' at least a hundred times on each page.' He looked her up and down. 'Ever thought of posing for some fashion shots yourself?'

'You call that a fashion shot?'

'Very much in fashion nowadays. But we could add clothes if you were so inclined.'

His deplorably suggestive grin made her want to laugh. She felt ridiculously at ease with him, as if they had known one another way back and were getting fun out of meeting again.

'Anyway.' He was abruptly crisp and businesslike. 'Perhaps you'll bear me in mind for any photographic work you need during your campaign.'

'I'll have to discuss it.'

'But of course. Big discussions. Brainstorming sessions. That's how it works, isn't it?' At the door, he shook hands quite formally, then with unexpected intensity said: 'From what I know about that neck of the woods, there'll be people anxious to muck up whatever you're aiming for.'

'What people?'

'You're aiming to keep alive the memory of folk who had a raw deal all those years ago. And appealing to their descendants overseas to visit and contribute.'

'I thought that had been made pretty clear.'

'Just so. But don't forget the other descendants — the successors of those exploiters who did well out of that deal. They're still around. And still with their claws on a lot of the land. A few of them may not care to have old memories stirred up.'

'I think we can cope.'

'I hope so.' As he was closing the door he said: 'I do hope so. Now that we've met, I wouldn't want *you* to come to any harm.'

6

As a detective inspector, Lesley Gunn had never been easily intimidated. As Lesley, Lady Torrance, she was even less likely to be overwhelmed by anyone presuming to lay down demands too aggressively. Yet she had to admit to a tremor of defensiveness when in the company of Mrs Morwenna Ross.

Not that the woman was aggressive, or too vulgarly flaunting the fact that she had a lot of money to spend and wanted everything done exactly according to her own impetuous wishes. But the undertone was there — what Nick, with his musical background, would probably have categorized as a ground bass, implacable and not to be deviated from.

'Another interesting morning's work so far.' It was said flatly, without condescension but with no particular approval. 'At least we know a lot of things we needn't waste any more time on.'

They were sitting in the lounge of her suite at Drovers Court with a silver pot of coffee and a plate of shortbread fingers on the tray between them. The room was high-ceilinged and airy, its decor in pastel shades and slender lines skilfully stolen from the concepts of Rennie Mackintosh. Everything about the building was spacious and relaxing, even though it was crushed into a traffic-choked square. Lesley's own suite was smaller than Morwenna's, but in no way cramped. Unnecessarily plushy, she thought, for the limited use to which she would be putting it. Going home at weekends when it suited her — a proviso she had laid down from the start — would leave it empty for a large part of the time. But this was typical Ross. Money no object, as had been made clear in her retainer for the job. Drovers Court had been an over-large and fading hotel, taken over and expensively reconditioned by Ross Enterprises for visiting customers, distinguished guests, and key overseas staff on visits. A suite was kept in permanent readiness for any of Mr Ross's rare and unpredictable visits.

Morwenna Ross had an impressive memory for what they had seen this morning. She had made no notes, leaving that to Lesley as a sort of glorified secretary, but over their coffee she was quick to sum up the items worth considering. A clan exhibition in the Old Town had yielded copies of old plaids and the addresses of several useful contacts. Buying pictures and souvenirs was all too easy when the provenance was doubtful, probably phoney; not so easy when the items were genuine. Sellers were often unwilling to admit their financial need to sell, so it all had to be done discreetly.

'A few elderly folk may believe that selling us their trinkets will give us a psychic hold over them,' Morwenna reflected. She had been delighted with a horsehair sieve, some of its rotted strands dangling loose, and even more so by a corpse candle and curse stone, sealed in a jar of holy water to neutralize its power.

The back of Lesley's neck prickled. Did Morwenna herself believe in such powers?

'As for the painters,' Morwenna went on, 'most of the work was done in hindsight. We can use copies in the Interpretation Centre, of course. That one of distraining for rent —'

'Wilkie, yes. And Nicol's rural scenes.'

Morwenna moved the coffee pot out of the way and spread out a selection of prints.

'That one has a wonderful atmosphere. *The Last of England.* So melancholy.'

'Ford Madox Brown. Mm. But it's a bit late in the day. And they're fairly comfortably dressed. Melancholy,' said Lesley, 'but not embittered.'

'Where's that one of the old woman crouched outside her front door?' Morwenna shuffled through the prints. 'And the factor's heavies pulling the thatch down. Pretty compelling stuff.'

'I ... well, I ditched that before we left,' said Lesley warily. 'I'm sure it was a phoney. Contrived for the market. The dates are wrong. Too late to be a contemporary of those goings-on, and even as a recreation it's inconsistent. The background's authentic, but someone has superimposed figures of people into the landscape, and removed the roofs of some crofts in the background to make out they were burnt.'

Morwenna looked stony for a moment, as if about to challenge her. Then she said briskly: 'OK, I guess I have to defer to your judgment. That's what you're here for, right?' And to add emphatic approval, she went on: 'Like the way you brushed off that cocky little runt who assured us that sad scene of an old man being thrown out was authentic.'

'Oh, the lousy copy of a Landseer? Yes, that was a bit much.'

Lesley had always been fond of that touching scene of an ageing drover getting ready for what would probably be his last tryst in Crieff. All too easy to twist its meaning when trying to impress a gullible client.

Morwenna reached across the scattered scenes for a shortbread finger. 'I guess we'll soon be getting a whole lot more from back home.' She laughed apologetically. 'I mean, what's home to me. People in our offices back in Canada, New Brunswick, all round there — coming up with the most evocative things carried away from the old country. You name it — flatirons, candlesticks, stoneware crocks, an axe or two.'

'Souvenirs stood a better chance of survival,' commented Lesley, 'than the treasures they had to leave behind. Or had them stolen before they left. So poverty-stricken, most of them, that they couldn't have left much of any value. No real value, either, in what they could manage to carry with them.'

'No commercial value, no.' Morwenna was suddenly fierce. 'But historically they'd be invaluable to us. D'you know, one Cape Breton family took with them a small crock of earth scratched up as they left. Two of the women died of smallpox on the voyage and were buried at sea, but the survivors clung to their last handful of the homeland. And it's still there.'

'Genuine? The original?'

'Oh, sure. But yes, I'll need to call on your expertise when we get some of the packages. Too many first-rate craftsmen in Nova Scotia go in for manufacturing mementoes of the old pioneering days, for the benefit of the tourist trade. And I'd guess you've got some right here doing the same sort of thing, all ready and waiting for gullible folk revisiting their ancestral lands and getting dewy-eyed about scruffy little souvenirs.'

'Kitsch has never been difficult to sell,' Lesley agreed glumly.

Their cups were empty. Morwenna had finished the last bit of shortbread. As if everything else had been merely a lead-in to the main meal of the day, she said: 'OK, then. The Ross Tapestry. Made any headway?'

Lesley's heart sank. Privately she thought the existence of the tapestry was as likely as the survival of Arthur's Excalibur in some Somerset fen. So many legends, none capable of being followed up.

'I've been taking soundings,' she said carefully. 'But everything's so vague. What exactly did it depict? How big was it? It couldn't have been all that big. Who worked on it?'

'It must have had a basic plaid pattern.' Morwenna's voice was confident, brooking no arguments 'Some of the older folk were highly skilled. Within their obvious limitations, sure. But they were used not merely to making and patching cloth but weaving and stitching ambitious patterns. Maybe they couldn't write, but they did their damnedest to leave some sort of testimony to themselves in handiwork — as a matter of local pride, with a distinctive thread through their patterns to establish their provenance. And' — she was becoming intense again — 'that's really the key to the whole thing. We have to find it. Make it the centrepiece.'

'I've been in touch with some helpful folk on the Art Loss Register in London. They cover a lot of ground — leading auction houses, art trade associations, the insurance industry.'

'And ...?'

Lesley could hardly tell her that her contact at the Register had wryly said how difficult it was to trace the movements of a missing work of art when there was no tangible evidence of that work having ever existed in the first place.

'It's not the sort of item,' she temporized, 'that shows up in most salerooms or house clearances.'

'It has to be *somewhere*. Somebody, somewhere along the line, must have got their hands on it. Stolen by some goddam factor? Or saved, hidden away ...'

Her fervour was making Lesley uneasy again. Rashly she tried to lighten the mood. 'Maybe we should go for a print of Winterhalter's portrait of the Duchess of Sutherland. Or Romney's painting of her husband, Stafford. May as well have the top villains as the real centrepiece.'

A cloud shadow across the sunlight pouring into the room fell across Morwenna's high cheekbones, and her eyes, already a deep sloe colour, grew darker than one would have thought possible. She was in no mood for any joky asides whatsoever. Very stiffly she said: 'We may as well have a quick lunch here, don't you think?'

The paintings in the restaurant were less controversial, though some diners might not have cared to eat under large studies featuring a Ross sawmill, a Ross-endowed technical college in a sylvan setting, and a touched-up, enlarged photograph of James Fergus's grandfather sporting a vast flowering of mutton-chop whiskers. The tables were occupied by what Lesley instinctively classified as 'men in suits' and a few intense, breathy girls she hadn't met but felt she had known before, in other places, showing up here in case they might miss something, or be thought not to be playing the corporate game loyally enough.

Simon Ogilvie was in a prominent position and audible across the room, showing off to a guest. He broke off and rose self-importantly to his feet to greet Morwenna. 'All going well, dear lady? Do let me know when we've got enough to send details to Toronto.' He nodded down at his companion, a sandy-haired man wearing a lapel badge which must mean something esoteric to those who recognized it. 'Wonderful nowadays, hm? Rattle off copies across the world in seconds.'

And make sure head office notices how scrupulous you are, thought Lesley.

Seated in the restaurant, Morwenna's manner changed again. Not condescending and with apparently genuine interest, she was politely asking her companion for more details about her specialist work — with no hint that this could be merely a sly assessment of her fitness for this present job.

'Forgeries,' she said, looking straight at Lesley with an inviting smile. 'They must make a fascinating study. You just have to let me know exactly when your book is due to come out.'

It was a subject Lesley wasn't reluctant to talk about. All the aspects of the research she had so recently completed, and now had seen laid out so clearly and convincingly in the proofs, were sharp-edged and real. She summed up the exploits of such brilliant craftsmen as Tom Keating, who had found himself so good at 'restoration' work that he attempted a fake Samuel Palmer, and succeeded so well that he went on to produce another eight which were accepted as genuine and brought in a tidy profit. Then there was the ingenious John Drewe, who contrived to get into the Tate Gallery reading room and the Victoria & Albert archives in order to insert phoney references which would 'authenticate' the provenance of works painted by a skilful colleague.

At end of lunch, before getting back to their researches, Morwenna said: 'You know, I reckon we do need to pay a visit to the site itself. And soon. We do need to establish exactly what artefacts are needed where. At the moment we've got just the bare bones of a croft. It needs to be filled with authentic echoes. How are you fixed?'

Lesley made it politely clear that she was going home for the weekend; unless, she added with what she hoped was a nice balance between amenability and scepticism, there was something urgent to be done. 'I do need to check one or two final references in my proofs before I send them back.'

Morwenna was swift to say that of course the weekend would be a refreshing break for both of them, giving them time to assess or reassess their priorities. And, smiling, she wouldn't dream of causing any troubles in the Torrance household.

'Your husband.' She made it sound chatty and relaxed. 'He's a Borderer?'

'From way back, yes.'

'And you — before you married, you were …?'

Lesley was instinctively sure that the woman had checked on every detail of this kind. But she said lightly: 'I was a Gunn. From the north-east coast. Some distance from the Borders. What you might call a mixed marriage, Highlander and Lowlander.'

'No sense of old antagonisms still smouldering?'

'If you're aiming to stir up a feud between my husband and myself, I don't think it'd work.'

'I wouldn't dare. As a matter of interest, a lot of Gunns settled in Ontario.' As they came out into the sunlight, she glanced at her watch. 'Right, what's next on the itinerary? Let's wrap up the week. I'm in your hands.'

They spent the afternoon in the Pentland Folk Museum. Morwenna's easy-going mood seemed to change as time went on. She sneered at a perfectly authentic linen mutch, complete with a wisp of string for tying under the owner's chin; but was attracted by what to Lesley was obviously a modern reproduction of a bannock spade, made from compacted wood shavings. At the end of the afternoon, without warning she came out with what sounded almost like a challenge which had to be answered.

'I've just remembered. I think I'm right. One of your ancestors who didn't bother getting to Ontario could have been George Gunn. Ex-Army type.'

'I'm afraid none of us ever dug very deep into family history.'

'This one stayed on as under-manager of the Sutherlands' properties in Assynt.' Her conversational tone hadn't changed, yet Lesley felt a chill accusation behind it. 'Head of the clan, too — though he did nothing to stop their evictions from Kildonan.'

*

A colour supplement in one of the Sunday papers had a feature about Morwenna Ross and her current researches in Scotland. It devoted two paragraphs to the search for a colourful piece of clan history — the Ross Tapestry, a tantalizing mystery.

'Makes a good story,' said Nick. 'But what's so mysterious about it?'

'I can't help thinking of it as one of those old wives' tales. A fantasy tradition like the fairy flag of Dunvegan, the predictions of the Braham Seer, that sort of thing.'

'If *you* can't believe in it,' said Nick affectionately, 'it probably never existed. Not exactly in the class of the Bayeux Tapestry, anyway.'

'That was a great work of communal art, celebrating a great victory. Any humble Ross needlework could hardly have been in that league.'

'Have any of your friends in London heard of this old treasure?'

'Fleeting references in books, yes. About as reliable as a volume of Scottish fairy tales.'

'Aren't things liable to get out of hand? You'll drown yourself in paperwork. This business of tracing your ancestors has become all the rage. Look at that page of ads.' He turned the paper over. 'All kinds of firms offering research in various magazines and on web sites. Modern technology bringing people closer together than we could ever have dreamed in the past.'

'Sometimes with unpredictable results.'

'Yes. Mind where you go, my love. I mean, this Morwenna female. Can it genuinely matter all that much to a well-heeled young woman with so many other activities all round her? Just playing along with her father-in-law's senile notions, waiting to inherit while making herself indispensable — playing it clever?'

'No, there's more to it than that. She really is driven by ... well ... *something*. I wouldn't want to be one to get in her way.'

The phone rang. She was the closer, and picked it up, though half expecting the caller to be ready to plunge into one of Nick's local problems.

Beth Crichton was sorry to interrupt her at home, but felt there was news she would want to think about before she came into the office tomorrow. Nick raised a quizzical eyebrow as Lesley said, 'But how much damage ... actual artefacts or ... oh, nothing *we've* collected so far then, but ... no, I'm sure she will ...'

As she put the receiver down, Nick said: 'There are few things in the world more irritating than listening to one end of somebody else's phone conversation. Now, do fill in the gaps for me.'

'Seems that somebody's already getting obstructive. There's been some damage to the croft and the study centre. And the workers on the site don't like the atmosphere.'

'Too windy for them? Or plagued by ghosts coming out of the glens?'

'Something more substantial than ghosts, by the sound of it.'

But she was haunted for the rest of the evening by the thought of spirits from the past — beings driven out bodily yet still somehow clinging with their roots in the soil, an earth from which they refused to be wrenched.

7

Walking up the familiar steps this morning, under the flutter of the Ross flag and in through the familiar side door beside the massive gilt-handled main door, Beth was at once aware of the equally familiar vibrations of an administrative panic. Instead of being in their usual offices, or the library or the computer room, key staff were clustered in the ground-floor reception room.

Ogilvie was in his element. Things going wrong were a justification for his innate pessimism about other people's competence. Like a general summoned to the front to sort out tactics in a military campaign that had struck an unforeseen pocket of resistance, he knew which subordinates to blame, which ones to liven up, and which general procedures to be urgently implemented.

'I've already briefed Pearce and McLellan and they'll be taking all preliminary legal measures required.' His voice rose half an octave on such occasions and he jabbed out each phrase emphatically as if to overrule objections before anyone had actually made any. 'I'm preparing an urgent visit to the scene of these depredations myself. See what security measures have been neglected. Or never properly applied.' Whatever the alternatives, he would predictably opt for the one which gave him most excuse to be peevish. 'These contractors nowadays ... security measures written into their agreement, for all the notice they ever take ... I was unhappy with that company from the start.'

Which was unfortunate, thought Beth, since he had been the one to engage them.

'What's happened?' She edged in beside Luke, and smiled a brief good-morning at Lesley Torrance.

Rather than showing impatience at having to go through the facts again for the latecomer, Ogilvie was happy to hear his own voice, shocked and denunciatory, cataloguing the outrage.

It appeared that the men at the restoration site had downed tools because their work was being systematically sabotaged. A section of wall put up one day would be reduced to a heap of stones overnight. The temporary access road needed for a JCB and supply trucks was repeatedly blocked by rubble or by a subsidence that could not have been natural.

'No such thing as a night watchman?' said Morwenna, tight-lipped.

'They had one, but he handed in his notice. Probably bribed by that cabal of local landowners. I've said all along we'd have trouble with them. That's why we had to engage a Glasgow firm to do the work. There aren't many skilled workers living in the region, and those that do are still as scared of the *gentry*' — Ogilvie spat the word out — 'as their old folk were. Haven't changed much over the centuries, these Highland layabouts.'

Beth felt Luke flinch beside her. He was waiting, as she was, for Morwenna Ross's reaction to this ill-judged slur on folk about whom, after all, this whole project had been set up.

Very coolly Morwenna said: 'I've been thinking it was high time for a visit to the site anyway. Now is as good a time as any for a full appraisal. Analyse the setting for artefacts we're accumulating, and at the same time see what these other problems involve.'

'Och, I'd not be advising *your* coming yet, dear lady. Not until we've sorted out this setback.' Ogilvie tried an avuncular smile. 'Mr Ross would never forgive me if I let you run into any unpleasantness.'

'Mr Ross has complete faith in my ability to cope with any situation which may arise. That's why he sent me. And he sure will want *my* appraisal of the situation.' She glanced about the room. 'Who do you reckon we should take? I guess we'll need Lady Torrance along to give her judgment on the placing of domestic objects — provided the basic structure hasn't been significantly damaged. And in view of this recent disturbance, her past police experience may prove most valuable.'

'I'm afraid I can't flash a warrant card at folk any more,' said Lesley.

'Luke, you have all the legal and historical records off by heart. We may need you to pick out relevant bits of them on site while we're evaluating the overall problem. And Simon' — it was a patronizing rather than friendly use of his Christian name — 'I'm sure I can leave all transport arrangements in your capable hands.'

'Naturally. But I do still think —'

'Shall we fix to leave an hour from now, say?'

As they all moved out of the room, Luke said to Beth: 'And what will you get up to while we're away?'

'Any excitement that offers. Such as checking on our regular full-page ads in the autumn tourist brochures, and sorting out the left-overs from that last trade festival. My life is all go!'

The Merciless Dead

*

The party had been gone less than half an hour when the switchboard asked Beth if she wanted to take a call from a Mr Randal Grant. She was surprised and a bit disturbed by her own readiness to do just that.

'Miss Crichton? Nice to hear your voice again.' His own voice was tinged with a mixture of friendly mockery and something mildly suggestive. She ought not to have found it agreeable, but she did. 'May seem a bit pushy,' he went on, 'but I was wondering if you'd like to see me at work.'

'I think you gave me a very clear impression of your work when we last met.'

'The results of some of it, yes. Not the actual creative bit itself.'

Shockingly she heard herself saying, almost like some pouting little starlet: 'We're not discussing your speciality of nude poses, are we?'

A faint intake of breath whispered in the earpiece. 'Not unless you want to make a definite date.'

'Which I don't.'

'A pity. But I wasn't having any such hopes, anyway. I merely wondered if you'd care to come along on an assignment I've got today. Get an idea how I go about things. Decide whether you want to use me. I mean, whether the mighty Ross empire would like to use me on its current project.'

Naturally he was following up his first approach. A nudge, a reminder of the reason for their earlier contact. Of course he wanted to contribute to the programme — and get paid for it.

'I've already made a note of your qualifications,' she said.

'Oeuvre,' he said. 'Please call it my oeuvre. Sounds so much more dignified. And expensive.'

'Look,' she said, 'just what did you mean by me watching you at work? I mean, I can't commission you to do anything specific for us. Not right at this moment, anyway.'

'I have a customer. One of my come-into-our-stately-home shoots. Glossy magazine feature, with gracious chatelaine allowing the hoi polloi a look at her family treasures. A pretty routine job, as far as I'm concerned. But you could come along and pretend to be my assistant. Carry a bag, flourish the light meter, look efficient — if the act appeals to you?'

'Why me? You've surely got your usual team. People like you usually work with a fairly close little group.'

'I just hoped to impress you with my skill. So you'd engage me forthwith.'

She knew there must be any number of off-putting answers. But again somebody else seemed to be using her reflexes. 'When would this be?'

'This very afternoon. Rather short notice. But I gather the lady prefers to have it done while her husband's away up north, or something.'

'And where? Some reconditioned castle in the Borders?'

'Not that far away. Lockhart House, off the Pencaitland road.'

'Just a minute.' A chill was tingling in the back of Beth's neck. 'That's a bit weird.'

'A lot of these old piles are.'

'No, I mean … isn't that the Ferguson home?'

'It is indeed. As you'll see, I deal only with the finest families.'

While the husband's away up north … She had a creepy feeling she knew where that husband might be right now.

'You do realize who the lady of the house is?' she said.

'Mrs Ferguson, not surprisingly.'

'Mrs Ferguson now, yes. Nadine Ferguson. Before that she was a Mrs Ross. *Our* Mr Ross. James Fergus Ross's second wife. A very nasty divorce. There'd always been bad feeling between the Rosses and this Ferguson character, and that didn't help.'

'I'm afraid I'm not up to speed on all these old dynastic feuds.' He waited a moment, then said: 'Well, then?'

'Well what?'

'I mean, this adds a whole new dimension to my invitation. Right now you're all busy tracking down Ross memorabilia. Wouldn't it help to snoop around his ex's place? Her husband his old rival, and wife-stealer, and whatever? Might even find something that's … strayed.'

Such as the mysterious Ross Tapestry? Beth gulped. 'That's crazy. I mean, we've no reason to suppose … that is …'

'But you're dying to have a look, aren't you?'

*

Lockhart House was set back behind a high stone wall following every curve of the road. Each stone gatepost was topped with a mythical creature which Beth did not have time to identify. Inside, the long drive curved more crookedly than the wall, cunningly withholding the view of the house itself until the last possible moment, when it spread out beyond a three-arched bridge over an artificial burn.

Nadine Ferguson was waiting for them on the terrace, a nineteenth-century addition of incongruous yet impressive Caithness slabs to an eighteenth-century Palladian house. She had posed herself against one of the columns of the façade, a gracious hostess who would have looked more at home outside an expensive London or Edinburgh night club than this East Lothian retreat. She was wearing a bright floral Versace silk shirt and white slacks tight enough to show that her hips were too wide. She carried a Louis Vuitton bag for which she could have had little immediate use, and which she ostentatiously laid on a gleamingly polished table in the entrance lobby through which she led her guests. Above the main door was a coat of arms of dubious provenance.

Beth had an apprehensive moment when Mrs Ferguson stared hard at her, and tried desperately to remember whether they had ever met on Ross premises or at some official function. But of course she hadn't joined the Foundation until after the divorce. The woman's stare of possible disapproval might have been due to her not having expected the photographer to bring a young woman along with him, distracting his full attention from his hostess.

All publicity photographs of James Fergus Ross and Nadine together had been discarded from the files on orders from head office after the divorce. But Luke, of course, had kept his own private little hoard. Beth recalled a couple of studies of the younger woman leaning forward to expose her cleavage while fawning up to Ross, who in turn had been caught with one of those simpering, silly grins that lecherous old men with younger partners produce for the camera. She was some years older now, but still leaned instinctively in that same way towards Randal.

Old habits died hard. Nadine Witherington had been a footloose Sloane, or its Morningside equivalent, whose father had given her a large packet of shares in a freight carrying firm which James Fergus Ross had intentions of taking over. She had done fashion shows for charity and featured regularly in the gossip columns of magazine colour supplements, once or twice in drugs investigations, once in and out of rehab, with bleary yuppies usually in attendance … until she began to realize that the endless partying was beginning to show. At a shareholders' meeting addressed by Ross on a flying visit from Toronto she made sure of a personal introduction. It was time to give up the raves and hangovers and settle down with a rich widower, provided the accommodation was up to her exacting standards. And when she grew bored of all that, there was the thrill of being back in the gossip columns with tales of an affair and a high society divorce: the sort of thing that so many of her fashionable friends indulged in.

Here, her second husband's residence was impressive enough. It had once been the home of the Keirs of Traprain, one of the few Lowland families to join Prince Charles Edward's forces when they reached Edinburgh on their way south into England. Dispossessed after Culloden, their estate was taken over by a Northumbrian Forster, and passed through several families over the years. Inside, the ceilings of the house were a riot of ornamental plasterwork, in one room with the rose and thistle of the Union, in others harp and fleur-de-lys motifs. Moving from one room to another, Beth had little time to inspect each one in detail, but was conscious of cracks and discoloration in ceilings and window embrasures, musty carpets, and an overriding dampness. In the main drawing room, a frieze of classical motifs was broken by pseudo-marble heads of Greek or Roman gods, chipped into what might have been deliberate copies of ancient busts or a sign of neglect. They contrasted oddly with heads of shooting trophies jutting out of walls in no sort of balanced sequence.

Each room had been adapted to accommodate a different aspect of Ferguson history. In the first were the inevitable sporting trophies, pride of place being given to a silver cup for some shooting achievement. Next door were photographs and maps of the original logging business in Newfoundland, and a display of Red Indian relics: totem birds, wooden deer masks, a prayer-stick trailing some bedraggled feathers, and a glass case of embroidered gloves and beadwork. 'Trophies collected by my husband's great-great-grandfather in the early settlement days,' Mrs Ferguson contributed.

Randal studied a section of totem pole, propped up in a window alcove with the raven head a dark silhouette against the sunlight. 'That would make a nice study, but the detail would be lost with that light behind it. Is it all right if I shift it a little this way?'

'By all means, Mr Grant. I leave it all to you.' As he lifted the section of pole further into the room and set it against the inner wall, she gushed on: 'My husband's family was one of the first to get on good terms with the natives. Accepted as honorary chiefs, you know. At one time they did get involved together in whisky running from Canada into the United States.' Her arch giggle was directed at Randal, not deigning to include Beth. 'So naughty, but it helped the family fortunes!'

The Merciless Dead

A book of fading photographs lay open on an occasional table. While Randal was taking his picture, Beth bent over it, and gasped. 'But that's ...' She stopped herself in time.

Mrs Ferguson looked at her sharply. 'You know the site?'

'No, no. It just reminded me of ... no, I must be mistaken ...' She lied quickly. 'I thought it was a sawmill where my grandfather used to work in Galloway.'

'Most certainly not. A lot further away than Galloway. That's near a logging site in Newfoundland. One of my husband's few triumphs,' she added with another laugh, this time with a sour edge to it. 'Managed to snatch the concession from under my first husband's nose. Jamie Ross, that is. Who never forgave him.' She looked complacent, as if the fact of having had two conflicting husbands was an enviable attribute.

As Randal replaced the totem pole, she changed tack and prattled happily about the family's distinguished record with the other kind of Indians, confirmed by the next room dedicated to a slice of colonial history.

'Distinguished colonial service,' she declaimed. 'It used to be in the Ferguson blood, of course.' *Used to be*? Beth found it disconcerting that Nadine Ferguson's tone veered so unpredictably between boasting and sneering. 'Or going at things bull-headed, anyway. Not terribly good at conserving their gains.' In front of a coloured print of a shikar party on a tiger hunt, dominated by a man who could well have been Ferguson's father in topee and full uniform, framed on the wall above a tiger-skin rug, she said with a throwaway laugh whose would-be sophistication failed to conceal another sneer: 'Some of his ancestors knew how to make money — and use it profitably.' She picked up an ivory croquet mallet and made an awkward swing with it. 'Such a splendid time they all had, until that dreadful Mutiny. Sholto loves to talk about it — almost as if he had been there himself.' Probably, thought Beth, one of those families whose mortgaged estates had been redeemed by the loot they had acquired during the carnage.

On a small lacquered table near the door a heavy gold bracelet and two glass bangles encircled an intricate figurine so small that one had to stoop to make out its contours. When Beth straightened up she saw the gleam in Randal's eyes. The carving was of an athletic position from the *Kama Sutra*.

'Exquisite, isn't it?' Nadine Ferguson put her hand on Randal's shoulder so that she could bend closer over the entwined figures. 'Do you know what a distinguished Indian visitor once told us about it? 'This position requires great holiness and the assistance of two other ladies.'' She took an inordinately long time to straighten up and take her weight off Randal.

As if to symbolize the worldwide influence of the Fergusons, halfway along a picture gallery of somebody's ancestors — it was difficult to see any consistent family likeness — was a massive trunk with huge brass locks and stickers from Africa, India, Canada, and the United States.

At nearly every corner were pictures of Nadine in silver frames, accompanied by a fluffy dog. The largest, shorn of the dog, was a wedding photograph of herself in a white off-the-shoulder dress — a photograph which, thought Beth cattily, must have been touched up to make those shoulders look glowingly enticing — clinging to the arm of her second husband in full uniform with a couple of medals. A sequence of ornately gilded frames enshrined groups of more impressive medals, each on a red plush background. The wall behind was dominated by a large painting of the same man in full Highland rig at an Edinburgh Tattoo.

'I think we ought to make a feature of that,' said Mrs Ferguson. 'He'll be furious if we don't get *something* of that kind in. At least he cuts a fine figure of a man, doesn't he?'

As Randal was setting up a flattering angle on the painting, she chattered on, making it clear that the arrangement of exhibits from room to room was entirely her own work. 'Such confusion when I married him. Held so many important positions, but no sense of organization whatsoever. Like so many men.' She smiled archly at Randal.

They went on room by room, stopping at intervals to take in features which Randal suggested or Nadine Ferguson demanded. As he worked out a composition featuring a large gong shining in a mahogany frame on the first landing, Beth wondered frivolously if the man of the house sent a servant to strike it when requiring the services of his wife.

Randal turned to her from time to time asking her technical opinion on an angle, and asking for items of equipment which she hoped she produced in the correct order. Mrs Ferguson glanced at each of her movements disparagingly. It was not, prayed Beth, that she suspected something phoney about this young assistant; rather that she would have preferred to have Randal to herself. In nearly every room she found an excuse to touch Randal's arm to draw his attention to some item, laugh in what she undoubtedly considered an infectious manner, and sigh admiringly at his skill.

Thinking it was time to make at least a polite contribution, Beth said: 'This must all need a lot of upkeep.'

Mrs Ferguson emitted something closer to a snort than a laugh. 'Upkeep? Without adequate staff? You really have no idea. Nobody you can rely on nowadays.' It was a feminine echo of Simon Ogilvie. 'We've had to cut down. Not at all what I've been accustomed to. At the moment I've got only one useless gardener and an odd-job man, and a wretched woman for the indoors. And I have serious doubts about the honesty of all of them.'

At the end, as they were leaving, she was all charm again. 'Well, Mr Grant. Your magazine will be in touch with me about the date of this feature, I trust? And you *will* send me the pictures for my approval first?'

'But of course, Mrs Ferguson. Leave it all to me.'

'And if you find there's anything that hasn't quite worked out' — her hand clasped his as they stood on the terrace — 'don't hesitate to come back. Preferably when my husband isn't here to get argumentative.' She produced another of her little giggles.

*

Back at Randal's flat, he said: 'Coming in for coffee?'

'Provided you really mean coffee.'

'For starters, anyway.'

She found the kettle and made the coffee while he unloaded his gear.

'Some interesting stuff in that place,' he said, his head on one side, waiting for her answer.

She knew which piece he meant to conjure up in her mind. And shamefully she would have liked to see an enlargement of that *Kama Sutra* figurine.

'Obviously Mrs Ferguson would be happy to inflame your passions.' And she found herself saying: 'I thought perhaps you were going to make do with *me*. Hurl me on that couch and have your wicked way with me.'

'Disappointed?'

'When it came to it, you couldn't really be bothered.'

'Not until you want it, too.'

'You mean you prefer your victims to be in the mood for rape?'

'In which case it's not rape.' He pushed some folders out of the way and put his coffee cup down on the bench. 'Right. I'll be sending you copies of what we collected today.'

'So that I can put in a good word for you with the Foundation?'

'Of course. And they'll want to engage me for a huge fee. Isn't that why I've been taking up your time?'

'I'll look forward to seeing them, anyway.'

'And before you go …' He finished his coffee, looked at her almost pleadingly. 'Let me add you to today's collection.'

'If you're hoping for a quick strip-tease —'

'I was thinking of taking a study of your face.' He was reaching for a small camera.

'My face?'

'It's so delightful.'

'But nothing like one of those Indian masks?'

He was clicking away as if taking a hasty set of seaside snapshots. 'Nothing like.'

At the door she said: 'Are you going to take her up on that invitation to go back — when her husband's not there, and *I'm* not there?'

'Jealous already? A promising sign.'

There was a flippancy in everything he said which made him easy to be with and yet more disturbing than Luke's earnestness had ever been.

8

The road narrowed and a breeze across a ruffled lochan plucked at the side of the Espace. Luke Drummond was driving, and from where Lesley sat she could see from the angle of his head and an occasional glimpse of his eyes in the mirror that he was enjoying himself. Not that he was smiling or muttering a song to himself, but his earnest concentration and the occasional odd twitch of his left ear fitted in with the way she had already sized him up. He took his pleasures seriously, but to him they were nevertheless pleasures. Getting things right without fuss was a constant gratification. Unlike Simon Ogilvie, who enjoyed the fuss as much as getting things right. Ogilvie had insisted on sitting beside the driver, to spell out each petty detail of the route, tell him where to turn and not to turn — 'I think we ought to go right at that crossroads coming up ... stick to the bypass ... do keep an eye on that soft verge' — all of which Luke blandly ignored.

Lesley was seated behind Ogilvie, with Morwenna on her right. Morwenna had not spoken at all during their first hour getting clear of the city and then the stretch of motorway and the A9 to Inverness. They stopped for brief lunch outside Tain, with Ogilvie supplying most of the conversation in the form of instructions about the care necessary on the twisting roads of Sutherland. Still Morwenna contributed nothing; but Lesley sensed an increased concentration in the woman beside her as they turned west across those lonely moorlands, broken by clumps of alder climbing the banks of shallow burns, and stands of birch and spruce. Her gaze was fixed for long minutes on the ghostly ridges and troughs of old lazybeds, as if gouged by fingernails out of the earth. Then she leaned forward and stared past Lesley at a drystone dyke around a fairly modern farmhouse. And this drew words out of her at last. 'Stones from the wrecked homes of the persecuted.' A few miles later, as they passed the outlines of an old croft with a collapsed lintel wrenched over like a dislocated shoulder, marked with a splash of bright white paint in the shape of a cross, she burst out even more bitterly: 'Isn't that just great? All smartened up by the local tourist board for the benefit of visitors with their cameras. Some guy even smart enough to add the laird's mark, to tell the poor wretches who lived there it's time to get the hell out, or else.'

What was so different, then, Lesley wondered, between that preserved shred of a banished community and the plans the Rosses had for their own contrived memorial?

The sky was darkening. Without warning, a sudden blast of hail scoured one side of the road, while the other stayed clear. Western skies shone a tranquil blue, with blackness to the east. And linking the two was a squared-off rainbow which Lesley would not have believed in if she had not actually seen it shimmering against that contradictory background.

'The rowan tree by that heap of stones.' Luke spoke over his shoulder, calm and explanatory. 'They used to plant the rowans by their crofts to ward off evil spirits.'

'Didn't work against the factors, eh?' said Ogilvie.

Morwenna stared for a long minute at the back of his neck.

The tree had been warped by the winds into a shape that to Lesley looked tortuously evil in itself. There was something weird about this whole landscape. They were here only on sufferance. There were things unseen, still waiting, shadows of something incorporeal, waiting for intruders to transgress. Then those true inhabitants would come to life again and deal out punishment. It was all more stark and disturbing than the historical and refurbishing discussions in Edinburgh. Lesley shuddered, and at once knew that Morwenna was aware of this.

As if to deride, or maybe reassure her, Morwenna said in a schoolmistressy tone: 'The cities have enough museums, you know. Just a jumble of unrelated material with no specific local or regional relevance. And they sure as hell don't have the atmosphere. That's what we're here to preserve.'

Whatever the traditions of this whole region might mean to her and old Jamie Ross, Lesley would have thought that many original inhabitants would in the end have been glad to get away from it.

The car stopped suddenly, with a scrape of tyres on the gritty road surface.

'This is ridiculous.' Ogilvie's voice was as petulant as an elderly woman's bitching at a careless young nephew in the driving seat. 'Drummond, how on earth did you get us into this?'

A clump of rowan had masked the sharp corner until they were right on it. Then Luke had to stamp on the brakes to avoid running into a heap of timber piled across the road.

'Somebody trying to tell us we're not welcome,' he observed.

'Ridiculous,' said Ogilvie again. 'That's illegal. Creating an obstruction. We have every right to use this route.'

Luke opened his window and leaned out. Beyond his shoulder Lesley glimpsed a couple of figures picking their way across the spongy ground, looking back at the Espace and apparently laughing.

Warily Luke backed a few yards until he had reached one of the narrow bulges laid out as passing places. After what became a jerky six-point turn, he drove back to a junction which they had passed half a mile back. While Ogilvie muttered some incomprehensible directions, Luke drove towards the rim of a small plantation of Scots pine. As the road slewed again to hug the edge of the plantation, a dark green truck with the lettering of The Reay Forestry Group on its sides emerged from one of the woodland rides, and slewed across the road in front of them. The driver leaned out and shouted: 'Sorry, ye can no go any further. This is a private road.'

'I've had enough of this,' raged Ogilvie. 'Let me out and I'll make a few things clear.'

'If I were you, sir —'

'You're not me, Drummond. Which is why, young man, I hold a top administrative position and you don't.'

Lesley glanced at Morwenna, who seemed uncertain whether to be amused or impatient.

Ogilvie got out and strode towards the truck.

'The other road is blocked, and it's essential that we get to Achnachrain without any more nonsense.'

The two men in the truck were grinning but not bothering to reply.

'You're causing just as much of an obstruction as that rubbish dumped on the highway over there.' Lesley was mildly surprised at Ogilvie's sudden switch to calm but self-righteously forceful speech. 'Please move your vehicle and let us pass.'

'I've already told you — this is a private road. Sorry.' He was clearly not the slightest bit sorry.

'According to my recently authenticated map, this is in fact part of the properties bought to form an integral part of the Ross All-Abilities Path through the wood.' He took out a mobile phone. To Lesley it seemed an incongruous possession for someone like Ogilvie, but he was flourishing it as if confident in it as a firearm. 'I shall ring the police.'

'They'll take a gey long time to get here.'

'Then we shall wait. And the longer it takes, the more serious the charge we shall lay.'

It could be only an empty threat. Morwenna let out a faint sigh of exasperation and stared silently past Ogilvie.

The driver of the truck glanced at her, tried a half-polite, half-dismissive nod, and sounded less certain than before. 'You'll no' find much of a welcome if you do get to Achnachrain. I'd no' be going further, if I were you.'

'You are not me.' Ogilvie seemed to be fond of this declaration. 'We *shall* be going further, so before I need to take official steps' — he brandished his mobile again — 'perhaps you will move out of our way.'

With grudging slowness the driver edged back on to the exit from the plantation. Ogilvie stumped back to the Espace and climbed back in with a self-satisfied smile, as if awaiting a round of applause.

It was left to Luke to consult the map he had marked up before leaving, and find an old drove road lurching in the right direction. The wheels squelched through the soggy ground, but it was just navigable. Lesley wondered if there would be any other deliberate yet paltry obstructions in their way before they reached their destination, but there was no further sign of opposition until they were approaching a large three-storey building which looked out of proportion in that landscape. As a defensive castle it might have made sense; but it was not ancient enough for that, and boasted no battlements or gun-loops. There was a web of scaffolding at the east end, and a collapsed heap of scaffolding poles halfway along the frontage.

Luke bumped the car at last on to a smoother, wider road and stopped in front of the central door. 'Used to be the girnel — the Rent House, where the tenants came to pay their rents in kind.'

'Before the rents were refused without reason,' said Morwenna quietly, 'and they were driven out anyway.'

'Under adaptation' — Ogilvie had been waiting to get his word in — 'as a Museum and Interpretation Centre to supplement the restored croft.' He opened his window and waved to a workman who had come round the corner of the building. 'A word with you, my guid man.'

The man approached warily. 'If it's that you're coming here to make more trouble —'

'We represent the Ross Foundation. We are paying you for the work you're supposed to be doing. And we've come to find out what the delays are. I have had reports of everything falling behind, and of some outside interference.'

'Aye. If you're really wanting to know, I'd say you'd have less trouble if you was to turn yon building into a distillery. Ye'd be doing a good trade with all the huntin' and shootin' folk.'

'Your opinion's not invited. We're here to talk about this job and how it can be speeded up.'

'Aye. Then you'd best be talking to Mr McAlister.'

The foreman was a well-set man with gingery whiskers and tobacco-stained teeth. His manner was courteous, but by no means deferential. You felt that while you might not like what he said, it would be well thought out and bluntly honest.

'We've been having trouble, that's the way it is. Things we've put up during the day get pulled down at night.'

'By some local ghosts?' Ogilvie sneered.

McAlister's tone remained steady. He pointed to the collapsed scaffolding at the end of the building. 'Something wi' a lot more strength than bogles. They'd not be wanting the work finished. Not wanting any part of it here.' Things got pulled down overnight, he explained. Sacks of rubble were strewn over the floors inside or tipped into the burn, clogging it so that it overflowed. Lorry tyres were slashed.

'Damn it, man, don't you have a watchman? With what we're paying you, you could afford a man to keep his eyes open all night. And report any intrusions immediately to the local police. Do you just sleep through any sort of noise?'

McAlister, keeping his temper in the teeth of Ogilvie's squeaky aggressiveness, explained that his workmen were accommodated in three caravans — 'near the hotel over yonder.' They all came from Glasgow. There were few local contractors of any size in this bleak region, and those craftsmen who did small local repairs and maintenance jobs wouldn't touch this one. Local landowners had made it clear that they might no longer employ anyone who worked on this site.

'I set a watchman over here to start with. Took it in turns. But one got badly hit, and there was no-one to pin it on. Told it was an accident, but we're getting the message.'

'Ridiculous, in this day and age. What are the police doing about it? You *have* bothered to get in touch with the police?'

McAlister's patience showed signs of fraying. 'Police? How many police d'you think they can let loose over this godforsaken wilderness?'

'There were enough in the old days,' said Morwenna quietly to Lesley. 'Enough police to beat up old men and women and children when they tried to resist being thrown out of their homes. Enough to smash in women's skulls and trample them into the ground.'

Ogilvie was blustering on. 'When you take on a job of this kind, it's your responsibility to install necessary safeguards. If you can't contact the police, it's up to you to adopt precautions of your own.'

McAlister took a long time to reply. At last he said, as if explaining to a confused child: 'I'll tell you how it is. We've needed protection once or twice on other jobs. Working on a ferry terminal last year, there was a wee bit of a dispute between two companies. Could gie ye the name of a security group in Ullapool, if it'd be of any help.'

Ogilvie harrumphed for a few seconds. 'I don't see we should allow ourselves to be terrorized into a position of having to commit further expenditure to the employment of mercenaries. Surely the responsibility lies with you and your —'

From the back of the car Morwenna said: 'Take the address of those security people. Get in touch the moment we reach the hotel. We don't have time to waste. Mr Ross is already getting very impatient with this whole thing.'

Lesley wondered how much bribery or back-scratching or hands in back pockets — call it what you like — there would be before this job was finished. She was growing fidgety about her own involvement in the project.

They drove on.

Luke smoothly resumed his self-appointed task of tourist guide as they came to the three caravans McAlister had mentioned and were approaching the Raven Hotel: a long two-storey white-harled building with a single-storey wing at the east end, sheltering a car park. 'Used to be a hunting lodge, set up after the strath had been cleared,' Luke explained. 'Sheep runs over to the west, shooting and stalking up through the north-east. Then it was tarted up a bit for the sporting types and passing tourists, and a small bar for the locals. Not all that many of those, I'd imagine.'

'And we bought it,' said Ogilvie smugly. 'Bought it a couple of years ago under the noses of the local squires and brought it up to modern standards. They still use it themselves — nowhere else to go — but they've hated every minute of being beholden to us.'

Four men in heavy tweeds emerged from the hotel and leaned on shooting sticks, sizing up the newcomers as if choosing the best angle from which to fire at them.

'Waiting to break in and tear out all the bedroom fittings, and disconnect the water and electricity?' said Morwenna.

'Well ... um ... I'm not saying they'd go that far,' said Ogilvie.

'Who knows what they may have inherited from their accursed forebears? *They* thought nothing of tearing a building apart. Or tearing up the bodies of those inside.'

The man at the head of the group waited for them to get out of the car, and then said: 'Come to see what a shambles this whole operation is? Got the sense to put a stop to it?'

'Colonel Ferguson, I think,' said Ogilvie stiffly. 'I believe we've met before.'

The man's face was a blotchy red: red with a permanent irritation, perhaps, plus a fair amount of drink taken in the hotel bar. His mouth produced a spluttering bark rather than a voice. 'So we have. When you've been up here trespassing on my land.'

'Using a right of way.'

'Load of nonsense. We're the people who keep this land fit for use, and we're the ones who decide on rights of any damn thing.' He sported a very English accent, with a little puff of breath sounding like 'wha' at the end of each heavily emphatic sentence. His thick lower lip had a permanent droop of contempt, as if it required a great effort of condescension for him to speak at all. For all the English assumptions of his voice, his clothing was demonstratively tweedy, with trews in a tartan which Lesley felt was trying to lay claim to some family relationship with the Campbells'. He was staring at her. 'And who might this be?'

'Lady Torrance,' said Ogilvie, his voice and his body somehow standing to attention. 'Colonel Sholto Ferguson.'

'Och, aye.' The man was suddenly overdoing a comic Scottish accent as if wanting in some way to caricature what was going on around them. 'I believe I've met your husband at some Border function. The baronet by the back door — that's him, hey?'

His bloodshot eyes took in Morwenna. Before he could speak, she said: 'I'm Morwenna Ross.'

'Ah, so the sad old goat's found another wife. To make up for the one he lost to me?'

'I'm Mr Ross's daughter-in-law.'

'Ah, yes. The one with the husband who couldn't even sail a toy boat.'

One of the men behind him mumbled what might have been a protest.

Ogilvie made a louder one. 'Whatever your pretensions, Colonel Ferguson, I'll not stand here and let you insult these ladies.'

'Don't worry, Mr Ogilvie.' Morwenna was still quiet and steady. 'We were well aware we could expect no courtesy from descendants of the rogues who took brutal pleasure out of the Clearances.'

'Oh, God, not that old story again? Clearances? There never were any. People were given their fares to clear off overseas and settle in lands that suited them better. *Clearances*? Sentimental claptrap.'

'Along this very strath, Patrick Sellars harassed families who for generations had —'

'Patrick Sellars cleared the region of layabouts, and was himself cleared in open court of any wrongdoing.'

'A court whose jury consisted of eight landed proprietors and a couple of livestock merchants.'

'Nitpicking,' bellowed Ferguson. 'The likes of you got nowhere then, and you'll get nowhere now.'

He stomped away, leading his companions to a 4x4 parked at the far end of the hotel.

Where his eyes had been blearily quarrelsome, Morwenna's had gone steely with a dark, cold hatred. Lesley experienced a sharp jolt as if some weapon had bruised her as it swung past — as if Morwenna really believed she might strike Ferguson down by the sheer force of that concentrated hatred.

'It was the ancestors of those scum who brought in police and the military to humiliate and destroy. Or hired bullies at short notice. Clearly we need to hire our own mercenaries to defend those properties we're reclaiming.'

Lesley was glad to be out of the car, easing her back and legs after the jolting along lumpy tracks and roads. She put her small travelling bag on the window seat of her single bedroom, looking out across a stark landscape made wildly beautiful under the glow of the setting sun. The sky seemed briefly to grow brighter rather than fade submissively into twilight, with the great leonine hulk of distant Ben Hope black against the glow.

The Merciless Dead

As she went downstairs again, Ogilvie was obediently phoning the security firm, to be informed by a recorded message that they would be reopening at nine o'clock the following morning, but if it was an urgent message regarding one of their present commitments there was a sequence of individual emergency numbers.

They had agreed to meet for dinner in half an hour. Lesley went out into the long-lasting twilight.

The wind which had buffeted the car on the way here had dropped, leaving an uncanny stillness. She took a few steps away from the bright windows of the hotel, and watched the light along the far horizon gradually seeping away below stretches of dark strips of cloud, some humped as if following the contours of the braes below. A few yards ahead of her on a low knoll was the even darker silhouette of a heap of stones.

'The cairn of the weeping stones.' A croaky voice came out of the shadow of a tree.

She gasped at the sudden sound, and peered into the gloom. An old woman was sitting hunched on a branch twisted down to ground level. There was just enough light from the side door of the hotel to pick out her bowed shoulders and narrow face with its short, jutting nose.

'I'm sorry. I didn't notice there was anyone —'

''Twas built by the family from the brae yonder. A large stone for each of the parents, and a wee one for each bairn. It stands right where they had their last sight o' hame. Disturb them now, and they'll weep blood.' The woman edged her way closer to Lesley and, her face still in shadow, peered at her closely. 'No, you're no' the one.'

'I'm sorry?'

'It has been said by the Braham Seer that a dark woman will come out o' the west and settle the scores o' the dispossessed.' It was an incantation that could have sounded embarrassingly silly; but in this weird dusk its resonances sent a chill down Lesley's arms.

She tried, clumsily, to keep it casual. 'There are plenty of legends around these parts, I can tell.'

'And if it's that ye're staying a while, ye'll learn they mean no good to incomers. There were folk who took away handfuls o' grass and soil from the graves of their kinfolk — and left behind them an undying curse on those as would meddle.'

Lesley was tempted to say this all sounded like a fine basis for a horror film; but at the same time she was conscious that it was no laughing matter.

Nick had made a joke of it at the weekend. 'Hey, all this rough stuff out there. Can't I come along to look after you — ride shotgun?'

She hadn't been over-worried by the sullen men at the road junction, or by Ferguson and his companions. But now they had arrived safely, she felt absurdly unsafe, more than she had ever felt as a serving police officer in the thick of violence. All of them here needed defending against something less tangible.

'You know what we're here for?' she asked.

'Och aye, 1 ken well what you'll be trying to mend. But there'll only be more deaths to add to those souls already destroyed.'

The woman struggled to her feet and walked past Lesley into the hotel. As Lesley followed, the manager came out of his office, said, 'Goodnight, Mrs Aird', and smiled at Lesley. 'You've met the old crone, I see.'

'Old crone? Not very complimentary.'

'Mrs Aird plays up to it, bless her. We have to keep her on. Done the cleaning here since the hotel was set up. A real character. They say she has the second sight, but she's not the only one round here. Our regular visitors love all that. Always call her the old crone, and she always has a fine retort for any of them.' He raised a welcoming hand as Morwenna walked through. 'You'll all be going in to dinner now?'

Mrs Aird had stopped for a moment by the service door. She and Morwenna stared briefly at each other. Then Mrs Aird shook her head and went on through the door.

Ogilvie was fussing in the dining room. 'You'll be sitting by me, Mrs Ross? We do have a lot to talk about. And first thing in the morning I'll check we've got that security matter settled, and then we can go to see the croft itself, right? That's what it's really all about, isn't it?'

Lesley glanced over her shoulder. Mrs Aird's shadow, uninvited, was somehow still with them, her voice still echoing. All part of the service — over-acting for the sake of visitors?

More deaths to add to those already destroyed ...?

9

Ten minutes after she had settled at her desk in the morning, Beth's phone rang. She assumed the call was most likely to be a chatty progress report from Luke or maybe a fussy demand for some piece of information from Ogilvie.

'Beth.' It was Shirley at the switchboard. 'There's a Mr Grant asking for you. A Randal Grant. Do you want to talk to him, or do I tell him you're in conference?'

'Conference, at this hour in the morning?' There was an odd tingling in her toes, but she kept her voice steady. 'No, I suppose I'd better talk to him.'

As he began speaking she conjured up an immediate picture of him sprawled languidly in that wicker chair in the corner of his studio. Yet his voice was actually crisp and businesslike.

'I've got a nice set of prints to show you.'

'What, already?'

'We aim to please.'

'Have you been up all night?'

'Nothing else to do with my nights.' This time laughter did creep into his voice. 'No, really, it's not that complicated a process.'

'Can you bring them round?'

The pause seemed interminable. At last he said: 'Naturally Mrs Ferguson will expect me to make a personal delivery. But for your batch ... well, your place is always so full of hustle and bustle. I thought perhaps you'd like to come round here again, where we won't be interrupted.'

Now she was the one to sustain a silence. But she knew all along what her answer would be. 'I've got a few things to sort out here.' Which was quite untrue. 'I could be round with you in about half-an-hour.'

'I'll have the coffee pot on the go.'

She then had to find a few meaningless things to fill in the time she had committed herself to. When she did leave the building she was walking briskly as she always did, but more breathlessly than usual.

The smell of coffee did indeed greet her as Randal opened the door. He was dressed in a grey shirt and fawn chinos, and his feet were bare. He smelt as if he had just stepped out of the shower.

'Hello. Nice morning.'

'Yes,' she said. 'Hello.'

A line of photographic prints had been pinned up on a wall board. One of the most striking grabbed her attention immediately. But her eyes strayed. Propped on an easel at an angle from the display was the portrait study of herself he had taken on her last visit.

'Attractive, isn't it?' said Randal. 'Beautiful, in fact.'

She did not remember having felt as wistful as that half-profile suggested. Nor had she deliberately parted her lips slightly in that amused, provocative way.

'It's … flattering,' she said. 'But then, I suppose it's your job to make your sitters look more striking than they really are.'

'False modesty …' He waited for a long moment, then added: 'Beth.' It was the first time he had used her name. She would not have expected him to sound so shy. As if to make up for it, he rushed on: 'It would be nice to have the rest of you in the frame.'

'To add to your collection of conquests?'

'To keep apart. Very special.'

'I think we'd better concentrate on Mrs Ferguson's possessions. That's what I'm supposed to be here for.'

His prints made an impressive array. Somehow he had brought out a depth that, incongruously, hadn't existed within the rooms of the house itself. The large painting of Sholto Ferguson would have made a superb recruiting poster. The way Randal had angled his view on the Indian room made it look almost three-dimensional. But the most striking subject was that of a wooden raven's head, looking more like a Viking figurehead than what it really was — the head of a totem pole from the American Indian room.

'But what's that on the wall behind it?' said Beth suddenly.

Randal's chin jutted close to her shoulder as he bent over the print, studying the blurred shape. 'Sorry, I kept the background deliberately hazy in order to throw that head into nice dramatic relief. Why? Got some notions about it?'

'I was wondering … no, it couldn't be.'

'The suspense is killing me. Couldn't be what?'

'The Ross Tapestry. You wouldn't have heard of that, but —'

'Oh, I've heard of it. Vaguely. One of those clan traditions like the fairy flag of the MacLeods, right? Come to think of it, that thing there does look more like a tattered old flag — one of the Colonel's campaign souvenirs, maybe.'

It would be quite a coup to have identified the tapestry and established that Nadine Ferguson had carried it off, egged on by her husband's old enemy as he carried her off as well.

But where had it come from; how much of its history had she scraped together in that vacuous head of hers?

Beth moved along the display until at the end she found, half tucked away among a stack of large prints in the corner of the studio, the study of the naked girl which had dominated the room on her earlier visit. 'You like your women with large breasts?' she said.

'No, I'm not really into bulges. Preferably medium, nicely balanced but not obtrusive.'

'Good,' she said, then felt she must be flushing scarlet. 'No, I mean, I didn't mean …'

'Oh, but I think you did.' Very quietly he said: 'I don't suppose you'd let me take a picture of you?'

'To add to your gallery of conquests?' Hadn't she said something that silly only a few minutes ago?

'Just because I think you'll be very beautiful.'

As if hypnotized, Beth felt her fingers plucking at the buttons of her blouse, and finding absurd difficulty in freeing them. Until, as she was shrugging the blouse off, Randal said, with what sounded like a painful croak in the throat: 'No, don't. I'm sorry, I oughtn't to have … I mean, Beth, I'm not in the mood for taking pictures right now.'

There was a slow, intensifying pulse deep down in her stomach. 'No, neither am I,' she breathed as she eased her hips out of her tights.

Luke would have been meticulous in preparations for this moment. The bed would have been neatly laid out, the curtains half drawn, a soft light glowing behind a vase of flowers. Even, on occasion, a bottle of champagne in a bucket at exactly the right temperature for afterwards.

Here she was being pressed down to the floor, laughing a protest that was too ridiculously insincere, feeling the roughness of the tacky carpet scratching at her bottom, shifting to and fro not because of that roughness but because of Randal's insistent, driving force shaking her, shaking her from side to side. His beard scraped her breasts, and they rocked to and fro, and then his mouth was murmuring close to her ear until the murmurs became gasps and at last they were both singing almost in pain to the rhythm of his thrusts and her eager, throbbing response.

'Quite a duet,' he said at last, when they were sated and still. He pushed himself up on his elbows and looked down into her eyes. 'Beth, I think that really was what they mean about making beautiful music.' He tried her name again, like someone discovering an enticing new flavour in his mouth. 'Beth.'

They both laughed contentedly, and she lay in his arms and for a fleeting moment felt a spasm of guilt about Luke, wondering how he would feel if he knew what had just happened; and then stopped wondering, and waited for what she knew must soon happen again; and again.

*

Luke saw Lady Torrance slapping twice at the back of her neck, and then at her left wrist.

'That's something you're going to have to cope with,' she said to Morwenna Ross. 'Midges. They're famous round here, aren't they? Or infamous. Visitors aren't going to be able to concentrate on much else.'

'I've been going into this,' Ogilvie piped up. 'There's a new machine which has been devised to kill them. I've got the specification back in the office. It sounds as though they've found the answer at last.'

Yet another wonderful breakthrough, thought Luke, to add to all the others that had promised so much and failed so dismally.

The four of them walked from the hotel through a windbreak of trees towards the restored croft, Luke shifting the canvas bag he was carrying from one hand to another, hearing the occasional squeak and rattle from inside. Patches of raw ground alternated with small plantings of saplings. Shreds of timber and bushes were humped into the apparent makings of a bonfire on the edge of a small lochan, whose shallow yet dark waters were contaminated by builders' rubble.

'That had better be cleared up by opening day,' said Ogilvie threateningly.

The path was better laid than the old track which would once have led to the turf-roofed cottage. And that roof was now in better repair than it would have been originally. A few yards from the main building, a small barn seemed to be forcing its ragged stones up out of the earth. Between it and the squat front door a headstone in the grass looked garishly new, although an attempt had been made to rusticate it. Morwenna turned to Luke for guidance, but Ogilvie strutted forward. Carrying a clipboard, he

The Merciless Dead

was prepared to tick off one item after another as they proceeded round the site. Luke had provided every last little detail of those notes, swotted up from page and screen and simplified for Ogilvie's benefit. In his own mind they needed no explanations, though here everything was more vivid and immediate: here was the reality, in three dimensions. Why, then, should it all look so false, like a film set?

'That stone is in memory of a young son of the family who enlisted in the Countess of Sutherland's Regiment,' said Ogilvie solemnly, 'and was killed in the Peninsular War.'

Lesley Torrance looked puzzled. 'But if he was so loyal and remembered with respect, how could their family be thrown out?'

As Ogilvie turned over a page in search of more details, Luke added: 'If a crofter's son didn't enlist when called upon, the family would be evicted. Sometimes the man of the house would be offered a small patch of land if his boys would enlist — and then when they'd gone off to the wars, the factor reneged on the agreement and chucked the family out anyway.'

'Thank you, Drummond, *thank* you. I was about to come to that.'

The sun came out suddenly, igniting a golden blaze in clumps of gorse across the bleakness of the moorland.

Indoors, the croft was much darker until Ogilvie, consulting his clipboard, found a switch and some low-wattage light bulbs came on, set in ragged gaps between the calculatedly uneven stones of the wall, plastered and held together by plugs of clay to make them draught-proof. The exposed roof timbers were of crudely sawn bog fir. At one end of the building was a byre; the other end was living accommodation. The floor throughout was an uneven surface of hard trodden earth. There was a box bedstead in one corner, and opposite it a bench with several cardboard labels, including one rough sketch of a military medal of some kind.

Morwenna Ross turned to Luke. 'I think you've got some of Lady Torrance's wonderful finds in that bag.'

He set it on the end of the bench and groped into it like a lucky dip. The ribbon of the medal he produced was faded, but the medal itself had been polished and gleamed proudly as he laid it on the cardboard marker. Beside it he spread a number of rings and pins, and a small, battered teapot.

Morwenna smiled graciously at Lady Torrance. 'We'll link them with their appropriate captions in due course.'

Ogilvie went on reciting from his clipboard as if laying a blessing upon the display. 'Those who tried to call upon ancient rights and stay in their homes were continually harassed. Water bailiffs were paid handsomely to watch over lakes and creeks day and night, to keep the locals from fishing as they had been accustomed to do. From now on all fishing rights were reserved for wealthy visitors, many of them the Duke of Sutherland's friends from England. If the locals' animals strayed, they could be impounded and the owners fined. Few of them had any money, so had to hand over their pathetic little personal valuables, such as heirlooms like' — he pointed dramatically — 'medals awarded for gallantry in the Napoleonic wars.'

Mementoes, thought Luke, which had somehow survived to be passed down through the families of men who had wrested them from the downtrodden as punishment and kept them as trophies rather than as genuinely needed payment, to be gradually discarded through junk shops by their descendants.

'We shall need to get some hangings for the wall,' said Morwenna.

'A tapestry?' said Lesley Torrance.

Luke wondered whether Morwenna Ross had caught the tinge of scepticism in that remark. 'Not many families would have run to that.' He kept his voice respectful, which did not prevent Ogilvie from glaring disapproval at him. 'Though they would, of course, have had some sort of curtains round the bed.'

As they emerged, blinking, into daylight, a group of men like beaters came plodding out of a cluster of gorse bushes. But there was no shooting party to justify their movements. They could equally have been a gang of old-time cattle rustlers biding their time, sizing up the strengths and weaknesses of the land and its defenders.

'Waiting till we're out of the way,' Ogilvie snapped, 'until they start smashing things up again.'

Old Mrs Aird was waiting outside the hotel. Not specifically waiting for the visitors, thought Luke: just waiting, as part of the whole ambience.

Lesley Torrance moved away from the others to speak to her. Luke felt the old crone was not quite real. Somehow he was seeing an old woman in a shawl and rough skirts, crouching over a peat fire like some overdone character in a pseudo-historical film. Then, quite clear and present in front of him, shifting from one vision to another, the woman was in fact dressed in a plain dark blue blouse, an even darker blue skirt, and a heavy grey cardigan. Yet her eyes were staring not at anything or anybody here and now, but at something distant in time, in a less comfortable past.

The Merciless Dead

As he moved past the two women he heard Mrs Aird's doom-laden mumble. 'May a shroud be spun for the chief who runs after money.' Part of her repertoire of sayings real or bogus.

Ogilvie made one of those impatient little croaks in this throat that Luke knew all too well from interminable meetings in the Ross building.

'We really will have to find a way of getting rid of that insolent old woman. Quite out of keeping with our image.'

At dinner that evening he threatened to dominate the conversation with his summary of what they had found and what they hadn't found and what had to be tackled urgently. There was no break in the harangue until, when he paused briefly to draw breath, Lesley looked pleadingly at Morwenna across the table and asked in a rush: 'That loutish Ferguson character. Exactly what is the situation between him and Mr Ross — or Ross Enterprises in general? Simply some dispute about estate borders?'

Ogilvie looked eager to pontificate about this, too, but Morwenna beat him to it. 'More to it than that. It goes back further. The two families have been business rivals for more than a century. There were clashes in Newfoundland and Canada — much larger concerns than here. And twice in our own times Mr Ross has bought out Ferguson. Leaving him near bankruptcy. Made a poor deal of everything he put his hand to.'

'And round here,' Ogilvie interrupted, 'Ferguson was not alerted to the purchase of the hotel and the derelict croft, and enough surrounding land to make the restoration project viable, until too late. We did it very quietly through a holding company.' His audience was left with the impression that this had all been Ogilvie's skilful work.

Luke went on eating, wondering about the ramifications of the divorce and Nadine Ross's remarriage to Sholto Ferguson. Part of a tit-for-tat? How childish these captains of industry could get! Or maybe it went beyond mere spite. Maybe Ferguson had hoped his new bride would tell him some crucial Ross business secrets.

Luke felt contempt for all this, even for the firm he worked for; yet he had to admit he enjoyed keeping tabs on things, even the seedier things, adding to his store of knowledge, able to call up a relevant fact from his files or machine memory or even, most enjoyably, direct from his own memory.

What sort of bloody job do you call that, for Christ's sake? If you'd had to work your guts out with real men, the way I've had to ...

His father's voice was startlingly clear above the others' conversation.

'You all right, Drummond?' Ogilvie seized an opportunity to reassert himself.

'Fine, sir.'

'Thought you were looking a bit seedy. Food's all right?'

'Fine, thank you.'

'Not used to being out of the office, braving the wilds, eh?'

As bad as Luke's father.

He was glad to be up early in the morning, ready to drive back to what he had to admit would be the comfort of his chair, his table, his computer screen and his bookshelves.

Their departure was delayed by Ogilvie making some aggressive phone calls about security arrangements, growing more and more irritable as he was passed from one office to another, until he could slam the receiver down and say, 'Well, took some doing, but I think I've made *that* clear.'

Like some guardian spirit forever watching over the place, Mrs Aird was outside to watch them leave. As Lesley Torrance passed her, Luke heard the old woman murmur: 'You'll be the one to understand the way of it. You have the gift.'

She said nothing to Morwenna Ross, but the two of them stared at each other until Luke had turned the car out on to the road.

They passed the Rent House, where the workmen were tackling the collapsed scaffolding. A couple paused to watch them go, but made no sign.

As if Lesley Torrance's remark yesterday had rankled, Morwenna Ross said: 'One wall in there must be reserved for the tapestry when it's found.'

When? Luke glanced in his mirror and caught a glimpse of Lady Torrance's sceptically raised eyebrow, and knew what it was saying. *If*...?

But aloud she was saying politely: 'I'm still hazy about this whole question of the tapestry. How could anything of any size or complexity be woven in ... well, the conditions they lived in then?'

'A group of devoted women in the family,' Morwenna intoned with almost religious fervour, 'worked together in a communal effort. They must have felt the threat coming closer, and wanted to leave some memory of themselves as a community.' As the car came out of the shadow of a line of birches into sunlight, she added a virtual command: 'We shall find it. We must.'

*

It was mid afternoon when they slid into Ogilvie's parking slot behind the Ross building. Luke had dropped Morwenna Ross and Lesley Torrance at the hotel, but Ogilvie, as could have been predicted, wanted to round things off with his usual neatness.

'Must get a full report off to Jack, eh, Mrs Ross? He'll want to know just what I ... what we've made of things on site.'

Ogilvie was devoted to despatching reports, memoranda and bulletins to Toronto. He wanted to keep up a day-to-day, almost hour-by-hour, record of his dedication to the Ross cause. Never a moment omitted, never a breathing space.

Morwenna was staring quizzically at him. 'Jack? Oh, yes, of course.' She explained to Lesley, yet in some way was implying something to Ogilvie: 'Jacques Hunter, in charge of head office in Toronto. Mr Hunter's the real power behind the throne — or Mr Ross's wheelchair, I suppose one might say.' Her emphasis on the 'Mr' was undoubtedly for Ogilvie's benefit.

Beth was in the library, spreading out some photographs along the table. Luke looked at the pale gleam of her throat in the afternoon light through the tall west window, and wondered if she had been waiting for him to return, as in that not so distant past when she would have wanted his report on what had happened and gone over every exasperating or amusing detail, and then rounded the day off by going comfortably to bed.

He was temped to kiss the back of her neck — lightly, affectionately but without implying too much.

Instead he said brightly: 'Well, what have you been doing while we were away?'

She turned a couple of the photographs towards him.

Before he could comment, Ogilvie came bustling in. 'Hello, what have we here? What's been going on while I've been away?'

'They're the work of Randal Grant. A photographer who's been suggesting he work for us. Samples of his work. A magazine feature, taken in the sort of house that ... well ...'

'Wanting to work for us? You didn't commit yourself to anything?'

Didn't commit herself? Luke interpreted that quite differently; felt a jab of irrational anger; and knew Beth well enough to know that she was aware of it.

'I've simply sent copies to Toronto in the usual way. I thought you'd want that.'

'Well, I think you could have left that to me. As it is, I suppose I'd better follow up with a word to Jack' — he caught Luke's eye and hastily went on — 'to Mr Hunter myself. But I hope you haven't offered this person too much encouragement. We've always used one of the bigger agencies.' He began sorting through the pictures, and said reluctantly: 'Hm. Rather good. Where were they taken?'

Luke knew that Beth was having to make an effort at being innocent and offhand. 'I — er, I understand they come from ... from Lockhart House.'

'Lockhart House? Just a minute. Good God, don't you know ... isn't that —'

'The Ferguson household,' said Luke. 'Our old friend Colonel Sholto Ferguson.'

'Well I'll be damned. But this is ... I really must get on to Mr Hunter about this. Let's see, what's Canadian time? I think he'll be fascinated. Fascinated.'

He bustled off. Beth was trying not to meet Luke's gaze.

He said: 'You went round that place with him, didn't you?'

'What makes you think —'

'Come off it, Beth. I know you well enough by now.' He repeated it very slowly: 'You went round the Ferguson place with this character.'

'You're not going to tell Ogilvie that?'

'What the hell do you think of me?'

'Sorry, Luke.'

'And that's all there was to it?'

'What else should there be?'

But he knew her so well. Sensed things about her still. No reason to feel resentful. But such a short time ago he had been thinking nostalgically of Beth in bed, and now he wasn't at ease with the certainty that she had been to bed with someone else.

10

Black Knowe, a stark grey tower on its knoll above Kilstane, could look forbidding under grey skies, but to Lesley Torrance it was a warm, welcome sight as she drove home that Friday afternoon and saw it coming into view beside the familiar road ahead, climbing towards her own front door. When she reached it, she would have some days to organize things in a leisurely way that suited her. Morwenna Ross and Ogilvie would be away early next week in Inverness, sorting out a tough surveillance programme with a security firm. She was glad not to be present at negotiations where Morwenna and Slimy Simon would surely be treading persistently on one another's toes and on everybody else's.

Nick was waiting in the open doorway.

'Welcome back. Working woman returns after exhausting week.'

She kissed him, and held him tight, and his arms went round her and they clung together for a long time until he said: 'You feel as though you're glad to be home.'

'You could say that.'

'Sad to tell you, though, that your work isn't over yet. There's a sheaf of illustrations from your book to go through. Came yesterday.'

'That can wait till tomorrow.'

They had a glass of Chablis from a bottle which Nick had had chilled in readiness, and continued with the bottle over dinner while they talked. Talked about life in Kilstane, because when he asked her about news from the Ross empire she said, again, 'That can wait till tomorrow.' So he brought her up to date with the week's goings-on in the town and around the shire.

'A big fuss about the proposed windfarm. Our local democrat —'

'Rhuaridh the Red?'

'None other. Thinks the logical place for six windmills is a hundred yards to the west of us. About eighty metres tall — would overshadow our humble dwelling. Old Doctor Elliott, though, is all for setting the whole cluster on the other side of Carrach Rigg.'

'And the final decision?'

'When did our dear representatives ever reach a *final* decision? Further plans have been called for, one councillor suggests we bring in a consultant —'

'That would be Cameron, whose son happens to run a business consultancy in Peebles?'

'Glad that the hurly-burly of the great city hasn't dimmed your memory of real life in the outback.' Nick reached out to refill her glass. 'And then there's Sheriff Brown. He really is getting a bit past it. Admonished young Garvie for driving dangerously and using threatening language to the local police sergeant.'

'Admonished? High time that one was fined and given a hefty chunk of community service at the very least.'

'And of course Brown added his usual regret that he can no longer authorize the use of the birch.'

By the time they were sitting by the west window, the twilit sky was streaked with bronze-tinted streamers of cloud that nudged Lesley back to Achnachrain. But here she was so much higher, above the world in her tower, remoter than on those stark moorlands. Nick's arm went round her, and she rested her head on his shoulder and was happy to be there until all the light faded and left the sky grey and then darker, until a few stars came alive.

'I've just had an idea,' he said.

'Good.' She snuggled closer. 'Let's try it.'

'No, I mean an idea about the Ross project.'

'The only projection I'm interested in at the moment is —'

'I'm way ahead of you.'

They hurried to bed, and coming luxuriously to life in his arms she wondered why she had been silly enough to let herself be lured into working for the Ross fantasies, too far away from the home where she belonged. With Nick's hand still caressing her, she heard herself let out a little moan of repletion before drifting off into sleep.

At breakfast he said: 'Right, now it's your turn. What's going wrong in Edinburgh?'

'Who says anything's going wrong?'

'You're saying it. I can tell. That's what I was going to bring up last night, only we sort of got distracted. So let's be having it.'

'But I don't know. I ... that is, I get on well enough with the folk involved, and they don't expect me to come up with a dozen miracles every day. Right now, it's agreed I'll stay on here for a few days and check up on some leads through the internet, without distractions in the office or the hotel or anywhere. Can't complain about the working conditions.'

'But ...?'

'Well, it's hard to put a finger on it. In spite of all the to-ing and fro-ing, we don't really seem to be getting anywhere.'

'And where exactly are you meant to get?'

'It all seemed straightforward on the surface. But now I'm not so sure. Maybe it's all becoming one of those inflated PR things. Somebody had an idea, and at once everybody had to start brain-storming. Maybe old man Ross himself did genuinely start out wanting to leave some sort of memorial to his generosity in his old homeland. Something sentimental but genuine. Only, now the whole Ross machine has gone into overdrive and nobody's really steering properly or knows when to stop.'

'I thought you said this Mrs Ross was a pretty powerful operator.'

'Yes, but oddly I'm beginning to feel that she's ... well ... really thinking of something else. *Aiming* at something else.'

'No idea what that could be?'

'None. Just that ... well, there's something out of true. All this collecting stuff and digging into history. It's not from love — it's from hatred. As if something's waiting to go off bang. Or is it just going to be a feeble little splutter?'

'Do I detect the suspicious mind of the one-time CID girl looking for suspicious goings-on where there aren't any? Looking for clues when there hasn't actually been an incident yet?'

'That's what worries me — that 'yet'.' She began clearing the table, wanting something mundane to get her back to reality. 'There are too many things that ... well, I'd say weird was the word.'

'Way out in the wild?'

'Especially out in the wild.' She told him about Mrs Aird, and tried to laugh about it. 'A type-cast old crone. Going on about me being one of them, or close to it.'

'One of what?'

'With the second sight, or whatever.'

He caught her arm as she was carrying a tray away from the table. 'All right, sit down. Nothing there to worry about, surely? You always were sort of psychic. All those hunches helped no end in your old job.'

'No, this is different. Scary. As if that old woman knows what's going to happen, because of what did once happen somewhere in the past, and —'

'And she's trying to tell you something?'

'No. Acting as if I didn't need telling.'

'Then tell yourself to quit now. If it's going to get on your nerves like this, then pack it in.'

'I couldn't. Not really.'

'You're going to stick there until it blows up in your face, aren't you? Because you're so bloody-minded.'

'I think it's time,' said Lesley firmly, 'to deal with some realities. Like settling down with those pictures.'

Nick caught her arm and kissed it as she was moving past him. 'Reality? Pictures of art fakes — that's your *real* reality?'

She acknowledged the absurdity of it; but looked forward to spending the first hour in what she had come to regard as friendly company. Just as a crime squad officer couldn't help admiring the handiwork of a really professional burglar or con man, she had always appreciated the craftsmanship of the Keatings, van Meegerens and John Drews of this world.

'One thing occurred to me when I skimmed through your page proofs,' said Nick. 'What about your own work on the Brigid Weir case? That deserves a chapter, surely? And maybe with a passing reference to Alma Tadema and the Bareback Lass.'

'Not important enough.'

'Considering that between them they brought us together, I'd say they were important.'

'Not to the sort of reader I hope'll be buying this book.'

She spent a leisurely morning checking the juxtapositions of original paintings and brilliant copies. Three of the colour separations would need to be re-set, but otherwise they had made a good job of it. She was sorry to come to the end of the job and knock out a letter to the publishers; and reluctant to contemplate work on the Ross project which would occupy her afternoon.

After a light lunch she took a cup of coffee into her study. Nick had gone into town for a Probus luncheon which was to be addressed by a long-retired sanitary engineer who would, Nick predicted, bore them with self-congratulatory tales of saving whole townships from nauseating plagues and disturb their digestion with airy references to excrement and sewage treatment of various kinds.

Early in the afternoon Lesley turned her attention to the lists she had brought with her about supposed Ross mementoes. Here, too, was a fine collection of fakes. Morwenna's TV programme and reports in the Press had brought in a tide of memorabilia, all of it supposedly what the researchers were looking for, and each item worth a great deal, the owners were sure.

Genuine items had been few and far between. The best specimens were those she had taken to the croft at Achnachrain, and which Luke Drummond had then packed up and taken safely back to Queen Street. Sorting out her notes on helpful suggestions from various folk museums and family records from the Scottish Archive Network, she settled herself by the phone and began ringing round.

Her old friend Dr Smutek protested that Scottish history — 'Or speculation,' he added in that crackling Czech accent which he had never shaken off — was not one of his specialities. And when she pointed out that he was known for his expertise in Bohemian and other Central European tapestries, and suggested he must at some time have heard of the Ross Tapestry, he said: 'Peasants' — the word was not used contemptuously but sceptically — 'making a tapestry of any value? With what materials? And how would they have acquired the techniques and artistry? No, it is so unlikely, my dear lady.'

One dealer sarcastically suggested that to get really convincing material she ought to get in touch with some of her old pals. 'Toddy Maxwell ought to be out of stir by now. Probably he'll forgive you for putting him away if you shove some work his way now. Just the man to lift a few olde-worlde stockpots and milking stools from private collections.'

An undertow of unease surged back. Could the whole operation itself be just a scam to collect artefacts, choose the best, and then ship them to one of the Ross Museums in Toronto or Winnipeg? Was she being just a stooge, collecting Scottish memorabilia not for Scottish preservation but for export?

She shook it off. Nick was right: these were just the stock reflexes of a 'one-time CID girl'.

Next day, after they had driven into Kilstane to post her final corrections, he said: 'Right. For the next few days you do no more than an hour's fretting and phoning each morning, and then we go out visiting.'

'Visiting what?'

'Local beauty spots. And hostelries. A couple of days away in Melrose pottering around the gardens will clear your head marvellously.'

Each morning she checked on antiques dealers and historic collections, and set up various dates for the following week; and without fail Nick arrived at the end of an hour and insisted that she stop immediately, switch that bit of her mind off, and come out into the open air.

As she was packing, ready to drive back to Edinburgh, he perched on the end of the bed. 'Look, my love, are you sure it wouldn't be best to get out of the whole thing here and now?'

'I can't just give up with the job half-finished.'

'I'd say you've probably given them their money's worth. Politely leave them to shove it into whatever shape suits them.'

'And give loudmouths like that Ferguson character a chance to make snide remarks about the team cracking up?'

'Ah, yes, Ferguson.'

'When we were at Achnachrain he spoke as if he knew you.'

'And not favourably, I'll bet. No, it's all right. Don't tell me.'

'Seemed to think you ought to be on his side about things. But you're not.'

'Decidedly not. One of the old style of landowner. Thinks the entire country should be manipulated for the benefit of his pocket and pastimes. I've been at the most godawful meetings of the Caledonian Estates Protection Association, with Ferguson and his cronies plotting to stymie every little bit of legislation in favour of crofting tenure reform and the work of nature conservationists. I was one of those who had the nerve to challenge his manoeuvrings.' Nick grinned. 'Never was much agreement between Highland lairds and the Lowlanders. As bad as the Scottish and English riding families along the Border — always at one another's throats. Though, mark you, this Ferguson character is more bluster than genuine indignation. Very few of those estates of his and his friends were ever handed down by families native to the region. They've all changed hands over the years for sums no real local could afford, with all sorts of tax dodges built in.' He half closed his eyes. 'What was it I read somewhere — 'A rural economy dependent on tweedy gentlemen coming from the south to slaughter our wildlife.' The last thing they want is a symbolic re-creation of the real world they thought they'd successfully crushed.'

The Merciless Dead

'The intensity of it,' Lesley marvelled. 'And all over things that happened so long ago.'

'You should be in the crowd at an Old Firm match in Glasgow. None of the past is really over yet.'

*

She had just reached the reception desk to collect her room key when she knew, without even looking round, that Morwenna was coming towards her from the cocktail bar. When Morwenna was in a room, she was instantly, vibrantly, in it.

She was not alone. As she came to greet Lesley, she was gesturing with her left hand towards a tall man at her side.

'Lesley, this is Mr Hunter. Jacques Hunter, from Toronto.'

Was that respect in her voice, or a challenge?

'Jacques, this is Lady Torrance. Lesley Torrance. She has done invaluable work for us.'

'So I've heard.' His handshake was firm, almost fierce. 'Lady Torrance, a great pleasure.'

His voice was deep and confident, with what Lesley supposed was a Canadian accent, though she had never had any cause to make comparisons between American and Canadian intonation. Or was there something faintly French running through it? He was a couple of inches taller than Morwenna, with dark parchment skin and slanting lozenges of sloe-coloured eyes suggesting Red Indian blood not very far back.

'Jacques arrived on Wednesday.' It ought to have been a simple, matter-of-fact statement; but Lesley had become familiar with Morwenna's different intonations by now, and in those clipped words could feel a cool wariness. 'Descended on us like an avenging angel.' Was she resentful of a senior figure suddenly showing up to take charge? 'It seems that Mr Ross is getting impatient.'

'Perhaps, Lady Torrance, you'd care to join us for a drink while I put you in the picture?'

'If I could just go up to my room first and —'

'But of course. Stupid of me. Too anxious to make your acquaintance, too quickly. Please, whenever you are ready to come down.'

Lesley went up to her room. Her case was brought up two or three minutes later. As she unpacked and went into the bathroom, she wondered about the new arrival. He and Morwenna — rivals within the Ross hierarchy, or manipulative accomplices?

When she got down to the bar, the two were talking amicably enough; but there was a stiffness in Morwenna's shoulders. In contrast, Jacques Hunter was relaxed and in full control. On his administrative level, he must have learnt to be a skilled manipulator. Every move was graceful and unhurried, one arm sweeping Lesley towards a chair, stooping a few deferential inches to ask what she wanted to drink, smiling as the drink arrived and he could begin to explain his presence as a courtesy rather than a necessity.

'Mr Ross' — the name was like an incantation — 'is anxious to come over much earlier than was planned. As well as his chronic muscle problems, he has over the last six months been having serious trouble with his eyes. Macular degeneration — a slow process, but recently there has been a complication with posterior capular opacification. Mr Ross has undergone laser treatment, but his eyesight is now deteriorating rapidly. You'll understand that he is anxious to see the fulfilment of his dream before it's too late.'

'So Big Chief Jamie is getting impatient.' The flippancy was awkward, unlike Morwenna. Were she and Hunter used to joking amicably together, or was this a snide provocation? 'And Jacques the mighty Hunter is here to arrange a big pow-wow. Right?'

'I'm here,' he said to Lesley, 'to speed things up so that Mr Ross can come over just as soon as possible.'

She glanced at Morwenna. 'It's not going to be easy to rush things, is it?'

'No, it's not.'

Decidedly not, thought Lesley. Skimping the job just in order to put on a dramatic charade for the sake of a feeble old man.

Or not so feeble. An old man still keeping a strong grip on the purse strings. A lovely old phrase. When did any of us last have a purse with strings on it?

'You are smiling, Lady Torrance.' Jacques Hunter was warm and attentive.

'Thinking of the panic in the office when the pressure comes on,' she said quickly.

The proclamation resounded in the air around them. Red carpets had to be found and rolled out. Mr Ross would soon be coming.

*

On Monday morning, Simon Ogilvie was less adept at keeping his feelings throttled down than Morwenna had been. Lesley could hear him holding forth to an audience of one, as she went into the library and saw Beth nodding with weary politeness.

'First we have Mrs Ross to take charge. Then Mr Hunter shows up to override her and me. Can't I be trusted to do my job any more? And as to what that couple may be up to, between them —'

He gulped, stopping himself in midsentence as he realized that Lesley was in the room. A moment later they were joined by Luke, breathless.

'You've heard the news?'

'That Mr Hunter himself has come to join us. Oh, yes, we've heard.'

'No. About that Ferguson character.'

'Ferguson?'

'Sholto Ferguson. That bossy bastard who made threats to us at Achnachrain. It's just been on a local news flash. He's been murdered.'

'Near our properties?' Ogilvie was immediately shrill, ready to accuse or throw up defences. 'There hasn't been some sort of confrontation on site? He wasn't trying to —'

'At home,' said Luke. 'His place down Pencaitland way. Apparently he was found by a photographer visiting the place. Now helping the police with their inquiries, as they say.' He was staring intently at Beth. 'Name of Randal Grant. Isn't he the one we've been ... *involved* with ... recently?'

11

DCI Rutherford picked his way cautiously over the jutting leg of a broken table and some shards of broken glass, and stared down at the head of a totem pole and the human head beside it, savagely smashed in by that wooden raven.

Leaning over to have a good look at the man's twisted neck and the blood from his shattered skull seeping in a dark snail trail across the floor, he took care not to reach out for something to hold on to. Forensics were on their way. There simply had to be prints, marks of shoes, or telltale threads from a coat or jacket somewhere within a tight circle round this crumpled body.

'Sholto Ferguson, right? The owner of this property?'

'That's right, guv.'

'Any idea yet about troubles with anybody?'

'Traffic have had dealings with him quite often.'

'I can't see Maxwell's team pursuing him home and beating him up because he was doing a ton along the ring road. Charges of drunk driving?'

'A couple of speeding charges. But he was a great complainer. A traffic jam outside his gates, blocking his exit. Too many large lorries using the road out there as a short cut. Trespassers joyriding round his estate. A squad car hogging the road and not letting him pass. Complaints direct to his old friend the Chief Constable.'

'Oh. One of those. Well, he can't complain this was a hit and run. Or I suppose it is, in a way. Only not by some car driver with evil intent. Who found him? One of the family?'

'No, guv.' The sergeant, standing well back in the window alcove, as wary as the DCI of trampling over evidence, jerked a thumb downwards. 'We're holding him downstairs. A Randal Grant. Youngish chap, says he's a photographer.'

'Here to do a family portrait? Don't think I'd fancy *this* framed on the mantelpiece.'

'This chap Grant says he came back to tidy up some loose ends.'

'Back? A regular visitor, then? Any family on the premises at the time?'

'As far as we can make out, Mrs Ferguson, the wife — widow — seems to have come in later. She's pretty hysterical right now. Not making much sense. We've got a WPC with her. If you want to see her, she's —'

'No. I'll start with our Lord Snowdon.'

To Rutherford, as with many of his colleagues, it was almost a matter of faith that the person who claimed to have found the corpse was most likely to be the one who had made it a corpse in the first place. They could rarely keep quiet about what they'd done. Wanted to draw attention to it, make sure somebody knew without delay what had happened. He went downstairs to find Randal Grant chatting earnestly about his photographic techniques with a detective constable who seemed to be enjoying the break — maybe acquiring tips for his next holiday snaps.

'Mr Grant. Detective Chief Inspector Rutherford. Perhaps you'll be kind enough to fill me in on what exactly happened here this morning, and how you came to be here in the first place.'

He never did like these hippie types with their scruffy beards and laid-back pretensions. But the young man spoke straightforwardly enough, with the right sort of respect for the arm of the law.

'I had taken some shots of the house — interiors, special aspects of the main rooms — for a magazine feature. A few of the shots were clouded over. I wanted to take them again, get them right. So I rang Mrs Ferguson, and she said to come over.'

'Right there and then?'

'No. It was yesterday evening I phoned her, and she said to come round this morning, about eleven.'

'And when you got here, she was waiting for you?'

'No. But the main door on the terrace was open.'

'And you just walked in?' Vaguely he remembered gossip column stuff about Nadine Witherington's goings-on both before and after she became Nadine Ferguson. 'Really familiar with the premises? Used to strolling in and making yourself at home?'

The younger man's agreeable manner chilled. He had understood the implication. Stiffly he said: 'I'd visited it just the once before. As I said, on a picture shoot. It's part of my regular job. You can check on that.'

'I will. And this particular shoot — what brought it about?'

There was a fractional hesitation. Then Grant said: 'It was destined for *Historic Interiors*. One of a series of stately home features. You know the sort of thing. Flattering angles on family treasures — and on the lady of the house, against a suitable background.'

'But today, although she had agreed to meet you here, Mrs Ferguson was not at home? So you met her husband instead.'

'I *found* her husband. And rang you lot.'

'He was upstairs. You wandered upstairs — or did he *call* you upstairs?'

'How the hell could he call me? You've seen what state he's in. Well past communicating with anyone.'

'Quite so. That's how he is now. But at the time you arrived …?'

Before Grant could come up with the sort of indignant reply which might be genuine or contrived, a uniformed officer put his head round the door. Forensics had arrived. Rutherford went up to join them for a quarter of an hour, and then returned to Grant. Never did any harm to keep them waiting — and twitching.

'How much longer are you going to need me?' The question was predictable. 'I do have other work to do, you know.'

'Now that one of your clients has other things on her mind, yes, I suppose you would have. Hoping your next visit doesn't end quite so violently?'

'The violence had been committed before I arrived,' said Grant acidly.

'Ah, yes.' Rutherford was as well practised as a barrister at sounding sceptical without risking any accusation of harassing a witness.

'I've told you everything I know. Is there any reason why I shouldn't go now?'

'We shall need a formal statement from you, of course.'

'Of course.'

'Perhaps you can give it to my sergeant before you leave. And if you remember something else, later, you can get in touch with him at the nick. And we can get in touch with *you* when we need to. You're not thinking of leaving Edinburgh for any length of time?'

'No, I'm not. But I can't imagine anything useful I could add to what I've already told you.'

'In these cases one never knows. But very well, Mr Grant. Thank you for your co-operation.'

'I hope you'll find out who did this. And soon.'

'Oh, we'll do that all right. Have no fear.' He made the last three words sound threatening rather than reassuring. 'Thanks again, Mr Grant. We'll be in touch.'

The Merciless Dead

It was time to turn his attention to the widow.

*

Nadine Ferguson had disposed herself picturesquely on a chaise-longue below a portrait of a portly man glaring out across some remembered battlefield, his uniform bristling with medal ribbons, and his red face adorned by a sumptuous moustache.

Rutherford gave a matter-of-fact resume of what Randal Grant had told him, which she accompanied with sad little nods and the occasional dab of a lace handkerchief at her eyes. When he had finished he said, in a more considerate tone than he had used with the young photographer: 'It's true, then, that you'd agreed Mr Grant should come round here this morning?'

'Yes. It wasn't really convenient, but I did agree he should come.'

'Not convenient?'

'My husband was at home. He's been very annoyed since I told him about all that photography. He would never have allowed it if he'd been here.'

'You mean he was absent when you agreed to the original session?'

'Yes.' Mrs Ferguson allowed herself a pathetic little whimper. 'You'd have thought he'd be glad to have his family achievements featured in a reputable magazine. But he ... well, he has his moods, and ... oh, dear, he was very angry with me. Came storming in halfway through the morning from one of those meetings he has — just a lot of drinking, if you ask me, and then spending the night at his club getting over it. And coming home in a filthy temper. I'm afraid we had a terrible row. Said he wasn't going to let any bloody little snapshotter — that's how he put it, typical of him, so vulgar — a bloody little snapshotter, wasn't going to let him set foot in the house again. Should never have been here in the first place.'

'You didn't think to phone Mr Grant and tell him not to come?'

'I did try, but there was no reply. He must have been on his way here by then.'

'But you weren't here when he got here? He says he just walked in — and found your husband's body.'

'Oh, dear, I suppose I ought to have stayed in. But Sholto had made me so cross. I'm sorry, Chief Inspector, but I did what I often have to do when he's in one of his moods. I went out shopping.' She tried a courageous, winsome little smile at him, appealing for the understanding she could surely expect from a man of the world. 'At times of stress, you know, one does. I decided to go and buy some shoes.'

'And when you got back?'

'Found one of your policemen here. And that clumsy young man.'

'Clumsy?'

'That dreadful wooden thing. That bit of totem pole. He moved it when I was showing him round the house, so that he could get some sort of clever-clever angle on it. He couldn't have replaced it properly. It must have fallen on poor dear Sholto.'

Poor dear Sholto? Who had been so angry with her that she had scuttled out of the house to get her own back by spending some of his money?

Rutherford said: 'I don't think it fell, Mrs Ferguson. Somebody lifted it and bashed it into his skull. Forcibly. And more than once, I'd say.'

'Officer!' she shrieked. 'Do you have to put it so crudely?'

'It was done crudely. There's rarely anything polite about murder.' He allowed himself to look patient and long-suffering while she collapsed back into fine dramatic sobs, involving the use of several more flimsy handkerchiefs and convulsive jerks of her shoulders.

When he had allowed her as long as he thought was reasonable for a stricken widow's histrionics, he said: 'How long have you known this Randal Grant?'

'Only a week or so. It must have been ... oh, let me see, it can't have been more than ... it was that Monday, or ...'

'You haven't known him long, then? Purely a business relationship?'

'Of course. What else?' Rutherford felt a flicker of suspicion at her immediate indignation. Everything about what he had heard of her past and her mannerisms right now suggested that the attentions of any presentable young man would be welcome. 'What do you take me for?' she was ranting on. 'He was here purely as a photographer for a magazine wanting to do a feature on the beauties of our gracious home.' She seemed about to lapse into offended silence, but abruptly added: 'Anyway, he had a young woman with him.'

'A young woman?'

'An assistant.' She sniffed. 'Or so he said. She didn't seem to me to be doing much assisting.'

Rutherford added a question about this additional character to those he was already trying to sort out in his mind. And it was becoming increasingly clear that one question underpinned all the others. What were the exact times of Ferguson getting home, Mrs Ferguson going out in a huff, and Grant arriving?

There couldn't have been much time for someone to murder Ferguson. Someone? Mrs Ferguson, in a temper, or even in self-defence? She didn't look as if she would have the strengths but it was amazing what reserves the frailest human being could summon up when in a murderous rage. But had her husband really been so outrageous that she was driven to smash his head in and then go out shopping for shoes?

Or there was Randal Grant. Had Ferguson not only snarled at him, threatened him, but actually gone for him? And Grant had fought back in self-defence ...?

Was the time gap large enough for somebody else to have come in, beaten Ferguson to death, and left, with just enough margins for nobody to have seen him come and go?

Mrs Ferguson was still sniffling, but peeping at him over the crumpled edge of her handkerchief, uneasy about his silence.

Rutherford said: 'Servants? Would anybody have been here to answer the door, let visitors in, see all the comings and goings?'

Unexpectedly she laughed. It wasn't the laughter of enjoyment.

'Servants? For all his big act, we don't run to much in that line.'

Rutherford looked up at the curlicues of the ceiling, and down at the spread of Persian rugs. 'This place must take a lot of keeping up.'

'Propping up,' she corrected him. 'With two useless part-time men and a woman who comes in three times a week to do some half-hearted dusting. Just for the showy bits. Oh, and sometimes we hire a cook for an evening if we're having a dinner party.' The laugh became a derisive rasp. 'Not that we often run to that. He's all show, and then only when he can't avoid it. Most of the time the place is a pigsty. Not at all what I've been used to,' said Nadine Ferguson loftily. 'God, if I'd known what a phoney it all was ...'

'Phoney? All those showpiece rooms up there?'

'Oh, *they're* genuine enough. Handed down by his precious ancestors. There must have been some Fergusons who worked hard enough back then. But *him* — he's just lived on the name and made a lot of noise about it.'

When forensics had finished their work, there would be the routine matter of removing the corpse to the morgue. Rutherford left it to a well-trained WPC to explain sympathetically the necessary rituals to the widow, and also explain why the body could not be released for a memorial service and burial until police inquiries had been finalized. He had a feeling that

Nadine Ferguson would be disappointed by delays: already she would be adjusting her mind to a vision of a fine funeral with military trimmings and the presence of distinguished figures from Edinburgh society and Highland estates.

Back in his office, he set a constable phoning around to check on certain points. Starting with Historic Interiors.

The response was unequivocal. 'Randal Grant? Oh, yes, he's done some first-rate stuff for us. But we never commissioned that particular subject.'

Rutherford contemplated postponing any further questioning until tomorrow; then decided to round off his afternoon with a brief visit to Grant's studio. Catch them on the hop — it was often the most rewarding approach. And he could fit it in neatly before going for a pint with a contact in the pub round the corner. That might wrap up one run-of-the-mill drugs bust he had been working on with the Drugs Squad for weeks. He had a feeling this other case wasn't going to work out as a run-of-the-mill one.

He was greeted with a mock welcoming smile. 'Come to tell me you've solved it already? Quick work, I must say. Don't tell me — Ferguson slipped and banged his head, and we're all in the clear? Or it was the butler after all? With a bit of lead piping in the Indian room. Only I don't remember the Fergusons running to a butler.'

'For a brutal killing, you're taking it all very lightly, Mr Grant.'

'He wasn't one of my favourite characters.'

'Oh, so you have some personal grudge against the deceased?'

Grant did not reply, but gestured towards a chair for his visitor to sit down. Rutherford took his time, summing up different angles on the studio, with its array of gadgets which he had seen in different settings — photographers crouching above dead bodies, taking shots of drug hauls, cracks in floors, crumpled vehicles in head-on smashes. Only here the subjects seemed less grim. There were some landscapes spread on a pegboard, a few half-profiles of children, and, propped on an easel more like a painting than a photograph, a large portrait of a young woman. Did Grant supply pornographic magazines as well as architectural and society ones? But there was nothing suggestive in the girl's face. She was simply a very pretty girl. And, oddly, Rutherford felt he had seen her somewhere before.

'I've heard a lot about Ferguson's background,' said Grant. 'And none of it appeals to me. I've come across too many men like him.'

'And you think the world should be rid of them?'

The Merciless Dead

'No, that won't work. I don't go around rubbing out people I disapprove of. You'll have to do better than that, old lad.'

Rutherford disliked being addressed as 'old lad' as much as he disliked being called Jock. He plunged vengefully in: 'Why did you say that you'd been commissioned to do that photo session by Historic Interiors magazine? They deny all knowledge of any such arrangement.'

'I don't remember telling you any such thing.'

'But you did tell Mrs Ferguson. Why? In order to gain access to the premises? Because of some hostility towards Mr Ferguson which you planned to sort out?'

The response was a faintly derisive grimace. 'It's *Colonel* Ferguson, actually.'

'So you really are quite familiar with the ins and outs of this family.'

'When I have a commission to fulfil, I check background facts as far as possible.'

'But you didn't have any commission in this case.'

Randal Grant sprawled back on his couch. Rutherford would have preferred to have him sitting upright in one of the calculatedly uncomfortable chairs in an interview room. Maybe that would be the next step. 'All right, I was being a bit devious.' Grant seemed to be airily addressing the ceiling rather than the detective. 'I was angling for a contract with the Rosses. I wanted to have something to show them — a whole shoot that would convince them I was the one to handle things at their Achnachrain project.'

'A bit complicated, wasn't it?'

'Not really. I was pretty sure I could sell the Lockhart House feature to one of the glossies anyway.'

'Except that Mr — ah, Colonel — Ferguson was opposed to any such idea. Very much so, according to Mrs Ferguson.' Rutherford was determined to disturb the young slouch enough to bring him sitting up straight. 'You must have run into him in a pretty foul mood when you got there.'

Grant did sit up; and his flippancy was dropped. 'I've told you. I found him dead.'

'You've told some porkies about being commissioned to go to Lockhart House that first time. We have to be sure you're not still telling them.' He timed his pause the way he had practised it many times, calculated to plant unease in the mind of the interviewee, then added: 'You won't object to coming to the station so that we can take fingerprints and do a DNA test? Doesn't take long.'

He had half expected a flurry of indignation and self-justification. But Randal Grant said calmly: 'If that will clear things up, of course I don't object. Eliminate me, and get on doing the job properly. I'll be very surprised if you find anything that connects me with that mess out there.'

'Oh, and one more point. Who was the young woman with you?'

He was glad to see that this had rattled the young man. 'There was no young lady with me today.'

'No. But on your earlier visit —'

'On my earlier visit I had a part-time assistant. She wasn't with me today when I discovered the corpse, and I wouldn't want her upset by something that in no way concerns her.'

'Some sensitive matter?'

'She wasn't there the day Ferguson got killed. And that's what we're talking about, isn't it? No need to clutter it with irrelevant details.'

That remained to be seen, thought Rutherford.

On his way down the stairs, he remembered where he had seen that girl before — full length, smartly dressed, in the company of people he had recently had dealings with.

12

Beth hoped, as she came into the office and exchanged the usual good-mornings and platitudes about the weather, that everyone was too busy to detect any apprehensiveness in her manner. The inquiries into Sholto Ferguson's death had so far passed her by, but the fact that she had been on the premises earlier with Randal Grant, who had discovered the body, must surely bring them round to her sooner or later. She had nothing to feel guilty about — not really, had she? But a dozen fidgety thoughts had plagued her during the night, and she had wondered whether to ring Randal, and longed to be near him, in his arms again — and then wondered whether to stay well away from him until things were clearer or, maybe preferably, not too clear.

Right now she wanted to avoid meeting Luke's gaze too directly. He knew her too well; could sense things that others would miss. Already she had caught a look in his eye, a few snide notes in his voice: he knew that she and Randal were lovers. Unlikely that he would ever come straight out with it, but it was there. Along with all her other waking worries during the night had been the nagging question of how she could explain to him what made Randal so different. She wouldn't have wanted to hurt him. But he wouldn't have been happy, or even philosophical, about her trying to explain Randal's warmth. Certainly none of that post-coital tristesse stuff.

Luke would certainly not ask outright. And what the hell, she didn't actually owe him any explanations.

Lesley Torrance said: 'Good morning, Beth. Miles away — dreaming up some wild new ideas for the campaign?'

'Still trying to fit the present ones into some sort of shape,' Beth improvised hurriedly.

'I've brought a few new things in for Morwenna to see. Like to have a look while we're waiting?'

She led the way into the library. Having her there made it easier for Beth to smile quickly and, she hoped, normally at Luke.

Lesley's finds consisted of a number of pencil sketches on unevenly sized scraps of paper, followed by a few prints taken from woodblocks, all protected within six plastic display folders. To Beth's relief, any suspicions

Luke might have had about her were immediately overridden by his interest in these transparent files laid on the table before him.

'Bewick,' he said eagerly. 'Thomas Bewick woodcuts, surely?'

'And original sketches for some of them,' said Lesley.

'But these ...' He pored over the scraps of crumpled paper which someone had tried to smooth out before inserting them in their covering. 'That one of the croft — he must have got there just after the roof timbers had been pulled down. You can see where the turfs on the roof have collapsed in on themselves. It's so intricate. And somehow it's more real than a photograph.'

'According to my friend in Newcastle who found them in the Cherryburn archives, they're what's left of material Bewick collected on his tour of Scotland in the late eighteen-hundreds. His woodblock of a Cheviot ram is famous; but at the same time he was horrified by the way that creature was already taking over the Highlands. Talked about the despotism of the early Clearances. And wherever he went he made sketches on any old scraps of paper he could get his hands on, and sorted them out when he got home.'

'This is a gem,' said Luke reverently, poring over a small drawing of a woman sitting by the doorway of a croft, bent over a spinning wheel. 'But there's no print from a finished block to go with it?'

'A lot of the sketches were never used. Put on one side and dipped into only when he needed tailpieces for chapbooks, chapter headings, handbills, that sort of thing.'

'The relevant ones here could be blown up and displayed in the museum. Look at this!' It was a tiny yet vivid study of two women leaning on either side of a drystone wall. 'You can almost hear the gossip about their neighbours.' He was turning them over avidly, feasting on them. Beth felt a moment of absurd fondness for him: in such matters, at least, he could never restrain his enthusiasm. 'What's this old woman doing?' The spindly figure was bent over what looked like a small wooden picture frame or an embroidery stretcher. 'Oh, and this one ... it's almost too graphic. Beautifully symbolic, but I don't believe it could have been sketched on the spot. He'd have been chased off by the factor.'

This larger drawing was of a man raising a whip and a woman cowering before him, incongruously framed in a garland of the foliage Bewick was so fond of.

Lesley leaned past Luke and turned the file over. A note on the back identified it as having been done for a Newcastle newspaper which had then decided not to print it.

'Oh, yes.' Luke was almost purring. 'He was up there only in the early stages, but the exploiters were already censoring what the world outside was going to be told.'

The phone buzzed. Luke reached for it, said 'Yes, she is,' and looked across at Beth with the beginnings of a malicious grin. 'There's a Detective Chief Inspector in reception asking for you. Been caught shoplifting, Beth?'

*

The senior officer in the hall was large and imposing — not fat, but disconcertingly solid. 'Miss Elizabeth Crichton? I've got the name right?'

'Yes, that's right. How can I help you? Something to do with parking near Drovers Court?' There had been a few problems there because of roadworks in a side street, but she had an awful feeling that this visit had nothing to do with those incidents.

DCI Rutherford confirmed that. 'Not my pigeon, miss. I'm here about the Ferguson case.'

'I'm sorry, but I don't know how I can help you.' Beth was aware that Shirley in reception was making a big effort not to look inquisitive, and failing. She waved towards the small conference room on their left. 'Shall we talk in there? I'm not sure why you're here, but …' She was trying not to sound breathless.

The room had a high ceiling and high windows looking out on Queen Street, but at the moment its walls were closing in more and more oppressively.

She pulled one of the small, comfortable chairs away from the conference table and nodded to the sergeant to find himself another. 'Please. Not quite up to the standard of one of your interrogation rooms, I suppose, but we do like to make visitors comfortable.' She wished she could stop blethering on.

The sergeant remained standing, impassive, occasionally bracing his thigh against the edge of the table.

Rutherford sat down in the chair offered, and waited until Beth was seated a few feet away from him. Then he said: 'Miss Crichton, why did you accompany Mr Randal Grant on his first visit to Lockhart House?'

'I … I don't understand. What visit?'

'The visit he made to take photographs of the Ferguson residence.'

Absurdly Beth wanted to giggle at the word 'residence': it was something out of the dialogue in a bad play. Butlers answering telephones uttered it solemnly. 'Mrs Ponsonby's residence.' Surely nobody used it seriously nowadays?

Rutherford looked very patient and in no mood to be amused. He sat waiting.

She fumbled: 'Who told you ... I mean, did Mr Grant say something ... or you mistook something ...'

'Miss Crichton, were you or were you not in Mr Grant's company when he made what I believe is called a shoot of those premises?'

'I ... oh, dear, I don't know why my name's been dragged into it. But all right, yes, I was there. Just that once.'

'Can you tell me why? In a private capacity, or a business one?'

'Mr Grant has been keen on us engaging him as photographer to the Ross Foundation's restoration work at Achnachrain. If he's told you I was with him, he must have told you why he invited me along. He wanted to impress me with the way he worked, and the results he could get.'

'Actually, Mr Grant didn't tell me he'd invited you along.'

'Then who ... I mean, where did you get this from?'

'We try to keep our sources confidential, miss. Just as this discussion today will be kept confidential. Unless circumstances eventually dictate otherwise.'

There was a faint squeak, almost like the sound of a quickly repressed snigger, as the sergeant's shoes scuffed the floor while he transferred his weight from one leg to the other.

Beth had a momentary stab of fear. Was that lovemaking of Randal's a direct consequence of his killing Ferguson — like a wartime victory running on into physical exaltation, the exuberant sexual aftermath of a killing? But no, that was all out of order. That first visit of theirs had been well before Ferguson's death, and his second one, when he found Ferguson ...

But had the time of death been established?

She wasn't going to let herself dwell on crazy speculations. Leave that to the police.

Rutherford was saying: 'That was a purely professional matter, then? You haven't seen Mr Grant since?'

The Merciless Dead

'I ... er ... well, I've seen him to go through the pictures he took. And sent copies to head office in Toronto so they could assess his work.'

'You seem to be doing quite a lot on his behalf.'

'I think his work is first-rate.'

Rutherford smirked. 'Yes, he's pretty good at portraits too, isn't he? I was very impressed.'

He'd have been even more impressed, thought Beth dizzily, if Randal had actually got round to taking one of those nude studies he had joked about.

'But,' Rutherford persisted, 'you didn't accompany Mr Grant to Lockhart House on that later visit — the one he claims he made in order to show Mrs Ferguson those prints?'

'No. That was of no further concern to us.'

"Us'?'

'The Ross Foundation. Where I work,' said Beth with exaggerated emphasis. 'Right here in this very building.'

There was a rap on the door, and Lesley Torrance came in.

'Finished the third degree?'

Beth half expected Rutherford to protest at the interruption and insist on continuing with his inquisition. But there was an odd rapport between these two, and with a dour grin he said: 'I don't think I need detain Miss Crichton any longer.'

'Just as well. She's needed in the library. Beth, Morwenna wants us to go through that Bewick material in detail. I'll be with you in a minute.'

*

Lesley perched herself on the corner of the table and confronted Rutherford.

'You can't seriously think that girl's involved in any way in your latest murder scene?'

'No, I don't think she is. But her and that Randal Grant character — don't tell me there isn't something going on between them.'

'There may well be. But she's not an accomplice to murder. She really is devoted to this firm and the work she does.'

'You, too? I mean, how the hell did you come to get involved with these weirdos?'

'That's what I've been asking myself every now and then,' Lesley confessed.

'All those museums, and awards, and endowments and whatnot. I can imagine you being interested in the arty side, but when it comes to all this stuff in the papers, and that weird woman on the telly raking up the past ... I mean, isn't it about time all that was forgotten, all the old feuds and whatever?'

'Shame on you, Chief Inspector. None of your unfinished business is ever written off, is it? No inquiry is ever closed until the problem's solved. At least, it wasn't in my day.'

Rutherford made a face at her. 'All right, all right. But I still don't see what hope you've got of any way of wrapping up all those old loose ends so everybody's happy.'

'Oh, there won't be anything tidy, no. No single clear-cut verdict, neatly rounded off with a judicial sentence, and forget it. Old vendettas never die. Remember the old cattle wars in the Wild West, and families hating one another for generation after generation? Or our own Border reivers — the Armstrongs and Eliots forever at one another's throats, so that even now they never have their reunions in Liddesdale in the same year. Clan wars ... and still they're at it. Blustering braggarts like that Ferguson creature.'

'Speaking ill of the dead, are we? Against proper procedure, Detective Inspector Gunn.'

'If you'd been there at Achnachrain. Listening to that lout sneering at my husband.'

'Ah! So you're one who hates his guts.'

'I don't care for pretentious loudmouths denigrating people finer than themselves.'

'Least of all your husband.'

'All right, yes.'

'Must add you to our list of suspects. Motive, yes. Opportunity?'

'Oh, come on, you can't seriously believe —'

'Unfortunately, no. A pity. Such a neat tie-in.' Rutherford sighed. 'But it's not you, is it?'

'You know damn well it's not.' Lesley thought for a moment, then asked: 'How did you get on with that odd business down in Leith?'

'Oh, what we expected. Coroner's verdict, death by misadventure. What else could it have been?'

'And Morwenna Ross is off your list of suspects? Theories of lethal hypnosis abandoned?'

Rutherford sighed. 'If looks could kill, we'd have our hands full in every Grassmarket pub every Friday and Saturday night.'

As the two of them walked to the front door, with the sergeant plodding behind like an obedient sheepdog waiting for the next command, Jacques Hunter strode across the foyer, staring straight ahead as if to confront some troublesome situation.

'And who might that have been?' asked Rutherford.

'Name of Hunter. Jacques Hunter. Big shot from Toronto. Second in command to old Jamie himself.'

'Seems to fancy himself, the way he strides out. Like he owns the whole joint.'

'I fancy there's a clash of personality here, somehow. Morwenna Ross has an executive position because of family. Our Mr Hunter's got there by sheer force of personality. Or because of old man Jamie's sentimental feelings towards the original Canadian natives.'

'Certainly looks like a Red Indian on the warpath.'

'Actually, I understand he's the descendant of a Scottish settler and an Indian woman. Quite common. And the Rosses were well into it. One of them became a fully accepted chief of the Cherokee.'

'Another oddball. That woman, and now this one.' He sighed again. 'But no reason to be killers, would you say?'

'Not unless there was something getting in the way of their ambitions,' said Lesley, mock earnest. 'Promotion, or whatever. It's only fanaticism of one kind or another that gets people into top jobs. And then they're susceptible to every wind that blows, hot or cold.'

'And *you* weren't fanatical enough to go for promotion to DCI?'

'I got distracted, remember?'

'Yes. Bloody waste.'

'Now you're the one getting disrespectful towards my husband.'

'Lucky sod.'

Lesley watched him stomp out with that familiar lopsided gait of his, then sauntered back into the library for another study of the Bewick sketches.

Beth had gone, but Luke was stooped over his laptop on the long table with its usual stacks of papers and printouts. As Lesley came in, he jolted backwards and banged his right hand on the table, while grabbing a sheaf of yellowing documents in his left fist and waving them in the air — for

Luke, an incredible misuse of hallowed paper. His sudden cry was like an explosion in the hush of that sanctum.

'It's the wrong Rosses!'

Before Lesley could ask what this was about, Jacques Hunter appeared in the doorway. 'We've got to get busy.' His voice, unlike Luke's hysterical outburst, was powerfully magisterial. 'Mr Ross doesn't feel he can wait any longer. He's coming over.'

13

James Fergus Ross's private jet was due to arrive at Prestwick mid-afternoon on the Monday. All work in the Ross Foundation was sidelined except for a weekend spent tarting up the Drovers Court facilities and the airing and polishing of the old man's personal office in the Foundation building. Ogilvie was in his element, fussing to and fro, checking and double-checking. By the end of the first morning he had grown hoarse, with every three or four words coming out in sudden high squawks. Then Jacques Hunter would sweep aside his orders and substitute others.

Beth had gone through sessions like this before, though without Jacques Hunter and Morwenna Ross to add to the turmoil. Years ago, old Jamie had heard of a Greek shipping tycoon who maintained a permanent suite in a Park Lane hotel in London and paid a full-time assistant with the sole duty of getting out of storage whichever of his art works he fancied having around him during a stay, all set in the exact spots he favoured. Beth had been appointed to this post on top of her other duties, and although there had been no explicit instructions this time she thought she could guess well enough which treasures he was likely to favour.

As she was supervising the setting up of two Renoirs and a Dufy above three ormolu tables carrying a Fabergé egg and an assortment of Jacobean glass she became aware of a tall man standing at her shoulder, as if in turn supervising her own movements. Ogilvie had already fussed in and out twice. This man was calmer, almost a statue which old Mr Ross might have decreed should be installed here.

Jacques Hunter said: 'Very efficient, Miss Crichton. We can just hope it's not all wasted on him this time.'

'He's usually been quite happy with the way I lay things out for him,' said Beth frostily.

'I don't doubt that. But he's not the way he was. I'd hoped we'd be hearing his laser treatment would have cleared up that opacification, but it seems there's been an infection. Endophthalmitis.' The words came out like an incantation learned by heart and repeated with a religious finality. 'And now a sharp decline. Too damn sharp.'

'And he's even more impatient to see how the restoration work's going, while he's still got *some* vision left?'

'You've got it. But already, Mrs Ross and myself have been learning to act as his eyes and ears.'

And being very selective about what he sees and hears, for your own good. Beth hoped her thoughts weren't too resonant to be picked up by this all too well organized executive.

'I think,' Hunter went on, 'we must set up a reception for Mr Ross. Give him a couple of days to settle in, and then — let's say this coming Thursday, OK? He'll be expecting some kind of big hello, even if he doesn't recognize half the faces any more.'

'In spite of that recent murder?'

'What's that got to do with us?'

'Well, I don't know.' Beth was flustered. Too many questions still hung over it, especially questions she still couldn't ask herself about Randal Grant. 'The victim ... that Ferguson man ... he'd been involved in lots of business troubles with Mr Ross. And with his wife once being Mr Ross's ... I just thought maybe ... well ... people might think it's not really a good time.'

'A thoroughly lousy character.' Hunter was emphatic. 'Nothing to do with us. Right, young lady. When you've finished here, perhaps you'd best be getting on with a guest list.' It was not a suggestion but an order. As if to soften it, he added: 'It's on record that you're very smart at knowing who's who and what they can contribute.'

Ogilvie was determined to shoulder his way into this, at any rate. The moment he came across Beth drawing up her list he was full of suggestions; but lacked Hunter's authority to make them a direct order.

'We've got to have the Canadian commercial attaché. He'd never forgive me if we —'

'I think a personal note from you would do the trick,' Beth said cunningly.

'And someone from the cultural side, of course. To tie in with the Nova Scotia and Cape Breton pipers, and the Clan Societies we're in regular touch with.'

'Yes,' said Beth. 'Yes, of course.'

She let him drone on about a television feature and the possibility of getting the local MP to attend while in her mind she ran through the names of business leaders who had met Ross on earlier occasions, and the Ross employees on both sides of the Border of high enough status to be invited into the awe-inspiring presence.

'Must go and check we have the proper Canadian whisky everywhere. Always insists on Valleyfield Schenley. You know, of course, that one of the Ross enterprises has been supplying staves to the cooperages of Nova Scotia and Quebec distilleries.'

'Yes, of course,' said Beth again. She had included the information in enough publicity leaflets and handouts at trade fairs to need no reminding.

When Ogilvie had gone off to harry some other members of staff, she had a quiet moment to draw up her own mental list.

Including the matter of a photographer to record the entire proceedings.

Monday lunchtime she bought a few sandwiches from the delicatessen round the corner from Randal's studio. As she pushed his door open he tried to put his arms round her, but she brushed him aside.

'I haven't got long. We've got to talk.'

'With our mouths full?'

'The big boss is on his way over. Arriving this afternoon. And there's to be a big reception for him on Thursday.'

'Ah.' He looked oddly distant for a moment, as if trying to drag events into focus. Then he turned away to get a bottle of Meursault from the fridge, and two glasses from the shelf in the cramped kitchenette. When he came back he sounded his usual airy self. 'So you're in charge of the festivities.'

'Television coverage, yes. The press, the VIPs, all my usual routine.'

'Including photographic coverage?'

'That's what I'm worried about.'

'I thought we had a deal.'

'Yes, but ... well, there's this awful business about that man Ferguson. I mean, with you involved in it, and involving me —'

'Sweet Beth, you're not involved in anything you don't want to be.'

'Why did you tell that policeman I was with you when you did the shoot for Mrs Ferguson?'

He put his glass down very slowly on the table. 'I never so much as mentioned your name.'

'Well, somehow he knew.'

Again he tried to put his arm round her, but she edged away. Then she felt a rush of something she couldn't control because she didn't know what she was most upset about. 'Randal, doesn't this make things too difficult?' It came out in a desperate wail. 'I mean, if some reporter wants to make a story out of you being at the reception and it's known you were ... oh, you know, 'helping the police with their inquiries' over the Ferguson murder ... doesn't it complicate things?'

'Not so far as I'm concerned.'

'But if someone wants to make a thing about the dead man being an old business rival of Mr Ross, *and* having stolen his wife away from him? And here we are, the Ross Foundation, employing a suspect in the murder case.'

'I don't think I'm a serious suspect. I was merely taking photographs.'

'And was it true that that magazine commissioned you to do that particular feature?'

He tried one of his relaxed, impish grins, but it lacked conviction. 'No. I thought it up myself. Convinced the divine Nadine, anyway.'

'But why?'

'Because I thought it would make a good feature and I'd be able to sell it easily enough.'

'But why drag me into it?'

'To impress you with my talent, of course, and get a commission from you. That was the real reason behind the whole shoot.' He waited a long moment, then said forcefully: 'Oh, nothing of the kind. I wanted to see you again. And Beth ... I want to go on seeing you. Over and over again. All the time.'

She looked at him, longing to forget Drovers Court and the Ross Foundation building, and all the hassle of it, and spend the rest of the afternoon here with him.

He sensed it, and again reached out for her, and for a brief eternity she let herself collapse into his arms. Then she pulled herself away. 'It's time I was back at the treadmill.'

'Beth. Darling Beth, forget them. Let's forget the wThole picture deal. What matters is us. Does that sound too corny?'

'Yes, it does.' Now they were both laughing, and she was saying, 'But I'll bear it in mind. Only before I go, let's fix the time for you to show up on Thursday.'

'So the job's still on?'

'You know perfectly well it is, damn you.'

On the way back, she tried to talk herself out of wondering if it really was true, after all, that she was being used as just a pawn in his career game. Against the chill of that, she was wrapped in the warmth of his nearness, still with her, still tantalizing.

The library door was open. Luke was sitting on the far side of his table, staring out like a timekeeper checking on employees' punctuality. 'Just time for a quickie, was there?'

'Luke, please. Let's not —'

'It's all right, Beth. You don't owe me any explanations. But I still ... I wouldn't want you to get hurt.'

She went on, to find that most doors were like Luke's — open, waiting for the first sound of Mr Ross's arrival.

*

Everybody had rehearsed the appropriate level of enthusiastic welcome, according to status in the hierarchy. But everybody was shocked.

James Fergus Ross, for all his philanthropic activities, had once been a fearsome figure. His entrances were always awaited with shivers of apprehension about his possible mood. His mere approach was enough to frighten any members of staff into wondering which of their possible mistakes had come to light; what irrational mood could make him fire a dozen men and women at one go; what abrupt, impossible demands he might make within seconds of arriving. But today was different. Voices were awkward, there were some shocked whispers, and some shuffling from side to side as he approached.

The imperious autocrat had shrunk.

He moved slowly, hunched over a walking stick almost as gnarled as himself, as if imitating an arthritic old shepherd or drover from some Wilkie painting. On each side he was supported — almost literally supported — by two six-foot heavies who might have been battle-scarred discards from the Royal Canadian Mounted Police. Shrivelled as he was, he looked as if he needed medical carers rather than pugnacious minders. And close behind the stooped figure, Morwenna Ross and Jacques Hunter looked unreasonably tall and healthy — ready to seize power immediately it became necessary, thought Beth. And then do battle with each other for final command?

Hunter made a long, grave survey of the groups of employees assembled in the hall and on the main staircase. 'Mr Ross is tired after his flight. But he'll want to talk to all of you — all of us — as soon as he's got his breath back.'

Ross shuffled towards the lift, on his way up to that holy of holies, his office at the top of the building. When the lift doors had hissed shut behind him, there was an echo in the querulous whispers that ran around the hall.

'Doesn't look too bright ...'

'Remember the way he used to storm in through that door and let fly when he was halfway across the hall?'

Each department expected a summons. Always there had been an inquisition. Sometimes grudging praise; more often searching questions and sharp condemnation. This time, the long-awaited, apprehension-loaded arrival had fizzled away into a nothingness almost as disturbing as the usual immediate confrontations.

Luke Drummond had anticipated a grilling over the updating of worldwide records of Ross Foundation activities, and had prepared a folder of key information. Beth Crichton was ready to show her own display file of PR material, and was wondering uneasily whether old Jamie had been shown Randal Grant's photographs of the Ferguson interiors and what questions he might throw at her.

There was no summons; no grilling.

Ogilvie, the only one to be summoned to the presence for any length of time, emerged to pontificate about Mr Ross's keen interest in the progress made on the croft reconstruction, his immediately helpful comments, and his wonderful grasp of each little detail. Ogilvie's interpretations were never altogether reliable.

Later Mr Ross was escorted to Drovers Court. No word came back as to whether he approved of the layout of his treasures which Beth had prepared; but neither was there a word of disapproval.

A television interview she had set up showed the old man in a more impressive aspect. Skilful lighting and a flattering camera angle made him look not so much shrunken as taut, coiled up ready to strike, his eyes bright as if staring a challenge rather than trying to bring things into focus. His voice was filtered and boosted to emerge as a confident, domineering growl. Yes, he was delighted to be back in the country of his ancestors, involving himself personally in this historic project. No, in spite of some trouble with his eyesight and the usual stiffnesses of old age he had no intention of retiring. There were still too many things to do.

'You'll remember, sir, how John D. Rockefeller was asked towards the end of his life whether, looking back, he would prefer to have had good health rather than all that money?'

'Sure, I do seem to have heard that someplace. And he said the money, right?'

'That's right, sir. And yourself?'

Ross scowled down at his knees. There was a delay, long by TV interview standards. When he raised his head again his voice was shaky and less assertive than usual. 'A family,' he said. 'A real family. That's what I'd have liked to have. Someone to follow on.'

Watching beside Beth in his studio, Randal Grant muttered something she didn't catch. She said: 'What was that?'

He turned the volume down. 'Just thinking. From what I've heard, he had a family, but managed to break it up. Old hypocrite.'

'I thought the trouble was that the older son died in an accident. Hardly old Jamie's fault. And wasn't there something about the other son —'

Randal turned the sound back up as the old man finished the interview on an assertive note, boasting about Ross Enterprise's big investment in two new biofuel programmes within their forestry operations in Quebec.

'Now,' said Beth, 'let's wrap this up. About tomorrow's big do —'

'We could talk about it in bed.' Randal put the remote control down. 'Afterwards.'

'We could talk about it first.'

'No. First things first.'

She had been sitting too close to him as they watched — too close to be able to pull away now.

*

Lesley Torrance had been in the library at the time of old Jamie's arrival, and caught only a glimpse of him limping past the open door. Nobody had bothered to call her out to introduce her. She was not greatly concerned, yet there was something slipshod about the whole set-up: a sense of let-down, things not quite coming together in spite of all the bustle and build-up.

Still, she and Nick had been formally invited to the reception in Drovers Court. Perhaps here the threads would be pulled together into a coherent pattern.

*

Standing beside her on a balcony above the ballroom, Nick said: 'All right, fill me in. That fussy little twit with the shiny cranium must be Simon Ogilvie.'

'It is.'

'After your description, I could have picked him out on any identity parade.'

Ogilvie had arrived early, and was dodging from one fresh arrival to another like a sheepdog rounding up groups of individuals and chivvying them towards different corners of the room.

'And that fantastic female just coming in,' said Nick. 'That couldn't be the Beth you've told me about?'

Lesley leaned past him. 'Indeed it couldn't.'

The female in question was dressed in a lime green two-piece with blouson sleeves which didn't really belong to the outfit but which, Lesley thought cattily, were probably meant to disguise flabby pink arms. Her bouffant hair was a wildly improbable apricot colour.

'I don't know, but I'd guess ... yes, there she goes.'

The woman looked around and then headed purposefully for Simon Ogilvie.

'I'd heard of her,' said Lesley. 'Now I know why they always refer to her as Mrs Apricot Ogilvie.'

The next arrivals were Morwenna Ross and Jacques Hunter, coming in together almost like a married couple yet maintaining a few unvarying inches between one another.

'That has to be Hunter,' guessed Nick. 'Married?'

'Only to his work, they say.'

The two were followed, as if their appearance had been a signal, by six waitresses carrying silver trays of drinks. For a few minutes the guests made a pretence of being mildly surprised by the array of glasses; then three or four accepted a drink as a polite gesture, and conversation grew louder.

Nick began humming to himself.

'Just a minute,' Lesley protested. 'You've not been commissioned to write the incidental music without telling me, have you?'

'Just playing around with a suitable theme. Not too brash. No signs of them being ready for a highland reel so early in the evening.'

He spoke with the easy authority of one who had acquired trophies in the days before he was surprised by his baronetcy — two statuettes on a side shelf in Black Knowe, commemorating rewards for a film and a TV series.

'A wistful folk song to make them cry into their wine?' he suggested.

'Most of them seem to be on the hard stuff.'

There was a change of grouping below. A little knot of guests near a closed door came apart, drifting in twos and threes to either side of the room, with Ogilvie almost dancing around them as if driven by sprightly

The Merciless Dead

music transmitted to him from Nick. Well back from them, a larger group began forming a semicircle, staring at the door, waiting.

'Cue leading man,' muttered Nick. 'Fanfare. And ... *action*!'

The door opened. James Fergus Ross was framed in it, hunched forward in a wheelchair. His two hefty attendants, each with a hand on the back, moved him into the room at a solemn, steady pace.

At the same time there was a blast of sound a few feet away from Lesley's left ear. A piper had appeared at the end of the balcony, and now began pacing along it, launching into the complex flourishes of a pibroch.

Nick took his wife's arm. 'Shall we go down?'

A man and wife were being introduced to old Jamie. Some insignia on the man's chest suggested that he was a figure of some local consequence. His wife was very tall and sleek, having to stoop at an awkward angle to shake the old man's hand.

Ogilvie nodded and half bowed them away, ticking them off his mental list, and beckoned Nick and Lesley forward. They might have been next in line on the New Year's honours list for a royal accolade.

'Mr Ross, this is Sir Nicholas Torrance. And Lady Torrance, who has been doing some admirable research for us on the project.'

'Torrance? Don't think I've had dealings with any Torrances.' Ross's head tilted towards Nick, his eyes squinting vainly. 'Property up in Sutherland?' he barked suspiciously.

'In the Borders,' said Nick.

'Ah.' Ross grunted what might have been a grudging absolution. 'Not a part of the world I've had much dealings with.'

'You've given the most generous donations to the Roxburgh Junior Orchestra,' Ogilvie hastened to intervene.

'Learning the pipes, hey?' Ross raised an arm in the vague direction of the player still pacing to and fro along the balcony.

'Mainly strings, actually.'

'Oh.' The two bodyguards moved in unison, edging the wheelchair with heavy precision a few feet towards the next waiting group.

After ten minutes, old Jamie suddenly heaved himself up a few inches in his wheelchair. 'Ogilvie!'

'Yes, Mr Ross?'

'Who the hell brought all these people here?'

'I thought you'd want to meet some of the outstanding members of our community who —'

'That's enough. Tell them they can all relax. And get me a drink.'

Ogilvie raised his arm, and a waiter carrying a tray with one large tumbler of whisky on it approached reverently. Ross held the glass between his two hands, shaking slightly, and took a long, appreciative sip.

'Got one thing right, anyway.'

The guests swirled about like leaves puffed into new huddles by a breeze. Old Jamie's minders steered him into the bar with a long plate glass window overlooking the indoor swimming pool.

Lesley and Nick drifted in behind them, watching swimmers beginning to appear with a regularity which might almost have been scheduled by Ogilvie. Some attempt was being made to create an atmosphere of family friendliness, with old man Ross as a benevolent grandfather who would enjoy watching his large family enjoying themselves.

Lesley nudged Nick, nodding towards a splash of colour on the far side of the pool. Mrs Apricot Ogilvie had clearly decided not to risk exposing too much of herself, but was determined to make another dramatic entry, this time appearing from one of the changing cubicles into the pool area in a long towelling robe in colours reminiscent of a tropical fruit juice packet. Smiling regally at the others along the edge of the pool, she sprawled onto a lounger of further clashing hues.

'I must say she's made a pretty quick change,' muttered Nick.

Ogilvie himself, in dark red trunks, hurried past his wife and poised himself with all the hand-rubbing and swagger of someone who has never much cared for swimming but is determined to be one of the gang. After a few moments he jumped noisily in. From her vantage point, Lesley wouldn't have put it past him to kick water in the women's faces and honk at them like a grampus.

Morwenna Ross stood on the edge a few feet away, statuesque rather than hesitant. She wore a jet black one-piece with a broad strap and a small bow just touching the end of that swathe of black hair which narrowed down the nape of her neck. Her nipples were large and thrusting within the taut fabric. Lesley guessed they must be as purple as the depths of her eyes.

Abruptly Nick said: '*That's* Beth, right?'

There was a startling contrast between the darkness of Morwenna and the slimmer, pale beauty of the figure moving past her.

'Right this time,' she agreed. 'Try not to steam up the glass.'

Beth's pale blue one-piece clung to each unselfconscious move, emphasizing the slight sway of her hips as she headed for the edge of the pool. Her hair was almost golden in the light from above, and runnels of light gleamed down her arms as she reached up with them, swayed, and dived in, a shimmering streak under the surface.

Morwenna seemed for a moment reluctant to follow. Haunted by her husband, drowned those thousands of miles away, all those long months away? Then she launched herself, and Lesley had a ridiculous vision of her as a dark killer in pursuit of its pale prey.

Randal Grant had been crouching at the end of the pool in maroon swimming trunks, taking a sequence of pictures. He waited for Beth's head to emerge from the water, wiping water from her eyes and smiling up at him; then set his Canon carefully on the corner shelf before plunging in beside her.

Suddenly Ogilvie's arms began to thrash wildly. It was difficult to tell whether he was in genuine difficulties, suffering a sudden cramp, or whether he simply wanted an excuse to grab the nearest shapely woman. He clawed at Morwenna Ross, and got his fingers snarled in the strap of her costume, wrenching it off her shoulder. She dragged herself free, colliding with Beth. Together they floundered away from Ogilvie and hauled themselves out of the water.

Close to Lesley's ear, Nick said: 'Do those two get on together?'

'Part of the team. Morwenna's senior, but Beth has belonged in the Edinburgh office a lot longer, and knows the local ropes. Seem to get on all right, anyway. Why?'

Morwenna did seem to be turning impatiently, angrily away from Beth. Even from this distance Lesley could see Beth flinch; see her eyes widen, while Morwenna reached up with the sort of affronted modesty you wouldn't expect between two women, dragging the strap over her breast with her right hand and hurrying into one of the cubicles. Beth stood very still for a moment, then looked down into the water as if to plunge back in again. Instead, she went off to change.

Behind the spectators in the bar there was a sudden flurry as two drinkers were pushed aside and a newcomer arrived, even more extravagantly dressed than Mrs Ogilvie. Nadine Ferguson came to a standstill before James Fergus Ross with her arms spread wide, pleading.

'James. Can you ever forgive me? I just had to come. After this dreadful business, I simply had to come and see whether —'

'How much did it cost you to have that phoney rubbed out, Nadine?'

'James, it was nothing to do with me. I swear it. But I can swear, too, that there's many a time I've wished it. I felt so guilty. He only wanted me in order to undermine you.'

'For God's sake get this creature —'

'Please, my dear. Please. Can we just get away somewhere private, just for a few minutes? Just so we can talk?'

'Who the hell let her in?' Ross's clenched hands struggled to push himself upright in his chair.

'There's nothing I'd like more than to look after you, my darling, now that you'll need —'

'Where's Ogilvie? Never around when you want him.'

It was difficult to look tactfully away, but Nick and Lesley edged closer to the far end of the bar. A tall figure strode past them and loomed over the group, just fractionally taller than even old Jamie's minders.

'Jacques Hunter,' murmured Lesley to Nick. 'The real power behind the throne, I think.'

It was only a matter of seconds before Nadine Ferguson was escorted, waving her arms and crying out in spasms like a hiccupping seagull, out of the bar. A few more seconds, and Ross was clutching his second tumbler of Valleyfield.

Beth appeared quietly beside Lesley, followed by Randal Grant with his camera. 'Did you see ... from where you are, could you ...' She shook her head, at a loss for words, and took Lesley's arm to steady herself.

'Girl talk?' said Nick. 'All right, I'll turn a deaf ear while I get you a drink. What's it to be?'

As he headed for the bar and Randal moved towards old Jamie, raising his camera, Lesley said: 'Just what did go on down there? That clumsy oaf Ogilvie doing a grampus act — or was he having a bit of a grope?'

'Just doing one of his hearty acts to impress his wife, and slipped. But ... from up here, could you see?'

'See what?'

'Morwenna. Just above her left breast. A great purple bruise. A dreadful blotch, poor woman. The clear outline of a horseshoe.'

'Just a minute. You mean, like —'

There was a sudden shout from old Mr Ross, further along the bar. 'And who the hell are you? D'you work for me?'

'Not on your regular staff, no, sir.'

'Then who are you? And what are you crouching down there for?'

'Randal Grant, sir. I've been contracted to take the photographs for this occasion. Now, I'd say this was your best profile.' Randal was down on one knee, tilting the Canon upwards.

'I'll bet you've got a profile just like it.'

'If you'll just look up at the bottles on that top shelf —'

'Looks like you've grown a beard. Your brother tried it once, but it was just one hell of a mess. Remember?'

'I don't have a brother.'

'Not any longer, no. Went overboard. Look, son, my sight may not be too good any longer, but there's nothing wrong with my hearing. I know that voice. Ought to. Heard it whining and complaining often enough. Grown up now, are we, David?'

14

This time DCI Rutherford felt that the questioning would be better done in a proper interview room rather than in surroundings too comfortable for the suspect. Not that the man was, technically, a suspect. Not quite yet. Just still helping the police with their inquiries. But Rutherford wanted those inquiries pressed a bit less courteously.

Starting with one shifty aspect of the whole business.

'Right, Mr Grant. Or is it Mr Ross?'

'I've got used to being Randal Grant for a long time now.'

'We may have to apply in due course for confirmation of the name under which we … well, call you in court as a witness, or whatever.'

'"Whatever' meaning being charged with murder?'

'We hope not,' said Rutherford insincerely.

The interviewee was provided with a chair as uncomfortable as possible, its seat just narrow enough to make it necessary to clench one's buttocks in order not to slide to one side or the other. And although the phrase 'interrogation room' was officially frowned on, everybody in the nick privately favoured it over 'interview room', and behaved accordingly.

'This revelation of your real identity,' Rutherford went on, 'does cast an interesting new light on the case, doesn't it?'

'In what way?'

'Well, are you going to tell me that Mrs Ferguson didn't know full well who you were when you photographed her house?'

'She certainly didn't. Didn't recognize me.'

'Odd, wasn't it? I mean, maybe that beard of yours is recent, but —'

'I'd left home before my father was stupid enough to marry that creature. And just before my brother married. Until now I've stayed well away from the lot of them. I preferred a different way of life.'

'But now you're regretting it. You want to win your way back into your father's good books. And your stepmother was finding out *she'd* made a mistake, and wanted to get back with your father. Both of you could have agreed to sink your differences and get Ferguson out of the way.'

'I've told you, we didn't even know one another.'

'Then what's the alternative? For some reason you wheedled your way into her house on the pretence that a magazine had commissioned you to do a feature. But it hadn't, had it?'

'I wanted to wheedle my way, as you put it, into getting a commission from the Ross Foundation. Impress them with my talent.'

'And get back close to your father. Maybe not just pictures, but hoping to please him by removing his hated old rival?'

'Do stick to one accusation at a time, Chief Inspector. If you're going to charge me with murder, go ahead and stop wasting time. Yours and mine.'

'All in good time, Mr … mm … Grant. Now, while you're on the premises, would you have any objection to our taking those finger-prints?'

'None whatsoever. I'll provide you with the DNA and urine samples as well, if that'll amuse you.'

'Murder's a serious business, Mr Grant. Not at all amusing. What's the betting we find your fingerprints on the murder weapon?'

'Meaning the totem pole head?'

'So you know that was the weapon.'

'Of course I know. I was the one who found the body, and saw that right beside it. I didn't need to be a detective to see which blunt instrument had done the deed.'

'And you handled the wooden head? Picked it up?'

'No, I didn't. Not then.'

'Ah. But earlier?'

'Much earlier. When I was taking pictures in that room. I had to move it into a better light.'

That, of course, would be what any competent defence counsel would say on his client's behalf. Rutherford groaned inwardly. It would be difficult to refute.

'So,' Grant went on, 'of course there'll be my fingerprints on the damn thing. As well as somebody else's, maybe.'

'Maybe.'

'And your experts will no doubt be able to decide which are the more recent.'

Rutherford longed to jolt this know-all out of his complacency. Yet at the same time he couldn't disagree with anything he had said so far. Forensics would have to sort out where the prints were in relation to one another and to the bloodstains and strands of hair, maybe superimposed one on the other. Whatever the results, there were still the imponderables: the whole tie-up between this so-called Grant, old man Ross, the widow Ferguson, and maybe somehow that Crichton girl, all seeming suspicious, but all too vague. He wasn't confident of pushing this much further; yet couldn't see any other direction worth pursuing.

There was a rap at the door, and a uniformed officer leaned round it. 'Sorry to interrupt, sir, but there's a lady in reception says she's got something from Lockhart House that'll interest you.'

Rutherford debated whether to let the young man sit here and stew for a while, and then come back to him. But Grant — or Ross, or whatever — was getting to his feet. Short of charging him, Rutherford had no means of preventing him leaving.

He came up with at any rate an implicit warning. 'You're not thinking of leaving Edinburgh?'

'I've already told you that. Right now, I'm just printing out my pictures through the computer, and I aim to go round and see about collecting my fee.'

'Don't spend it on any holidays abroad, Mr ... er ... Ross.'

'I prefer to remain Randal Grant.'

They walked out together. Rutherford had half expected the lady waiting for him to be Mrs Ferguson, and was bracing himself for hysterical demands as to why he had not arrested the murderer, whoever it might be. Instead, it was Lesley Torrance. As Randal Grant nodded politely and headed for the street door, she said: 'No, don't go. Please. You may be able to confirm something for us. Do you remember this?'

She was holding a small silver brooch in the palm of her left hand. Grant bent over it, and then made way for Rutherford.

'What's all this about?' asked Rutherford.

'Yes, of course.' Grant made another inspection. 'It was in the Fergusons' collection. It's at the side of one of my close-ups. In the ... let's see ... the North American room, I think.'

'Odd place to put it. I'd have thought it belonged —'

'Could have been taken over by emigrants from Wester Ross, maybe, and later brought back to Scotland by one of the Ferguson family.'

'Just what the hell is it?' demanded Rutherford impatiently.

'A witch-brooch,' said Lesley. 'To keep witches and child-snatching fairies at bay.'

'An expensive piece for a crofting family to own, if that's what you're suggesting.'

The Merciless Dead

'Just possible for a skilful relative to make for them in the days when they were still working the land and saving up over a period of time. It would have been a family treasure.'

'Look, what made you think I'd be interested?'

'A robbery from Lockhart House is pretty interesting, isn't it?' said Lesley. 'Especially as it obviously took place *after* Ferguson's murder. Because it was still there beforehand, when this gentleman took those photographs.'

'How did you come to get your hands on it?'

'It was offered to a dealer friend of mine who knew I was acquiring material for old Mr Ross's project.'

'And *he* got it — how?'

'He was a bit hazy about that.'

'I'll bet.'

'I fancy it could have been one of the staff at Lockhart House nicked it.'

'One of the staff?' Randal laughed. 'From what Mrs Ferguson said, there were precious few of those.'

'Then it shouldn't take long to round them up and interview them,' said Rutherford.

*

'You bastard!'

Beth was heading for the library as Randal came up the steps and into the foyer. He shifted the large leather display folder under his arm to get a better grip after shouldering the door open, and grinned.

'Absolutely not. Parentage vouched for very recently. In front of reputable witnesses.'

'All those pretences,' she seethed. 'And all the time you just wanted to wheedle your way back into the family firm. That's what it's been about, hasn't it?'

'Where *do* you people get these deplorable ideas?' Randal protested. 'That's the second time today I've been accused of that. The first time, it was linked with a picture of me as a murderer. Wheedling — what a word! But speaking of pictures, wouldn't you like to see the stuff from the reception?'

'Not particularly.'

'Come off it, my love. Of course you would.'

'I'm not your love. And I'm not sure I ought to have let you con us into taking on that ...' Her voice trailed away. Reluctantly she said: 'Did you get a clear picture of Morwenna and me? Of her shoulder and ...?'

'Better let me show you.'

She held the library door open for him.

It might almost have struck a spark triggering an explosion. Crouched before his computer, stabbing at the keyboard and glaring spasmodically at the monitor, Luke let out a furious shout. It was quite unlike him. He could remain calm and methodical over the most complex analyses, and even when there was a glitch he usually confined himself to a shrug and a derisive sigh. Today he was out of control.

'Damn clodhoppers. There must be a way of separating these family strands. Has to be. But I've got to be *sure*. And here we are, stuck halfway between paper and online records.'

'National Archive hiccups?' said Beth sympathetically.

'Switching all their records from files to this.' He gestured a challenge at his computer screen. 'And taking their time about it. The online version's running two years behind time. I've tried the microfiche, but some of it's too blurred to be any use. I'm told the Statistics Office can access its own files digitally, but the rest of us are going to have to wait another couple of years, sod it.'

He became aware of Randal Grant behind Beth and stiffened, the way a dog might stiffen when a dubious newcomer edges onto its territory.

'Special delivery,' said Randal. 'Ready to see my pretty pictures? No porn, I'm sorry to say.'

'What about that business with Morwenna and me?' Beth could not restrain herself. Like Luke, she was desperate to grapple with a question plaguing her. 'There was something very nasty there. Does any of it show up on your shots?'

Randal opened the folder and riffled through the transparent pockets. There were scenes of Ogilvie, looking even more of a pompous clown than he did in reality, Mrs Ogilvie sprawled out on her lounger, Sir Nicholas and Lady Torrance in several relaxed poses, and several long shots covering the whole pool. The camera then zoomed in on Morwenna and Beth, favouring Beth, with Morwenna half turning away and Beth staring, blurred by flashing ripples of light across the water.

'That's as close as you got?'

'Sorry. I didn't know there was anything special going on. We didn't have time to discuss it afterwards. Things took rather an unexpected turn.'

'Quite,' said Luke sourly. 'Family revelations. Wonderfully dramatic timing, Mr ... er, Mr Ross, isn't it?' But he must have felt the need to soothe Beth. 'What's worrying you about that scene?'

'Morwenna. On her shoulder, where her costume got pulled away, there was a weal just above her left breast. The shape of a horseshoe. She was very upset. Didn't want me to see it.'

'A riding accident back home?'

'No, it was ... I don't know, it was somehow worse than that. I was telling Lady Torrance afterwards, when ... oh, we got interrupted by that business about you and old Jamie.'

'Apologies, I'm sure.'

'It was frightening. I've been trying to tell myself it must be a tattoo, but people aren't usually in a hurry to conceal those. Tend to flaunt them.'

'Don't tell me she's got a ring in her navel as well?'

'No, it wasn't like that. It was ... well, the only way I can put it ... that mark was almost burnt into the flesh. As if with a branding iron. Or a red-hot horseshoe trampled into her shoulder.'

Luke very quietly said: 'Like Margaret Ross of Strathcarron.'

'They called that a massacre, didn't they?' said Randal.

'You've been doing your homework, Mr Ross. Yes, all those women attacked by the police. Truncheons splitting their heads open. Dragged off to Tain gaol dripping blood. Nailed boots stamping on their breasts. And Margaret Ross knocked down while a mounted officer's horse trampled on her.'

They looked at one another and then at the photograph of Morwenna and Beth as if to zoom in on that shoulder under the torn strap. It was Beth who broke the shuddering silence. 'You can't *inherit* the shape of an injury over the generations, surely?'

'You might feel so strongly about it' — Luke had slid back into being his usual quiet and implacably matter-of-fact self — 'that you develop sympathetic stigmata.'

Randal raised a sceptical eyebrow. 'Inheriting stigmata?'

'Psychosomatically, maybe you can *believe* yourself into inheriting it. If your feelings are intense enough.'

Intense, yes, thought Beth. But Morwenna was a Ross only by marriage. Could she possibly have taken on a weird inheritance along with taking on her Ross husband?

There was a bumping noise from the outer hall. A mutter of voices, one of them suddenly becoming harsh and impatient. A door thudded shut, the door into the library opened again. James Fergus Ross was wheeled in by one of his heavies, who came to a stop and stared blankly above his employer's head.

The old man squinted in an attempt to focus on some recognisable features out of those already in the room.

'Whatever you're doing, you can stop right now.'

Beth glanced down at the photographs. No point in showing them to him, even if he had been in the mood to study them, which sounded unlikely.

However poor his sight, old Ross seemed to have sensitive antennae. 'Getting bored, young lady? Losing a taste for the Edinburgh fleshpots? And the whole job?'

'No, sir. I've felt all along that we were actually achieving something with this project.' It sounded as if she were buttering him up, but that was just too bad. She was telling the truth.

He seemed to have picked that up, too. 'Meaning that you usually spend your time promoting some very dubious causes?'

'No, I didn't mean —'

'Of course you did. And quite right, too. Chopping down trees, running fleets of container ships, and telling the world what noble deeds we're doing. Why do you think I'm trying to make up for all that? Glad you're with me.' He twisted his wheelchair to one side, while his bulky attendant lowered over him, trying to interpret which direction he wanted to go. 'David, I know you're here. I can tell. And you'll be joining us.'

'Joining you?'

'Since one of my staff has, I understand, engaged you to make a photographic record of our entire project' — he directed a crooked grin into space, hoping to hit either or both of them — 'you'll be coming along with us to Achnachrain tomorrow.'

'Rather short notice, sir.'

'You haven't got any other engagements.' It was a statement, not a polite query. The peremptory old Ross was still there within that shrivelled frame. 'I want this whole thing wrapped up. Send for Ogilvie, someone, and check on how soon we can fix the official opening. And David —'

'I keep telling people I think of myself as Randal nowadays.'

'Too bad. I don't. Anyway, let's see you contribute something useful.'

'I'm not sure I —'

'Not sure you won't be in the cooler waiting trial for murder?' Ross winced as he shifted awkwardly in his wheelchair. 'Doing you a good turn, getting you out of the way. And if you *are* guilty, I could get to be quite fond of you in spite of everything.' He grunted, wriggled again. 'Come on, all I'm asking for is a few pretty pictures. That's your line, isn't it? Pretty pictures of landscapes? Damn it, I've *created* whole landscapes.'

'And ruined others.'

Beth waited for the explosion. None came. Instead there was a guttural sound in Ross's throat which might have been a laugh.

'That's settled, then,' he said. 'Better buy yourself plenty of film.'

'Nobody uses film nowadays. We just feed our results into the computer, juggle with them a bit, and pick out what we need.'

'I'm always willing to learn,' said his father. 'Hope you are, too.'

15

Luke was informed by a busy, bustling Ogilvie that his services as a driver would not be required this time. One of the bodyguards took the wheel of the specially adapted minibus into which Mr Ross's chair could be lifted. So far the man had been nameless. Now he became known to the rest of them, in his employer's crackling tone, simply as Waldo. His own responses consisted of monosyllables grunted in acknowledgment of instructions.

Those others on the trip were Ross himself, Morwenna Ross, Luke Drummond, Simon Ogilvie, and Randal Grant — referred to by his father occasionally as David, but then correcting this emphatically as 'young Grant', as if it were the sort of ridiculous joke which would enliven the whole journey.

Ogilvie's appearance threatened to add another frivolous note. He had abandoned his usual starchy office gear in favour of a light blue tam-o'-shanter, open-necked shirt and tartan trews, and carried a navy blue blazer draped over his left shoulder. Wanting to seem one of the gang, out for the day? Luke wondered what Mr Ross's bleared vision would make of that rig.

He wondered, too, why the old man had agreed to let Jacques Hunter go on two days ahead to familiarize himself with the whole set-up, but leaving his daughter-in-law to follow with the main party. It raised the question again: were those two collaborators or rivals? Nothing specific had been said, so far as Luke knew, other than one passing remark to Jacques Hunter as they set out: 'I need a fresh mind to set alongside what I've already been told. And this is strictly a research trip, not a holiday — not for anybody.' He turned on Luke with a sour smirk. 'Sorry we've had to cut out the female companionship, Drummond. Single beds all round, hey?'

Randal Grant stiffened. His quick, questioning glance at Luke showed him in no mood for suggestive jokes. And Luke was in no mood to admit that his own affair with Beth was over. Keep the bastard on the wrong foot.

'Your job, young man,' Ross went on, 'is to keep me informed about every significant site along the way, right? And I do mean every single one. I have these pictures in my mind, and I've read plenty, but I need you to sharpen my eyesight. You with me?'

'Yes, sir.'

Luke had brought along his laptop loaded with every detailed reference he could foresee being called on to explain. He was pretty sure he knew most of the historic sites off by heart, confirming them on that previous visit, but in case of any awkward questions he wanted every exact little detail to hand. You didn't take any risks with Mr Ross.

For a while there was nothing for him to do. He was like any day tripper, looking out of the window, apart from the fact that he knew so much about the landscape, even those parts of it that had no particular bearing on Ross interests. Only now it was becoming three-dimensional again. This was reality, somehow less reassuring than the files and documents and old prints which he enjoyed browsing over in his comfortable library.

Two hours into the northwestern Highlands, Ogilvie became brisk and authoritative. 'Turn left at the T-junction coming up, and slow down. There's a tight little bridge immediately round that corner.'

Waldo stared straight ahead and went on driving steadily without saying anything.

Ross said: 'Check the satnav and see how it squares with young Drummond's route map.'

'Should tally with what Mr Ogilvie says,' Luke confirmed.

'OK. First left at the roundabout, then.'

Waldo grunted. That remained the pattern for the rest of the journey: Ogilvie fidgeting and piping eager instructions; Waldo waiting until his boss had confirmed them before acting on them.

When Luke said, 'Stop by that stand of alders half a mile ahead,' there was the same wait for confirmation: the same words, but in Ross's cranky voice.

'This was where the Macdonalds reneged on their emigration deal,' Luke explained.

From the corner of his eye he saw Morwenna Ross's head jerk, the way a dozing traveller jolts abruptly awake. She stared intently out of the window. At the same time her father-in-law pressed his face to his nearest window, straining to see. Not that there was much to see: the trees shuddering slightly in the breeze, a lochan rippling under those same gusts, and a heap of stones like jagged teeth jutting up from the whin.

A brief rise in the pitch of the breeze might have been the voices of ghosts lamenting their life that could never be restored.

Here the widow of the Macdonald clan chief had ordered that because of arrears of rent her tenants should be driven off the land to make way for sheep. She assured them that she had their welfare at heart, and offered to pay their passage to Australia. Then at the last minute the destination was changed to Canada. Several families refused to move, declaring that the lady's late husband had promised that after the recent famine no rents would be collected until times improved, and no one would be ejected. One elderly widow, scared of facing such a journey alone, declared that rather than leave her native land she would prefer a grave to be dug beside her daughter's, even if it meant them throwing her in and burying her alive.

'When the factor and his heavies arrived,' Luke recited in a solemn monotone, 'she wouldn't move away from her fireside. So they doused it with water and dragged her out, while she grabbed at everything within reach. When they had dumped her outside, they threw her stools and bed, her spinning-wheel and her dishes, out on to the grass. Then they tore the house down.'

'A house of the Chisholms,' said Morwenna in little more than a whisper.

An echo came as another whisper from the back of Luke's mind. Of course. Morwenna's maiden name had been Chisholm. Not that it would have made any difference to the Macdonald widow had the other old woman's name also been Macdonald: she was quite determined to drive her own clan folk off the land to make way for a prosperous Lowland grazier.

Old Jamie sighed a dramatic sigh acknowledging the validity of all his deepest sorrows. It was all real and vivid to him. Just as intense as his moneymaking had once been. All those old energies were now concentrated into one knot deep inside: a sick man physically restricted but mentally all the more fervent because of that; hating every moment of his dependency, but suffused with a burning obsession as powerful as all his entrepreneurial obsessions had once been.

As they drove on, a mobile's ring-tone squeaked a few bars of *Annie Laurie*. Ogilvie, flustered, was trying to decide whether the phone was in his jacket pocket or back trouser pocket when Ross shouted: 'Turn that damn thing off. I should have told you before we set off —'

'We need to keep in touch with Queen Street, sir, in case of —'

'Turn it off. And keep it off. *I'll* tell you who we need to be in touch with and when.'

Wretchedly Ogilvie fumbled and managed to drop the mobile on the floor. Fortunately for him, Ross was distracted by a sudden vista of Swedish-style timber chalets above the sheltered arm of a loch.

'What the hell are those things doing here?'

Luke was prompt with explanations. 'Started out as a holiday complex, then a time share. Now some of them have been sold off as permanent residences.'

'They're a damned eyesore. Don't belong. All the genuine clachans were stone-built.'

Again Luke felt himself back in his library, looking through the company archives with all their references and cross-references to Ross activities in Canada, the profits they had made from timber and the company housing and stores monopoly for so many full-time and part-time employees working in the forests. He was careful not to allow himself even the flicker of a smile.

'Ogilvie, the moment we're back, set about buying those properties. For demolition. Give the occupants notice to quit.'

'There may be some problems, Mr Ross. It all depends on the terms of the —'

'Problems? Problems are for getting over, man.'

Nobody, thought Luke, was likely to draw any embarrassing parallel between the arrogant evictions of the distant past and the present intentions of James Fergus Ross.

Until Randal Grant came out with it. 'It's still in the local tradition, then? The exploiter from far away drives off the irritating local residents. What were you thinking of putting there instead, father? Sheep are just too, too last year. Not much call for a library. Maybe there's room for yet another of the celebrated Ross sawmills, right?'

'Very amusing,' said Ross. 'All right, Waldo, drive on.'

Luke resumed his stint as guide, pointing out hillocks which half covered old homesteads, and two places where wells had been closed up and the factor's teams had pulled up saplings which people had planted to shelter the homesteads they were struggling to maintain.

'Stop!' snapped Ross at one point, where a ruined croft had been converted into a sheep-fank. 'Got your gear at the ready, Mister Grant? A few shots of that. And you could have been a bit livelier over some of the sites we've just passed. Make sure of getting them on the way back.'

Randal Grant scrambled out on to the soggy ground, and obediently paced round the crumbling remains. Luke thought irritably that he already had file upon file of similar views neatly annotated in his archives. Later he would have the pleasure of sifting through this intruder's resulting prints and discarding the lot.

As they were approaching Achnachrain, he said: 'On our right, down by that burn, that's one of the late Sholto Ferguson's plantations.'

'Not any more it isn't,' said Ross.

'No longer in this world to irritate us,' said Ogilvie eagerly, to show that here he was in the know.

'There's always you around to fulfil that function.' Ross grinned an evil grin in what he calculated must be Ogilvie's direction. The old man might have mellowed in some ways, but he still needed a cringing subordinate to vent his spasmodic irritations on. 'And for your information, gentlemen, Ferguson lost that property while he was still alive. Though he didn't know it.' He was sounding gleeful now, like a small boy tipping a hated school bully into a pond. 'We bought it through his creditors while he wasn't looking. I'm thinking of establishing a Timber Research Centre there.'

'A wonderful idea, Mr Ross,' Ogilvie fawned. 'It'll bring so much into the region.'

'Might bring *you* here for a holiday? A week or two's outdoor exercise would do you a world of good. Roll up your sleeves and saw a few logs. Find out what real work is.' The main reason for Ogilvie being brought along was still clearly to be the butt of the old man's rancour.

'One of the Sutherlands' factor's nastiest efforts.' Luke was pointing out a clachan within a crumpled ring-dyke. 'When he'd set the place on fire, the stocks of butter and cheese the family were trying to save melted and ran down the slope.'

'Just the same as the American settlers treated the food stores of the Ojibwa,' commented Randal Grant.

For the last few miles Luke had been anticipating a few blockages and hostile demonstrations. Instead, stretches of road were being trimly repaired, and a gate was being set up with a bright new signboard at the entrance to the spruce plantation. Two men, dressed smartly in matching shirts and denims, unloading pallets from a truck, straightened up and gave a casual but respectful salute as the Ross contingent drove past.

'Those security men I recruited seem to know their job,' smirked Ogilvie.

'Or Mr Hunter's achieved a lot in the couple of days he's been here,' said old Mr Ross tartly.

They passed the old Rent House, still bristling with scaffolding, and arrived at the Raven Hotel.

Mrs Aird was waiting by the main entrance as the travellers got down. She looked each one up and down, nodding and ticking them off in her mind, until she came to Luke. He smiled, expecting that knowing little nod of hers in return. Instead, as she stared into his eyes the blood drained from her dark little face, leaving it as blanched as her voice. 'No, oh no.' She stumbled to one side, looking away from him and shivering.

Waldo was lowering the wheelchair out with Ross fidgeting in it. Mrs Aird moved towards him, still avoiding Luke's gaze and staring into the old man's face.

'It's true the way it was promised. Ye'll be bringing them back.'

Old Ross craned forward as he had been doing so often, striving to get a hazy picture into focus. 'And that'll be a great day, right?'

Ogilvie, on his way to the hotel entrance, turned back and tried to urge Mrs Aird away. But Ross barked even more imperiously and groped a friendly hand towards her.

She said: 'The burning is nae finished. The embers will be breathed on.' Without further explanation, she hobbled round the side of the hotel.

Old Ross chuckled. He was caught up in the atmosphere, longing to believe in second sight, the evil eye, the prophecies of the ancient seers, all part of the atmosphere. 'Now *that's* what I call a *character*.'

Almost, thought Luke, a TV sitcom character with a catchphrase. Only those catchphrases, repeated down the generations, had become sad, not comic.

Indoors, Jacques Hunter was waiting, rather like Mrs Aird, to count them all in. Also he had an urgent message for Luke Drummond from Edinburgh. Ogilvie risked a plaintive glance at Ross. 'That would be what they were trying to tell me on my mobile.'

It was a message relayed from Luke's sister. Their father was very ill. She thought Luke had better come immediately.

Ogilvie was decisive. 'Go ahead and phone home, Drummond. Explain that it's impossible for you to get away right now.'

'I'm pretty sure I don't need to go anyway. He's always having these turns, and none of them ever turns out to be serious.'

When he rang, Dorothy was insistent. 'It really is serious this time, Lukie. I don't think he's got long.'

'It really won't do,' Ogilvie fretted.

'What's going on?' Ross was wheeled up beside them. Luke was only halfway through an apologetic explanation when the old man interrupted. 'Nonsense. Of course you must go, laddie.' The word 'laddie' sounded incongruous in that accent, all part of an image which Ross was belatedly acquiring. 'It's right and proper,' he said emphatically, with a glance over his shoulder in Randal Grant's direction, 'that a son should be at hand when his father needs him.'

'And if you're feeling guilty about it,' said Jacques Hunter with a seriously friendly smile he had not shown before, 'on the way back you can drive round some of the remoter Clearance sites and give us a report on the state of their maintenance. Croick, Inchbeath, those sort of places. We could then assess how they mesh in with our work so far.'

'Unfortunately,' said Ogilvie with quiet triumph, 'we don't have a spare vehicle here.'

'Then find one,' said Ross. 'By first thing tomorrow morning.'

*

Rutherford nodded to the constable to start recording, and said: 'Right, sir. Your name and present address, please.'

'Look, I told ye all that oot there when ye brought me in.'

The man was in his fifties, but the lines of resentment bitten into his face made him look older. His shabby tweed jacket might have come from a charity shop, or been snatched from the back of a pub chair.

'For the sake of the tape, please,' said Rutherford patiently — as patient as a bird of prey awaiting the moment to swoop.

'Och, of all the ... aye, well, I'm Ali Murdoch.'

'Ali?'

'Alistair. Alistair Murdoch. Of no fixed address. That's the way you put it, isn't it?'

'No fixed address? You were found at your brother's in —'

'Och, aye. Only because that bastard threw me out, and I'm with Jim and the bairns until I've ... well, found another job.'

'Also present,' Rutherford added in the direction of the recorder, 'Detective Chief Inspector Rutherford and Detective Constable Mackay. Now then, Mr Murdoch, what was your occupation until you were thrown out, as you put it?'

'Ye ken fine that I worked for the Fergusons o' Lockhart House.'

'In what capacity? On a regular basis?'

'It was never what ye'd call regular. When it suited them. Or when there was a panic and the place had to be cleaned up. I had a cottage at the bottom of the grounds, so they could yell for me when they wanted something doing. Usually at the last minute, when madam had one of her fits on her.'

'And when in the end you were dismissed, you decided to take a souvenir or two?'

'I took nothing.'

'You were paid off, and —'

'That I wasnae. Just yelled at, and kicked out like some mongrel. As if it was *my* fault his woman'd had some pictures taken and I ought to have been there stopping it or something. No reasoning with the bastard.'

'So on your way out you felt you'd help yourself to a few pieces to make up for it.'

'I told you, never touched a thing.'

Rutherford put the witch-brooch on the table between them.

Murdoch licked his upper lip. 'And what would that be?'

'That would be the property of the Fergusons of Lockhart House — your employers, who you've robbed.'

'Never seen it in my life before.'

'Stole it,' said Rutherford implacably, 'after you'd had a big row with Ferguson and smashed his head in.'

'I never ... I ... look, I never laid a finger on the man.'

'Maybe you could plead self-defence. You claim the Colonel was in a bad temper about something. He went for you, you fought back —'

'It wasnae like that.'

Rutherford admitted to himself that the likelihood of this crumpled little wimp of a man tackling a man of Ferguson's build and reputation was improbable. But he persevered. 'After your set-to, you got out quickly, grabbing whatever you could.'

'There was only that one wee thing.'

'Ah, *this* thing? You're admitting it now.'

'All right, then. Just that one thing. But I didnae attack him, I just got oot as fast as I could — fast, the way he'd been ranting at me — and I just ... och, so I did just grab that one wee thing as I went. So fashed wi' the way that man treated me ... wouldn't pay me what he owed me ...'

'You could have taken him to court for non-payment of wages.'

'Me? Taking a sodding Colonel to court? Och aye, an' who'd be paying any attention to the likes of me?'

'So you decided to steal —'

'I wasnae myself. It just came over me, I ... well, I helped myself as I went past. Just that one thing,' Murdoch insisted plaintively.

'And never raised a hand to Colonel Ferguson?'

'I keep telling ye. Look, why not find about that other one?'

'What other one?'

'I wasnae the only one there that day. There was that car came in as I was leaving. Belting up the drive, spraying gravel all over me.'

'Who was it? A regular visitor?'

'Didnae see the face.'

'If you're making this up as you go along —'

'I'm not. I'm telling you. There was this car there. A hire car.'

'How d'you know it was a hire car?'

'I know where it came from. Expensive job. Johnson's by the airport.'

'That's something we can check on.' Rutherford took a deep breath. 'Now, let's get this straight. Think carefully. We're talking about the day of the murder, right?'

'I'd not be wanting to say that. I mean, I only heard afterwards about it, and I never got down to —'

'If you want to escape a charge of murder, or accessory to murder, as well as theft, you'll get down to some serious work on your memory right now. The date. The time of day. Every last little detail ...'

*

The closer Luke got to Thurso the deeper he drove into his childhood landscape. For some miles there had been a beautiful but bleak wilderness, shaped and limited only by the hunched hills of gorse to the north and a shadowy Ben Loyal to the west. But then, topping the slight rise three miles from home, he looked beyond the low ridge on to a gleaming sea, with the red-brown hulk of Orkney in a distant haze. To him the compact town was even more a wilderness — the dead land of his father's coldness and scorn at everything the boy had loved most. The rasp of that voice was always there to torment him, with no Off switch. *What sort of job is that, sitting in an effing library all day? Never find a woman who'd look at the likes of you twice.*

He had spent a good part of the previous evening extracting snippets of information for old Jamie from his laptop. The old man was in a mellow mood. He had reached his destination, he was pleased to be here and to be soaking up the atmosphere. 'You sure do have a command of that machine of yours.' Difficult to tell whether he was genuinely ignorant of the world of computers, leaving such things to subordinates, or if it was a pretence and he was merely in a rare patronizing mood. 'Got the whole history of the Rosses in there?'

'I keep adding to it. And finding all kinds of questions about different branches of the family. Some marrying into Indian families. Some descendants still proud of their mixed ancestry, some still not sure of the exact links.'

'You're enjoying your job?'

'I am, sir.'

'Good. Seems to me that with all you know about the past, you've got a good solid future with us. And on the subject of the Indians ... well, it's polite nowadays to call 'em Native Americans. Isn't that right, Jacques?'

'Only some of us happen to be Canadians.' Jacques Hunter loomed over them. 'Don't want to interrupt, but I thought before it gets too dark you might have a look at the ground that's been cleared for the Highland games and dancing.'

His smile, an oddly twisted smile in that dark uncommunicative face, lingered in Luke's mind, and was still there, haunting him, as he drove away early in the morning: not so much threatening as passing judgment. He wanted to settle down somewhere and chase up that worrying business about the two Ross threads, and maybe the Hunter involvement in the whole family pattern.

But right now there was the more distasteful confrontation ahead.

Rab Drummond had worked for years on the Orkney ferry out of Scrabster, retiring early after a dispute and claiming sickness benefit for a sudden onset of nervous spasms and an inexplicable pain in the left leg which went on plaguing him for years. In spite of this kind of disability he ranted almost without pause against his son for his lack of physical guts, lack of interest in maritime affairs, and ingratitude to the parents who had done so much for him. When he had a moment to spare from berating Luke he would turn on Dorothy and say, in various different ways, that you only had to look at her to see why she'd never catch a man for herself. Their mother's attempted reproaches and her soothing remarks to her children were gradually worn down, just as she herself was, until her death became another unreasonable burden on her husband's life.

Luke could almost, shamefully, hope that this time his father's illness was real. And lethal. But of course it wasn't. He had been right: just another self-indulgent false alarm.

'I'm sorry, Lukie.' They were sitting in the window of the parlour that had hardly changed since Luke's childhood, except that today his father wasn't sitting in that creaky chair of his, waiting to snarl and attack without warning. 'But it really did seem genuine. It got so bad after I'd rung you, they had him over to Inverness late last night. Operated. He had all the symptoms, the doctor said this morning.'

'Symptoms of what?'

'Gallstones. He was doubled up in pain, truly he was, Lukie. And the way he described it, they were sure it was at a dangerous stage, and they operated right away.'

'Remember his kidney trouble that wasn't kidneys at all? Just something he'd heard from another old soak in the bar.' More like an old woman, thought Luke sourly, than an old man, picking up stray items from gossip and inflating them.

'The surgeon said' — it was the first time Dorothy had summoned up a feeble little attempt at a smile — 'he's what they call a church-window patient: hundreds of small panes. You know, like —'

'Yes,' said Luke, 'I get it.'

'Do you want to go in and see him? I mean, if it's on your route back.'

He wanted no such thing. But if he failed to visit the hospital then of course there would be reproaches: a scrawled, self-pitying letter, a spiteful phone call timed to interrupt him in the office, and all the usual abuse on the lines of 'Call that a job?' and 'Running away from your responsibilities' and 'Don't suppose you're man enough to marry that little tart of yours and get down to real work and raise a family.'

The only guilt Luke felt was at leaving poor Dorothy to cope with their father's tantrums when he got back home.

Leaving Thurso today was like that first escape. Going to university, in the teeth of his father's scornful disbelief, had been a wonderful release into a world he soon fell in love with. And after his mother's funeral, and after obligatory visits to the increasingly malicious widower, it was bliss to get back into what had become his wonderful retreat, the Ross Foundation library. There he was in charge. There he organized things the way he wanted them, enjoyed his skill in responding to any request, however complicated, from all departments in the Foundation, and set a tempo which only the occasional barb from the wasteland of his family home could disturb.

And getting back to Beth. Always in the past she had been there, an essential part of his pleasure in getting back to warm, uncompleted routine. But this time, driving through the damp monotony of the flow-lands, the pleasure of anticipation abated. Something would have to be done. He had let her go too easily, too damned politely. He was suddenly angry with himself, suddenly determined not to let that creep Randal Grant, or David Ross, or whatever he cared to call himself, get his hands on her.

He wrenched his thoughts away from that subject. It was becoming more painful than he wanted to admit. He tried to make himself concentrate on speculation about that unexpected Ross discrepancy. Should he come out with his interpretation of that discovery, and throw the whole project into chaos? First thing back in his own world, he would really have to wrestle with the tangle between old documents, microfiche, and the still undisciplined online transfers.

If he had been really intent on dutifully visiting his father in Inverness, he would simply have taken the A9 and kept going. But Jacques Hunter's suggestion that he should call in on a few historic sites while he was in the region was a good excuse for dawdling. There were so many places whose history he knew from those archives he loved to pore over, but few he had ever had cause to visit until old Jamie Ross's pet project was upon them, becoming real and immediate.

He swung westwards towards Strathnaver, one of the most heart-breaking of the valleys.

The route took him past a neat little church, one of those built by Parliament to lure Highlanders away from their stubborn Catholic faith. It was a surprisingly squared-up building, almost a Lego toy, in a setting of low hillocks bare save for smudges of bell heather and some dark smears of forestry development. The unkempt churchyard was surrounded by a drystone wall gashed with a number of gaps where stones had fallen inwards. Headstones of uncared-for graves leaned at crazy angles. Luke knew he had let himself be drawn here to look for one particular burial, to confirm what he had read.

It took some finding, since the name on the stone had almost worn away, or been clumsily scratched away; and the outline of the burial plot at its foot was only a bare rectangle of earth. So the legend was true. Here the factor who had driven out so many families of the strath had gone on living and exploiting part of the resulting sheep ranch for himself, and in due course had been given a respectable Christian funeral. But one evicted woman travelled back from her family's dismal hovel on the coast and cursed his grave so that no grass would ever grow on it.

No grass was growing here.

A thin smirr of rain blew across the strath, swirling like a woman's skirt, swishing coquettishly from one side to the other in a grey dance before enshrouding the church in a chill embrace. Luke turned back toward the car. As he drove away he had to persuade himself that the shapes in the haze were not old phantoms drifting purposefully at him, demanding some recompense it wasn't his to give. 'Not my quarrel, old things,' he said aloud, and was ashamed of himself for half believing in them when really, in his mirror, the only hazy shape was that of a car following, then drifting off along some side track that must be pretty harrowing on its suspension.

He took the grimly named Destitution Road through a jigsaw of rills and bog to pick up the long road down Strath Kildonan, picking up the A9 at Helmsdale and stopping for a quick lunch and a few minutes bringing his laptop up to date. He could then turn south for Inverness. But if he was going to report on key sites as Jacques Hunter had suggested, two he really must visit were Badbea and Inchbeath, close together some four or five miles north. It would take no more than half an hour to give them a quick check, and add them to his report.

A car which looked briefly like the one he had seen out in the wilds moved out of the car park as he came out of the café. There were few enough cars around: it would be worthier of comment if he had seen three or four vehicles within the past hour or so.

A small signpost by a lay-by indicated Inchbeath. He parked the car and went down a rough path towards the glitter of sea and sky, blurring together with no definite horizon, and emerged on to a slope of coarse grass — a slope slanting down at a dizzying angle, with the gleam off the water slashing at his eyes. On this exposed height a keen breeze began to pluck at his jacket, groping inside it, forcing it out like a sail while he fumbled to fasten the buttons, urging him downhill.

The families driven on to this alien coastal cliff from their burnt-out homesteads had no knowledge of the workings of the sea, the fishing trade, or anything to replace their slow, steady way of life. They had been exiled here and left to make the best of it. There was little they could grow on this barren soil, and little enough fodder for more than a few animals. On that precipitous slope, animals and children had all to be tethered to posts to keep them from being blown over the cliff edge. Not just human cruelty but the savage elements were against them.

The posts to which they had clung were long gone. A few stones were all that remained of the few makeshift crofts, but other stones had been built up into a squat, ragged column with a plaque on it. Lettering almost worn away recalled the name of the last family to leave, driven at last to emigrate to New Zealand.

As he began groping round the column to get out of the wind, Luke was suddenly aware that there was somebody pressed against the other side. Instinctively he moved back from the pillar, and the wind caught him full strength. He groped for some handhold that wasn't there. Then there was an added thrust as hands tightened round his throat from behind and rushed him down the slope, kneeing him in the back as he stumbled, trying to fight free, trying to shout, desperately trying to get a foothold and fight back.

Until he was thrown forward with one last heave, and there was nothing under his feet, and he was in the air, falling through the wind towards waters thrashing up in a foam to engulf him.

16

'It's a tragedy.' Morwenna Ross, sombre in a high-necked black dress which one could almost believe she had brought from Toronto in readiness, was posed at the end of the library stacks. Her voice was a powerful contralto, a throbbing half-octave lower than usual. 'Such a gifted young man. So wonderfully committed to our work.'

Simon Ogilvie, anxious to assert himself, was more of a seedy baritone. 'Such a loss. Always regarded him as one of our key personnel. I like to think my encouragement was instrumental in helping him reach his full potential.'

'I'm sure Mr Ross will agree we should set up some memorial for him.'

'Perhaps endow a Luke Drummond chair at the Heriot Watt University.'

Or a natty little bust on the library window-ledge, overlooking his well-worn chair? Beth felt a twinge of distaste. The news of Luke's body having been spotted on the rocks below Inchbeath by a trawler from Wick had hardly been digested before being put to use as part of the Ross legend. It was all too sudden. She had not yet really taken it in. She felt guilty. But why? Even if she had been there with him, could she have saved him from falling off the cliff? And guilt about not being with him in the first place made no sense. Still she felt utterly miserable.

As she left the building at lunchtime, Randal was waiting for her. Which somehow made it worse. Perversely she had been longing for him to be there, while at the same time wanting him to keep his distance, because his mere existence made her feel even more guilty about Luke.

'Come and have an omelette and a glass of wine over the road there,' he said.

'I don't think I can manage to —'

'You don't have to talk. We'll just sit there and eat. And drink a quiet toast in memory, if that'll help.'

'I couldn't have a drink right now.'

'You can,' he said, 'and you will.'

She let him persuade her because she didn't have the strength to argue. Just by being there he was what she needed; while at the same time she resented that need for him and blamed herself for the way things had worked out for Luke.

'I'm not very good company,' she ventured. 'And look, I still don't know how I feel and whether I ought to —'

'Accidents happen every day.'

'It's not like Luke to do something silly. I mean, not let something like that happen to him.'

'Come on, you're not fretting about …' He reached out and took her right hand firmly in his. 'I don't care how brutal this sounds. You don't think he jumped off the cliff just because of his feelings for you?'

She tried to smile. 'More likely to kill himself over a wrongly attributed reference — some glaring error. But … oh, I don't know what to think. Maybe you and I … I mean, I didn't think about the way it might affect him.'

'Was there any reason why you should? You weren't engaged to him. Or living with him?'

'Only off and on. And that was over anyway.'

'Well, then. His death was an accident. Sad. But you'll have to get over it.'

She knew that made sense. But it was easier said than done. How long would it be before a clear memory of Luke faded away into a wraith and then disappeared altogether?

Back at the Ross building, he would still be too vividly present in the library. She would have passed it as quickly as possible on the way to her own office but for a call from Lesley Torrance.

'Oh, Beth. Just the girl. Maybe you can help us. It's about those pictures your … er … contact took. The young Mr Ross, I mean. You know where Luke kept his set?'

She forced her mind off the presence haunting the desk and into the old familiar working pattern they had established. Yes, she knew which long map drawer he used for storing large photographs, and had them out on the table within seconds.

DCI Rutherford, seated beside Lesley, had already opened a folder of prints. 'Comparisons here could be of great value. I'd like to confirm that that brooch was the only thing missing. And that everything else was in its usual place.'

'Looking for anything particular?' asked Beth.

Rutherford grinned at Lesley. 'We've been used to years of this, hey? Not knowing what we're looking for until we find it.'

Their heads were close together as pictures were shuffled to and fro. Some of the police shots had been taken from the same angle as Randal Grant's, others in close-up, including some clinically detailed ones around the smashed head of Sholto Ferguson.

Beth gulped, remembering the setting before the corpse was added. 'That man. He's ... still lying there?'

'For the time being,' said Rutherford, 'he's in the mortuary while our inquiries proceed.'

He reached for a cluster of the prints Beth had produced.

'Just a minute.' Lesley pointed at one. 'What's that?'

Beth stared into the background of Randal's picture of the totem pole head in the Native American room. She remembered the care he had taken to move it into the best light, sharp against that artistically hazy background. In contrast, the wooden head in the police version was lying on the floor smeared with blood and hair, close beside the more fragile head of the murdered man.

'On the wall?' Beth narrowed her eyes, trying to conjure a clear picture out of that blur. 'Looks like a drapery of some kind. A hanging.'

'Such as the longed-for Ross tapestry?' said Lesley sceptically. 'In *that* room?'

'Hold it.' Rutherford slid the police version of the scene alongside it.

'It's gone,' said Beth. 'Whatever it was, it's not there in the later picture.'

'Hanging on the wall before the murder. Gone after the murder — or at the same time. Looks to me like I need another word with a certain Ali Murdoch.' Rutherford pored over the two different studies as if they might suddenly turn into a movie and provide him with a dramatic revelation. 'Hmph. Oh hell, no, I still don't see that little runt having the know-how to nick a selection of things worth flogging. One quick grab and run on impulse, that's him. Whatever that thing there is, it was probably out of his reach.'

Lesley turned to Beth. 'Do you think your friend could have it blown up and brought into sharper focus?'

'I'll ask him.'

'When you were there with him, did you notice that wall hanging?'

'No. Sorry, it didn't register.'

Rutherford heaved himself to his feet. 'Can I take this with me? I'll get our lot to go over every possibility there. In the meantime, if your young man, under whatever name he's using this week, can do his bit, we'll get together.'

Beth was slotting the rest of the prints away into a file which she appeared to use as automatically as Luke would have done. 'Got to get back to my own little cell in the hive. Ringing round and assembling the troops. Making sure everyone's in place when the curtain goes up.'

In spite of the shock of Luke's death, thought Lesley fondly, Beth was still committed to the cause. How deflated would she feel when the pace slackened, ground to a halt, and it was all over?

She was gathering up her own papers when Jacques Hunter stopped by the open doorway.

'Miss Crichton not with you?'

'She went back to her office just a moment ago.'

His lips tightened in a thin twist of irritation. He was as bad as Ogilvie when it came to resenting any hindrance, no matter how petty, to a progression he had established in his own mind; but far more intimidating.

He forced a laugh. 'Ridiculous, isn't it? I go there, she's not there, I come down here, and she's back there.'

'It gets that way sometimes,' Lesley sympathized. On impulse, half regretting it before the words had even finished coming out of her mouth, she said: 'It's just occurred to me, Mr Hunter. Perhaps with your background you could solve the problem in one of those photographs.'

'I'm sorry. Photographs?'

'The pictures that young chap Grant, or young Ross, whichever ... the studies from the Ferguson house ... you would have been sent those in Toronto, just before you came over.'

'Of course. Yes, Miss Crichton transmitted a set.' He managed to be impatient and politely attentive at the same time.

'Did you notice a hanging on the wall among the Indian ... Native American collection?'

'I can't say I did. Has it any relevance to our Achnachrain project?'

'Not that I know of. But it reminded me of something.' Behind the sound of her own voice was another voice, telling her to give up now, that she didn't even know what sort of hunch she was stumbling after, and anyhow it wasn't leading anywhere. Yet Hunter's impassive stare somehow prodded her on. 'I once had to help catalogue a collection of property stolen from an exhibition in Glasgow, and I remember one interesting item — a ghost dance shirt. You know of them of course.'

'Of course, Lady Torrance. Symbol of an old tradition. But what concerns you about such things at the moment?'

'It does seem that the one in Lockhart House — if that's what it was — has gone missing. It was in that picture you saw, but it's not there any more.'

At last Hunter moved. It was only the slightest muscular relaxation, but it was as good as a clear, sharp dismissal. 'I can't say that I see any reason for us to be involved in the matter of any presumed theft from those premises. I fancy the police are seeking more tangible reasons for the distasteful murder there.'

Was there, thought Lesley absurdly, such a thing as a tasteful murder?

'You'll have to forgive me, Lady Torrance.' Hunter was at his most suave again. 'I really must track Miss Crichton down. We do have to set up a meeting of various key visitors tomorrow. That, frankly, is our immediate priority.'

Tomorrow's priority proved instead to be a sad visitor from Thurso.

*

Dorothy Drummond was a wispy woman of early middle age, but looking as if the years had worn her down more swiftly than most. She plucked spasmodically at the left sleeve of her dark brown coat, glancing at her wrist watch as if to check how long she had got, but apparently forgetting within a couple of minutes and needing another glance. Her whole attitude and her tone of voice were tinged with apology.

'I'm sorry I had to show up like this. So suddenly, I mean. So soon after Lukie ... I mean, that is ...'

Beth steered her towards the most comfortable armchair in her office, and rang through for a pot of tea and biscuits.

'I'm so glad you've come. It's good to meet you. But I'm sorry it has to be in these circumstances.'

'I couldn't think what was best. I've got Lukie's address down here, of course, but I don't know Edinburgh, and I haven't got a key anyway. Only I remember him talking about you, and I knew where he worked. The Ross building isn't hard to find.' She tried a thin, nervous smile and stared out at sunlight on the treetops. 'It *is* all right, isn't it? I mean, coming here where you work? You won't be in any trouble?'

'I'm glad you came. We're all shocked about Luke's death. If there's anything we can do ...'

'He did speak of you. Some while back, that is. Not lately. But I thought you'd be the one knowing where that address is, and' — her pale cheeks went a blotchy pink — 'do you ... that is, would you be having a key to his flat?'

Not any longer, thought Beth. She had no intention of going into details. She said: 'I'm afraid not. But the caretaker on the ground floor there will have one.'

Dorothy edged her coat over her knees, looked round the room, looked at her watch again, then sagged helplessly back into the armchair.

'You've seen Luke?' asked Beth.

Dorothy nodded. 'Yes. They took him to Wick. He was ... bless him, he didn't look too ... too awful. Just ... he wasn't there any more.' She stared pleadingly at Beth. 'I don't know where we'll go from here. Dad's in a right mood. Complaining about why Luke couldn't have gone straight to Inverness. 'Didn't have to go stravaiging about the countryside. Look where *that* got him.' She smiled apologetically. 'That's oor dad all over. He's gone lively all of a sudden, and in a hurry to get back home and start making a fuss. And I'm to collect Lukie's things together and take them home.'

'Of course. But you needn't have come yourself. Not yet, anyway. After the inquest, I'm sure we could have been given powers to look after any of his things on the premises here, and put things in store for you until everything's settled. In any case, you know, I think the authorities may want to check on his belongings before releasing them.'

'Oh. Oh, dear. Only dad said I was to come right away and make sure.'

'Make sure?'

'I was to get here just as fast as I could. 'Before they start helping themselves' — that's the way he put it.' Again she was wincing an apology. 'That's the way he is. I'm sorry.'

There was a pause while a tray was brought in and set on the table between them. Dorothy's hand trembled and the cup and saucer rattled as she reached for them.

'And he said' — she was shakily determined to get it all out in one rush — 'to be sure and check if there was anything in the car as well.'

That, too, was something which ought to be left to the authorities. But Beth could tell the poor woman needed some reassurance, especially when faced with having to report back to her father. While Dorothy sipped at her tea and nervously refused a chocolate biscuit, Beth began ringing around.

The car had been returned to the hire company in Lairg, who had handed over a small overnight bag to the police officer who had made the delivery.

'And that was all?'

'A bag, yes. On the back seat. That was the lot, according to the officer who returned the vehicle.'

She rang the Northern Constabulary, and was transferred from one office to another before reaching an officer who had been in the patrol car which spotted the hire car in the lay-by overnight and next morning, and stopped to investigate. Yes, it was routine. Logged the times they had checked on it, and a note of the contents when they took charge of it.

'And there was only an overnight bag?'

'That was all, miss. Name and address of the owner in a leather tag. And then of course we related it to the news about the body being found.'

Beth had a vision of Luke leaving the office to join that earlier trip, and then the one with old Jamie himself. As ever, like a violinist refusing to be parted from the precious instrument in its case, it was impossible to visualize Luke without his laptop. Particularly on that drive to Achnachrain with the old man himself.

So inseparable that he would have carried it down the slope of Inchbeath, and still had it under his arm when he plunged to his death? He must surely have intended to leave the car for only a few minutes, and if there was anything to record he would have done it when he got back into the driver's seat, not out on that windy hill-side.

She asked: 'Wasn't there a laptop somewhere in the car?'

'Hold on a minute.' There were a few mumbled comments and a rustle of paper at the other end, then: 'No, sorry. Not according to the report here.'

Dorothy had been trying to look as if she wouldn't dream of listening to somebody else's conversation; but as Beth rang off she blurted out: 'If it was something to do with Lukie's work, one of those computer things or whatever, I'm sure we wouldn't want it. Dad might, just to stop anyone else getting it. But we wouldn't really know what to make of it.'

'No, probably not. But where *is* it?'

*

Lesley took clothes from her wardrobe and laid them on the bed. A shaft of sunlight over the rooftops opposite Drovers Court stabbed down to show up the stains on her fawn slacks. She must leave them with the cleaners, and remember to pack another pair and some more tights after the weekend.

There was a tap at the door.

'Ah, Lady Torrance.' Simon Ogilvie came into the room with a deferential sideways movement, but with an almost masterful gleam in his eye. 'Just in time. Save you some wasted journeys.'

'I'm only going to Black Knowe. Home for the weekend, as usual. Or do you need me to help with all these things going on?'

'Not at all, no. Just the opposite, in fact.' He cleared his throat, and his tone became that of a Rotary chairman summoning up platitudes to thank a guest speaker. 'We've all been very appreciative of the invaluable work you have put in on our project. But rather than take up any more of your valuable time, it has been decided that we should terminate the arrangement with you. It would be greatly appreciated if you could let me have a list of any extra expenses you have incurred in addition to the agreed fee. And of course you will sign our usual confidentiality clause.'

'I understood I was still expected to advise on the placement of the material we've accumulated. After my visit to Achnachrain, I've been sketching some plans for —'

'Lady Torrance, we have all learned so much from you. And of course you and Sir Nicholas will be invited to the formal opening. But it has been decided that the time has come for us to assume full responsibility for implementation of the rest of the programme.'

Lesley stared into that smug little face. *It has been decided* ... She was not going to demean herself by asking: decided by whom?

17

Nick Torrance looked affectionately at the back of his wife's neck as she glared into her computer monitor, stabbed her fingers down at the keyboard like a pianist tackling a complex toccata, and then let out a wail of frustration.

He said: 'Do you want me to tell Mrs Robson to put lunch back half an hour?'

'No. I've done enough for one day. But I could do with a drink.'

'Come away from that fiendish machine and sit somewhere comfortable.'

They settled in the lounge with its view down the hillside towards the roofs of the town. Sun glinted on the church spire and the sham crenellations of the sheriff court. For a moment the picture was blurred by the recent memory of light slanting into her Drovers Court room, while Ogilvie delivered that smooth yet offensive dismissal. Damn them, it had all been so abrupt, so irrational. What lay behind it? Because there had to be something — maybe some remark she had made, some casual aside that meant more than she had realized. But what?

'Hey, m'lady.' Nick was offering her a glass of amontillado. 'Come back home, will you? Right back home, this instant.'

'Sorry.' She took the glass and risked spilling it as she kissed him. 'I'm still half there.'

'Having been shoved out, there's no point in you trying to keep one foot wedged in the door. Or pounding away at that machine as if it were some fortune-teller who might come up with the right predictions.'

Lesley knew he was right. She had done the work that was required of her, and if the employers who had commissioned it decided they had no further requirements, she ought to be glad to ease back into her home and her own routine.

'But there's something wrong.' It was still nagging at her. 'I don't know quite what they're up to — or even who's the main mover — but there's *something.*'

Nick sighed. 'The old hunches? Detective Inspector Gunn shedding the disguise of Lady Torrance and sniffing out misdeeds that nobody else has even noticed?'

'Oh, my darling, I'm a bore, aren't I?'

'Never. But a bit of a worry. And a worrier over things you ought to have ditched. How long'll it take before you're really back home? A week? Ten days?' He slid on to the couch beside her and put his arm round her shoulders. 'Anyway, one thing I do know.'

'Tell me. It may be the one thing I need.'

'I know,' said Nick, 'that after lunch you'll be back in front of your soothsaying screen doing battle with it for the rest of the afternoon.'

Over lunch she tried to draw him out on estate matters and the question of the windfarm. After ten minutes he said: 'You're not hearing what I'm saying, because you're still way up in the Highlands. Come on, what's really bugging you?'

'It's a silly bit of speculation. All because of one throwaway remark.'

'Ah. One throwaway remark? Enough of a spark to start a fire?'

'That thing that Luke Drummond came out with. 'The wrong Rosses.' That's what I'm trying to get at through the computer. If only I could link it with his own — in the office, or that laptop of his that's gone missing — then I might get a glimmering of what he'd stumbled on.'

'Is it really of any consequence?'

'Luke seemed shaken up. Something which maybe wasn't obvious earlier, because of scattered documentation. Only now all those records are being sorted out and gradually brought together and analysed online, so the real pattern can be picked out.'

'You're not eating. Be a good girl and finish off your greens, or I'll tell Mrs Robson you're to get no treacle tart.'

His prophecy proved true. As soon as they had finished, she was back in front of the monitor, calling up one Ross reference after another, seeking the threads which could form a coherent pattern. There were gaps; but by mid-afternoon she was beginning to suspect that Luke had been on the track of something that could prove catastrophic for the long-held beliefs of old James Fergus Ross.

Many courageous Rosses had indeed tried to stand up against the greed of their landlords and clan traitors. The womenfolk of Strathcarron had stood their ground against repeated baton charges until they were bloodied and trampled on; yet still they and others maintained resistance until they were utterly exhausted. Their cause was taken up and later recorded in grisly detail by another Ross, a Glasgow lawyer who wanted the world to learn the truth.

Hundreds of men, with Malcolm Ross of Alladale in the forefront, launched a counterattack, rounding up six thousand of the invading sheep and driving them south, aiming to chase them out of the Highlands and restore the crofters to their rightful homes. The army was called in, the sheep were chased back, and the landowners called on the magistrates to inflict vicious punishment on the rebels. A courageous young advocate, Charles Ross, put up a spirited defence, but the power of the lairds ensured that the Highlanders were sentenced to transportation, banishment from Scotland for life, fines which they could not pay, and to long gaol sentences.

James Fergus Ross could be proud of such an ancestry. Defeated they might have been, but their descendants had lived on, scattered throughout distant lands, never forgetting where their true roots lay buried deep. But with the pride, could there be lasting hatred — a bitterness so intense it had gone on living unabated?

'Congenital diseases can lie latent, skip generations. Porphyria, haemophilia, that sort of thing. D'you suppose old resentments can simmer below the surface of other obsessions — job, family, everyday life — until something triggers off what's been lying dormant so long? Something or somebody, breathing on embers and making them blaze up?'

She realized she had been talking to herself, aloud. And was interrupted by the remembered voice of Luke Drummond, now plucking at her attention.

The wrong Rosses?

There had been other families, other influential players on the scene. Twenty minutes ago Lesley had extracted the name of a procurator fiscal, a Hugh Ross, who had been a keen supporter of the Duke of Sutherland's ruthless factor, Patrick Sellars. Then there was a vice-president of the Association of Gentlemen Farmers and Breeders of Sheep, a Sir Charles Ross of Balnagowan, intent on putting as much as possible of Ross, Sutherland and Caithness into the hands of well-to-do graziers from the Lowlands and England.

In the middle of the afternoon Nick brought her a pot of tea and two pieces of Mrs Robson's shortbread.

'Having fun?'

'I've stumbled across something that'll interest Jack Rutherford.'

'The Ferguson murder? It was old man Ross after all. Got his ex-wife to let him into the house, wrestled Ferguson to the ground and then beat him up with —'

'Do shut up. Sometimes I wonder why I married you.'

'You found it easier for me to make you a lady than for them to make you up to chief inspector.'

'I learnt they did have every intention of doing just that.'

'So I'm glad I snatched the trophy away from them just in time.'

'In time for what?'

He let his fingers slide down and caress the back of her neck. 'For lots of things. And still more to catch up with when you can spare me some — what's the current jargon? — quality time.' His hand moved back up to tug a handful of her hair. 'But you're still miles away, faithless hussy. What's all this about inflaming Rutherford's passions?'

'The Macdonalds,' she said. 'And the Chisholms.'

'What about them? Come on, the suspense is killing me. Oh, and your tea's getting cold.'

'Morwenna Ross's maiden name was Chisholm. And that chap she was seen following on the building site in Leith was a Macdonald.' She nodded at the screen. 'I just happen to have stumbled across a snippet of information while I was looking for family connections. Chisholms and Macdonalds have been at feud for centuries over some grazing and harbour landing rights. Did Morwenna go looking for Angus Macdonald — or, more likely, see his name on the shop and decide to stalk him, to see if she could stare terror into him?'

'They all sound bonkers. And they're beginning to infect you.' He squeezed her shoulder. 'Look, next week I'm off for a few nights to that Travel Association shindig in Stirling. Come with me. Help me deal with present cock-ups, it'll take your mind off the dead and gone.'

'But *are* they? Gone, I mean. I'm sure poor Luke was on to something. And I think my ex-guvnor'll be interested, too.'

'Ex, yes. Remember I'm the boss now. And' — before she could raise an objection — 'I love you, and I know it's time you stopped fretting over other people's obsessions.' Nick sighed dramatically, and left her.

She tried phoning Rutherford, feeling disloyal as she did so. The fact that he was out could be taken as a symbolic hint. But Nick was right, damn him: she was still fretting. In the end she tried Beth Crichton.

'Is it all right for you to talk, now I'm no longer on your payroll?'

'Some question's arisen — or you've left something in the building?'

'It's just that I've been trying to follow up that odd remark of Luke Drummond's. About 'the wrong Rosses'. Do you know if he ever got any further with that before ... before his accident?'

'Not so far as I know. Certainly there was something bothering him, but he didn't confide in me.' There was a wistful note in the words.

'He didn't do a print-out of anything that might be relevant?'

'If he did, it hasn't shown up. Not that anybody's looking for it, as far as I know. There might be something in his laptop, but that's still missing. Why, what are you thinking?'

Lesley said, as casually as possible: 'I keep stumbling across oddities. One nasty tale, for instance, about a Ross who kept well in with the factor who was throwing all his relatives out. The young man was allowed to stay on in his croft, telling the clearance teams in advance what sort of defence his fellow crofters were planning to put up against their eviction. One or two instances of traitors like that. Sometimes they got what was coming to them — after helping to evict their friends, they eventually got chucked out themselves, and then they were unwelcome anywhere else at all.'

'You're not suggesting that Mr Ross's ancestors weren't who he thinks they were?'

'I'm wondering if that was what young Drummond was worried about.' Lesley waited for a reply, but there was none. Everything about Luke's death was probably still too close and painful for Beth to sort out her own confusions, let alone any that Luke might have had. She changed tack. 'And another thing. I'm trying to get in touch with the police about that theft from the Ferguson home. I think I can identify that wall hanging. You remember? It was there when you and that young man went round the place, but gone later.'

'There was some talk of it being the Ross Tapestry.'

'Nothing of the kind. From what I vaguely remember, and allowing for it being displayed in the Native American room, I'd say it was an Indian ghost dance shirt. Part of a cherished old ritual. Any dancer who wears it can see his ancestors in their next life, and call on them to help him restore the tribal lands stolen by the white man.'

'But what on earth has that got to do with the Rosses?'

'It just seems such a weird parallel. Reclaiming stolen lands ...'

Lesley was suddenly aware of a resonance too slight to be an echo or a voice in the background. Not even a sound of breathing. But somebody else was listening in on their conversation. Just an extra dimension, something she had known from past experience: no more than a tremor, a hinted harmonic below the pitch of their voices; but once experienced, never forgotten.

'All a bit bizarre,' she said brightly. 'But not really any of my business. Must get back to my own work.'

Nevertheless the parallels continued to fascinate her after she had rung off. Once you got down to it, there was so much interaction between Scots and the Indian tribes. Some of the settlers got on well with the natives of the new country. Some exploited the local tribes, some were exploited by them. A branch of the Ross family traded so amicably with the Cherokee that one of them married into the tribe, and his son Ross eventually became chief of the Cherokee, fighting with them against more rapacious white settlers. And along the way she had dug out fragments of a sept of the Gunn clan which had reached Ontario and then gone on to Dakota, where the Ojibwa tribe employed them as 'hewers of wood and drawers of water', and took them across the plains hunting buffalo.

Until the incomers considered themselves strong enough to turn on their hosts and drive them off their lands. The disheartening pattern repeating itself, thousands of miles away across the world. No escape from that predestined repetition?

And now the struggle had returned to its old homelands. Or was she reading too much into it?

She really longed to turn her attention to a query she had had from the Art Loss Register in London. There were awkward puzzles there, too; but she would be back on her own ground, unstable as that might sometimes be. She knew where to begin, whom to consult, and where to tread carefully. Yet still her mind refused to let go of the complexities of the Ross set-up. Way out front were Morwenna Ross and Jacques Hunter. And her abrupt dismissal rankled; but more than that, it provoked questions she could not dismiss as being no longer her concern.

Was it too melodramatic to conceive that those two were maybe planning that all the excitement of the Achnachrain venture would give old Ross a heart attack, so that they could take over the whole organization? Or were they subtly working against each other, each manipulating the old man to strengthen their own ambitions?

And did they have any plans for dealing with the unexpected reappearance of the younger son? Suppose Randal Grant decided to become David Ross again, and let his father coax him back into a seat at the top table?

*

Beth said: 'All right, what's the game? Just where do you stand?'

'If you care to move over to the couch, I'll demonstrate.'

'It's not funny. Nothing's funny any more.'

'Getting disillusioned with the Ross campaign?'

'It's all gone … well, sour. I did believe in the whole concept, and it felt great, going along with it. But now there's something shivery about it all.'

'Including me?' Randal tried to put his arm round her, but she edged away, tempted to run out of the studio and down the stairs, out into the street, back to … well, where? Her office, no longer a place where she felt confident of herself and what she was doing? Back to her flat, alone, still haunted?

'Ever since that Hunter creature came, things have gone twisted.'

'I thought he was quite pleasant to you when I was there.'

'Gives me the shivers even more.' Instead of fleeing, she surrendered and let herself sit down, trembling. Trying to steady herself, she said: 'You must have known him, way back. What did you make of him then?'

'A tough bastard. He hadn't been there all that long when I decided to quit, but I got the impression my father had taken him on as a real tough trouble-shooter. A man after his own heart.'

'Implacable,' said Beth. 'That's the word I've been looking for.' She lobbed him a question which had only just woken in her mind. 'Has he got a wife? It's hard to imagine.'

'I don't think so. Too busy with … well, business.'

'Yes. Cold, calculating … and implacable.' She came back to her earlier accusation. 'And where do you stand in all this? Waiting to pick up your father's offer? He really does want you back. You must see that.'

Randal brushed aside some prints on the bench and perched on the end of it. 'Giving battle to my fellow directors? Jacques Hunter and Morwenna Ross. One at a time — or in cahoots? Maybe getting married, even.'

'But then maybe your dad wouldn't fancy them getting too powerful together. Could be that he fancies you marrying your late brother's widow and keeping it all in the family. Tidy everything up nicely.'

'Tough luck. Because I'm not going to marry Morwenna. I'm going to marry you, right?'

Flurried, she glanced at her watch. 'Right, that's it. I've got to get back. Everything's being rushed through, it's getting quite absurd, but somehow we've got to get that show on the road. And I've got to keep on making the right noises, the right phone calls, the usual routine only three times as fast.'

'Why not engage the Rolling Stones and Amy whatsername and start an annual rave? Glastonbury, T-in-the Park. Why not Gaelic-in-the-Glen?' As she headed shakily for the door, he slid from the bench and blocked her way. 'Look, there's something more important in life than all those panics and presentations.'

'Not to the Ross Foundation there isn't. Not right now.'

'Right now,' said Randal forcefully. 'Beth, will you just take a few minutes off and tell me you'll marry me?'

*

Rutherford's sergeant steered the squad car into a parking slot between a Mazda and a gleaming Vectra. As they got out, Rutherford nodded ruefully at the muddy side of their own vehicle. 'We could do with the sort of wash-and-brush-up Mr Johnson gives *his* fleet.'

'That burst water main back there didn't give us the sort of power jet he can afford.'

The proprietor was waiting for them in the inner doorway of his sparkling, air-conditioned office. Apart from the sound of their footsteps there was a cool silence within the building, soundproofed against traffic outside and aircraft flying in and out above their heads. His main window commanded a view across the parking area and the main entrance and exit. A screen on the opposite wall flickered with pinpricks of differently coloured lights across a huge street map of Edinburgh.

'Mr Rutherford. Long time no see. Not bringing trouble this time, I hope?'

'We hope not, Mr Johnson. Unless you've got some useful information on that ram raid in Livingston.'

'Not one of my clients. Not this time. All cars returned safe and clean around … when would it be? … last Wednesday?'

'I'm sure your records are as accurate as ever. So we'd be glad of your help regarding the hire of a car on the twenty-fourth of last month. A Thursday that would have been.'

'What make of car? And who was driving it?'

'That's what we'd like to know.'

Johnson waved them to two chairs, more luxurious than any they were used to in interview rooms at the nick. Then he waved, less hospitably, at the screen on his left. 'We do keep an awful lot of stuff on the move. I'd need to have something a bit more specific. Then I can get our Miss Grieve to run through the records.'

'Can you give us any details about a rental for a journey to Lockhart House down the Pencaitland road on that date, the twenty-fourth?'

'People don't always tell us exactly where they're going when they leave here. As long as they pay their deposit and bring the vehicle back without scratching it or spilling beer over the interior, we don't ask all that many questions. But just a minute.' He leaned towards the microphone sunk into his desk, and rattled off a few instructions which Rutherford found quite unintelligible. But in a matter of seconds a girl was bringing in a sheaf of print-outs which Johnson leafed through confidently. Then he said: 'Oh, Christ.'

'Something doesn't gel?'

'No, it all adds up. But that was one of those bloody awful days. Bad weather over Iceland and the Atlantic. Planes arriving a couple of hours late. We're used to that, of course, but it does mean we have to pull all the stops out. We have to move cars around so that people who've booked them in advance can pick them up without too much delay. Only on a day like that there are dozens of others making emergency bookings on the spot and getting just a wee bit impatient.' He turned several sheets over. 'We certainly wouldn't have been asking anyone for details of where they were headed.' Johnson shook his head, then sat up sharply. 'Just a minute. Lockhart House, you said?'

'That's right.'

'Isn't that where ... hey, now just a minute ...'

'Where the murder of Colonel Sholto Ferguson took place on that date, yes.'

'But what's that got to do with us hiring a car out? I mean, out of all the stuff we had to-ing and fro-ing, why should you think one of our cars was there?'

'Because the odd-job man there says he recognized one as coming from here. You putting a sign on the roof nowadays?'

'A discreet logo on the back of the boot,' said Johnson indignantly. 'Very discreet.' Rutherford looked at DS Blake, expecting — and getting — a sag of the shoulders and a 'wild goose chase' droop of the mouth.

He said: 'You've no memory of anything particularly unusual? For instance, did somebody bring a car back after only a short time and ... well, act suspiciously?'

Johnson smiled dourly. 'There are times when I find everybody seems to be acting suspiciously. It's one of the hang-ups you get in this trade. But like I said, days like that you're too rushed off your feet to take note of anything very much other than getting stuff off the forecourt there in a nice steady stream.'

'Yes, I get the picture.' Rutherford saw no alternative to giving up his line, for the time being at least. 'But if anything does occur to you —'

'In the middle of the night, when I can't sleep?' Johnson nodded. 'That sort of thing does happen. I can lie awake for hours worrying about some little thing that I ought to have noticed — and then in the morning spend hours tracking it down and finding it as a false alarm.'

'I know the feeling,' Rutherford agreed.

'But yes, I'll let you know if anything does occur to me. Only don't blame me if I've set you off on a false trail. Wouldn't want to be accused of wasting police time.'

The two detectives left glumly. It had been too much to hope for one of those sudden revelations that simplify a case; but that never stopped you from hoping. Rutherford sent Blake off to check on progress with DNA samples from the murder scene, even though they so far had no other samples for comparison. On impulse he himself went to the Ross offices. There were still too many loose ends. Pleasant as that young Crichton woman had seemed, the whole relationship between her and the Ross son was tied up with the show pieces at Lockhart House — a tie-up whose knots might need more unravelling than he had managed so far.

No, Miss Crichton was not in. Busy setting up television coverage of the Ross project, an interview with Mr Ross himself, and visitors from Canada and Australia. Mrs Morwenna Ross was on her way to Achnachrain. And Mr Jacques Hunter? Already at Achnachrain.

Before Rutherford could slouch away, disgruntled, Simon Ogilvie appeared, his feet tapping briskly across the floor as loudly as if he had been a woman in high heels and in a hurry.

'Ah, Chief Inspector.' It was by no means a welcome. 'Didn't expect to see you back here so soon.'

'And I didn't expect to find everybody out. Except yourself, that is.'

Ogilvie picked up the insinuation immediately. '*Somebody* responsible still has to look after the shop.' He tried a man-to-man chuckle, but it came out resentful. He was obviously peeved at being left behind. 'Is there anything specific that I can settle for you? Or you've got some news about poor young Drummond's missing laptop? We're none of us happy about the thought of confidential company records falling into the wrong hands.'

'That'll be in the hands of the boys in Inverness. I'm sure they'll be in touch when there's anything to show. But as a matter of interest, do you normally let junior members of staff go wandering about the countryside with confidential material about their persons?'

'By no means. Unfortunately young Drummond had an emergency call about his father being taken ill, and it was arranged to hire a car and let him pay a visit on his way back here.'

Rutherford tried to think up a few words of routine sympathy to round off the conversation and get away. 'Must have been a blow to you, getting back here and learning what had happened to your colleague.'

'Dreadful. Oh, quite dreadful. But actually, we heard it while we were still at Achnachrain, the day the rest of us were due to start back. Mr Hunter was back here ahead of us, and he was the first to get the news and let us know.'

Rutherford was in no mood for hanging about any longer; yet something vague and of little consequence seemed to be growing disturbingly less vague.

'Mr Hunter wasn't with you all the time?'

'He preferred to drive up on his own, and drive back. You know what it's like with these top brass, Chief Inspector. Like to be on their own to make decisions without having to consult lesser mortals like us, eh?'

'Too true, Mr Ogilvie.'

'And not even our perfectly good company car,' said Ogilvie peevishly. 'Not good enough for him. Too impatient, from the start.'

'Impatient?'

'From the moment he arrived in this country. Always expect the world to run like clockwork on *their* behalf. I had personally made arrangements for one of our cars to be waiting for him *with* a driver at the airport. But the plane was a couple of hours late, and somehow the driver missed him, and off goes our Mr Hunter, couldn't be bothered to phone us, simply had to hire the most expensive car he could find and drive himself here — taking his time about it and losing his way, of course,' Ogilvie added with a smirk.

Taking his time about it ...

Rutherford said, slowly and very quietly: 'But charged the car to the firm, of course.'

'Of course. And a fine rental it turned out to be, with the extras.'

'Extras?'

'Mr Hunter decided he liked driving that particular model. He kept it on, and used it on the Achnachrain trip, and on the way back — and, for all I know, any other excursions he might have fancied.'

'But it's been returned to Johnson's now? Or is he still using it?'

The specific name of Johnson's might have been an alarm bell, jarring Ogilvie into realizing that he had been ranting on too indiscreetly. Flustered, he gulped and said: 'What on earth has this got to do with anything, officer? I really can't stand around gossiping like this. Short-staffed, expected to deal with every last little detail while the rest of them ...' He reined himself in with difficulty.

'While I'm here,' Rutherford, making a move to turn back towards the reception desk, 'perhaps I could see Lady Torrance. Unless, of course, she's out in the wilds with the rest of them.'

'Oh, no. Lady Torrance's work with us is complete, and she's no longer with us.'

'Completed? Paid off, just like that?'

'I'm just waiting for her to let us have her assessment of any incidental expenses she may have incurred on top of our agreed fee,' said Ogilvie stiffly. 'And look, Chief Inspector, you really must forgive me. I do have to be off.'

'Thank you for your help,' said Rutherford insincerely.

On the steps down from the building, his phone rang. He barked a 'Rutherford' into it as he sauntered away along the pavement; then stopped, and his bark became a gasp. 'Say that again. A *what*?'

'Started in a Facebook.' Sergeant Blake was more used to up-to-date jargon than Rutherford really cared to be. 'On the message wall, saying that 'a historic pile is open for a rave this very afternoon.' Open invitation for every young layabout within twenty miles to come in and help trash the place. All the rage nowadays, to fill in the odd hour or two. And they're at it right now.'

'We've got a squad there? Enough backup?'

'DI Muir's coping. But we may have to handle things carefully.'

'Carefully? For Christ's sake, a lot of yobbos run loose and —'

'It appears that the website setting the thing up belongs to the daughter of one Councillor MacPherson. Of the Police Committee.'

Rutherford swore loudly enough to provoke a reproachful glare from an elderly woman passing with a very small dog on the end of a very long leash.

'And just where is this whoop-up taking place?'

'Lockhart House.' Blake sounded apprehensive about coming out with it. As well he might.

Meaning, thought Rutherford despairingly, that both lawbreakers and law-enforcers would be trampling all over any evidence that still remained about Colonel Ferguson's death.

18

At short notice both the BBC and local ITV had spared cameras to cover the preparations for tomorrow's parades and the formal opening of the reconstructed croft at Achnachrain. The BBC programme was announced as a forerunner to a series over succeeding months covering preparations for the bigger event next year, the massive Gathering of the Clans in Edinburgh during what was already being publicized as The Year of the Homecoming. As so often on such occasions, the TV companies had chosen to go head to head, transmitting across the same slot, though in mid-afternoon there could hardly be much to gain from such contrived rivalry. Lesley, settling down after a late lunch with a mug of coffee, flicked the remote control idly to and fro, finding few basic differences other than interruptions for advertisements on the commercial channel.

Nick had left late the previous day. She had joked about looking forward to the break, so that she could tidy up her desk and files after wrapping up every last query on the proofs of her book, and fill the paper collection bin with scraps of notes and discarded pages; but somehow it wasn't working out like that. She felt too fidgety, unable to concentrate on the sort of tidying-up she usually enjoyed. Watching the comings and goings on the screen, she could almost hear Nick's voice beside her, doing a derisive running commentary in conflict with the platitudes being trotted out by the commentators on screen.

It was all too disjointed. Given time, the whole ceremony could have been most appropriately integrated with The Year of the Homecoming. Instead, James Fergus Ross's fear of total blindness and maybe even death had meant it all being cobbled together from fragments that could never quite fit.

A visiting group from a New Zealand Caledonian Club watched proudly as their piper went through his paces in the middle of the green square which had been levelled out to the trimness of a barracks parade ground. A small contingent of young men and women from the Gaelic College at Englishtown in Nova Scotia who had travelled across from Edinburgh, where they had been taking part in preliminary discussions of next year's major events, were being photographed by Randal Grant in front of a small, low building which at first sight Lesley thought was the restored croft. Then, as the visitors were shuffled to and fro and the dimensions of the building became clearer, it looked more like a cheap mock-up of a doll's house rural cottage rather than the real thing. It had surely not been there during her own visit. Just another last-minute gimmick?

Beth came in and out of shot, interviewing groups and individual visitors. Dashing from one part of the arena to another, she was somehow not her usual smooth self. Lesley wondered if she was reading too many of her own uncertainties into Beth's wan appearance on screen. Was disillusion creeping into Beth's veins as sourly as into her own?

On the BBC channel there was an interpolation of footage from a documentary made some years earlier about the Hudson's Bay Company, featuring the fortunes — and misfortunes — of a Macdonald family driven from Kildonan to seek work with the Company. Landing more than a hundred miles from their supposed destination, only a handful survived a dreadful winter, making their way at last to the Red River in Manitoba, where their leader married the daughter of a Chinook chieftain. As the scene switched from the film back to live transmission, there was sudden focus on a group of men so incongruous in this setting that for an absurd moment the viewer might have thought a snatch of a John Wayne film had been mistakenly substituted for an intended sequence. Eight bronzed men in full Red Indian warpaint, very dignified and statuesque, were standing in line as rigidly as guardsmen waiting for a command. Morwenna Ross, who had been staring at the cairn of stones as if conjuring them to weep, turned away to gaze even more intently at these implacable warriors, her face suffused with a silent denunciation.

Jacques Hunter came into the frame, smiling aloofly as he strode towards the group of Indians, as still as burnished wooden statues. He raised his arms in what might have been a symbolic embrace, and they all lowered their heads. Draped across his left arm was a muslin shirt with an ochre fringe. The camera zoomed in for a moment, catching a brief glimpse of what looked like painted birds or ghostly figures before Hunter filled the screen, mouthing a protest and waving the cameraman away.

'Not yet.' His voice was resonant and decisive. 'This is not yet the time.'

Lesley wanted to freeze the frame, hold the scene, explore its meaning; but there was a brief wobble of the picture and a hurried switch to something even less in keeping. A voice-over announced, with a touch of incredulity, the arrival of 'The South Dakota Lassies'. Two girl pipers marched out on to the main level, danced around by six sandy-haired girls

The Merciless Dead

with long legs and the shortest of mini skirts, twirling pom-poms at the end of plastic lances.

In the background there was an outraged cry from Morwenna. Lesley waited for a similar outburst from Jacques Hunter, but there was a sudden blackout. When she flicked the remote control, she found it was matched on the competing channel. Then on each an announcer read out a hurried news flash. A suspected terrorist attack on Prestwick airport was under way, with a rumoured involvement of US planes on rendition flights. The BBC was hurriedly apologetic: 'It is hoped to incorporate a further visit to Achnachrain during Woman's Hour. In the meantime, we shall be giving live coverage of events at Prestwick as they unfold.' ITV made no promises. In both cases it was obvious that camera teams were being rushed away to the airport.

Lesley sat back. Questions lingered, unanswered. Hadn't the Torrances been promised an invitation to the opening? Official opening was tomorrow, but they had received no invitation.

She watched the panic-stricken to-ings and fro-ings around the airport for a while, until it was reported that two mischief-makers had been arrested and there was apparently no serious threat.

After that she felt no taste for further news bulletins or for predictions about next weekend's football.

In the evening Nick rang briefly to report on matters just as muddled as those at Achnachrain or Prestwick, pronounced himself ready for a good night's sleep, and wished her pleasant dreams.

Lesley found it impossible to sleep. At best she sank into fitful drowses, with dreams irritating rather than pleasant. One minute she was involved in a meeting with some faceless dealer anxious to sell her some cracked porcelain which dissolved into a pyramid of broken crockery shards and began to ooze blood; then she came face to face with Jacques Hunter offering to contribute an Indian shirt to the Ross collection. She jolted awake, found that only ten minutes had elapsed, and tossed to and fro, half fighting off another silly vision, half trying to keep a hold on it and squeeze some sense out of it.

In the small hours she got up, made herself a cup of hot chocolate, and sat in front of her computer. It was a crazy thing to do. Her eyelids seemed gummed together, and she was tackling the keyboard as clumsily as that of an old-fashioned typewriter. What on earth did she imagine she was searching for? Normally she used her machine only for straightforward correlation of details or linkage with compatible reference sources. Now, in the middle of the night, she found herself seeking some response from Luke's missing laptop. Somewhere out there were the answers to so many exasperating puzzles. But it would take a more experienced operator than herself to make a connection in that way-out no-man's-land.

She wondered about ringing Nick first thing in the morning.

But if she did ring him, it would be to tell him that she had to drive to Achnachrain to see for herself. See what? She wouldn't be able to tell him that because she didn't know just what was dragging at her mind, and he was sure to get angry and tell her to stay where she was and have nothing more to do with that crowd. It would be unreasonable of her to interrupt his own commitments right now.

And why persevere, when they hadn't even had that promised invitation to the opening ceremony?

If anything, that spurred her on. Even as a polite formality, why hadn't the invitation arrived?

She ought to go back to bed.

And do battle with another swirl of nagging questions and visions?

Including a sudden clear vision of old Mrs Aird smiling at her with a knowing, fatalistic smile ...

It was no good. She simply couldn't hang around any longer, waiting for the night to end, when there would still be no answer. She dressed, hurriedly packed a bag, and drove away from Black Knowe into the night. She was well beyond Aviemore by the time the sky in her rear-view mirror became flushed with the dawn and she had to stop for petrol.

The filling station had the bleakness of an Edward Hopper painting. The attendant was half listening to a babble of radio news and pop music, and resented the need to say 'Thank you' as he tore off the receipt from the credit card machine. Not that she would have enjoyed a perky 'Have a nice day' from him.

She wondered how many people, groups summoned from overseas and members of the public looking forward to a colourful day out, were waking up or already on their way to Achnachrain.

*

Beth was woken by the sound of two trucks rattling to a halt at the side of the hotel. She moaned, turned over, and clung for a few minutes to the warmth of Randal's body before pushing herself up and out of bed. He groped vaguely after her, but she was on her feet and trying to persuade herself that it was going to be a wonderful, sunny, well-organized day which would work out exactly according to plan.

After breakfast, she stood beside Randal as he played around with a light meter and then watched him pacing around the arena, calculating, trying to anticipate any snags and any first-rate possibilities.

'Made up your mind yet, young lady?'

The voice might so appropriately have come out of her own head that for a moment she did not realize that old Mr Ross's electric buggy had bumped up alongside her. His two shadows — very substantial shadows — stood in their usual positions behind him, but looking forlorn with empty hands.

'I'm just having a last-minute check on what we might have overlooked,' she temporized.

'You're not one to overlook anything.' He chuckled, then raised a peremptory hand, which his two minders interpreted as meaning that he wanted to be pushed along the path for a closer view of the croft.

A group of security men arrived in a 4x4 and jumped out vigorously, making a great show of inspecting the exteriors of every building and spreading out along the perimeter of the site to check on the temporary metal fencing.

Another gang was finalizing the erection of two plinths for the return of the television teams.

Randal, swinging a camera over his shoulder, came back to Beth.

'They're going to make a complete cock-up of this, you know.'

It was something she didn't want to hear. 'I've checked on every detail I could,' she said defensively. 'It's always like this. I'd be worried if it all looked too smooth. Pandemonium until curtain up — and then somehow it all falls into place, and sheer determination carries it on. We've always coped in the end.'

'Only this time you're not in charge.' He put his hand on her shoulder and fleetingly kissed her cheek. 'You've sweated your guts out, OK, but somebody else is calling the tune.'

She wanted to snap out some indignant put-down; but it came out as plaintive appeal. 'After all we've put into it, it'd be a tragedy if it all went pear-shaped at this stage.'

'Not a tragedy. A farce. Farce noir.'

Before she could summon up a denial, a tall, domineering figure came striding across the grass towards them with the confidence of a man who had only to lift a finger for the orchestra to begin. Morwenna Ross, coming out of the hotel, was staring at him. Whatever work she had put into preparing the individual contributors, Jacques Hunter had taken on the role of conductor. Now her gaze seemed to be demanding that he turn and bring her in alongside him — or else, perhaps, be stricken down for his arrogance.

Hunter was at his most condescending, 'Ah, Miss Crichton. Everything going smoothly? Television, film cameramen, the Press — your usual efficient list, ticked off item by item?'

'One or two folk haven't shown up yet. But we've still got an hour' — she glanced at her watch — 'and twenty-five minutes.'

'Like I said, on the ball as ever.'

'But,' Beth ventured, 'there's nothing on my schedule about your friends over there.' She nodded towards the file of Indians who had silently appeared on the fringe of the arena as if conjured up by some incantation beyond the hearing range of ordinary mortals.

Hunter sounded loftily dismissive, deigning to bother with only the sketchiest explanation. 'They have their part to play, as they played it in the past. These are representatives of the true Americans who greeted the first Scottish settlers, fought with them, and then assimilated them. Our fates are interwoven.'

Assimilated?

'Just as Big Chief Prancing Bullshit proposes to assimilate my father's empire?' said Randal in an undertone as Hunter stalked away.

*

Early morning traffic was sparse, but police patrols were already in position along the main approaches. AA signs, some attached to the metal posts marking passing places on the narrower roads, directed visitors to THE CROFT REVIVAL. Lesley was thankful to arrive, at last, at the uneven line of steel fencing weaving its uneven line between the Auchenchrain site and an improvised car park on a stretch of lumpy moss. She would not have been surprised to find that the urge for pseudo-authenticity had driven the team to rush up a drystone wall in record time. Out of the car, she stretched to ease the stiffness in her joints, and made her way across the spongy ground to a gap in the fence. If the proceedings should be ruined by a heavy downpour, it was going to be difficult to get vehicles out of the inevitable quagmire.

Nobody was on duty yet at the entrance, taking tickets or offering directions. She walked through the gap with a confidence that made the cluster of men a hundred yards away assume that she was an authorized participant.

She stopped by the odd new building she had noticed during the television coverage. It proved to be no more than the shell of a croft, hastily assembled and topped with a turf roof, unlike the painstakingly reconstructed old homestead of the Rosses.

'A bit of dramatic spectacle the public are bound to expect.' Jacques Hunter had appeared silently beside her. 'Like a firework display, you know, to round off the proceedings.'

'No, I didn't know. I don't remember it being in the programme.'

'A dramatization of a screaming old woman being thrown out of her home, while it's set on fire and burnt to the ground. A dramatic set-piece to end the day for the benefit of sensation seekers.' Hunter had opened the door of the mock-up and seemed ready to wave her in. 'I must say, I'm surprised to see you here, Lady Torrance. I didn't think you had any more to contribute.'

'I understood my husband and I were to receive an official invitation to the opening. As it has failed to arrive, I decided to drive up anyway.'

'Sir Nicholas is with you?'

'He's at a meeting in Stirling.'

'Perhaps you would have been wise to go with him.'

She was seized by a crazy desire to wipe that arrogance off his face and out of that chilling voice. 'There are still some questions to be answered here. About the 'wrong Rosses', for starters. Haven't you worried about what Luke Drummond may have come across?'

'Such vague speculations are not what you were hired to investigate.'

'I was hired,' said Lesley, 'to track down and authenticate historic artefacts related to this reconstruction. I'm still interested. More and more interested, in fact, in some even deeper basic truths.'

Hunter's arm had seemed to be gently waving an invitation for her to look inside the mock-up croft. Now the gentleness ebbed out of it and was lost under an almost sadistic pulse.

'Recorded screams, of course, through an amplifier. Background noise of crackling flames. And over there' — his right hand was an iron clamp on her shoulder — 'a smoke generator, and a controlled flame-thrower.'

Lesley knew this had gone beyond a joke, beyond even a dramatic charade. Her old training had to come to her aid now. She braced herself, ready; but tried to stay very calm, still not quite believing that things could have gone this crazy.

'I don't know what sort of nonsense you're adding to the programme. So far as I was aware —'

'You have all of you been aware of so little.' She twisted down and under, slid from his grasp, but then he had both hands on her and she was lifted off her feet and hustled right inside the dark little room.

'Oh, no. You really mustn't leave, now that you've taken it into your head to come so far. Let's see if we can't calm you down until the real drama begins.' His laugh was almost friendly, sharing a joke with her. 'You wouldn't want to miss the grand climax, would you?'

19

Morwenna Ross, alone on the platform with a microphone in front of her and television cameras angled on her for the opening address, might have looked lost and vulnerable. Instead, she radiated enthusiasm. After all they had come through in such a short, harrowing time, the moment had come for jubilation — this moment she had been waiting for, planning for.

She held a dramatic silence for a long, brooding minute. Then she stared at some vision in the air before her, and opened her arms in greeting. Her eyes shone, her voice throbbed.

'So many of the workers on this land were shipped off without their consent, driven out of their wilfully destroyed homes. Now they are coming back. *You* are their embodiment. We are here on lands sacred to all of you. Welcome. To our cousins from Newfoundland, Cape Breton, Ottawa, the United States, Australia, New Zealand ... welcome.'

There was a spattering of applause. A man sporting the MacLeod tartan stepped up beside her, well primed in his part. He clutched the microphone as if to lift it from its stand and start singing — a traditional Hebridean lament, or, more befitting his stocky appearance and confident swagger, country and Western, hip-hop or reggae?

'I know I speak for all of us when I say that ...' He paused, took a deep breath, and bellowed: 'We always promised ourselves that one day' — another dramatic pause — 'we'd see Scotland. We'd be back in our homeland. And here we are. By God, here we all are.' The amplifiers added a whistle of protest to his booming delivery, but were drowned out by a genuine roar of approval. 'And in return let me offer all you good folk an invitation to visit *us*. In March every year we have Tartan Week in the United States, with the greatest parades you ever did see through New York City. We aim to be here with you again next year for the Gathering of the Clans around the great Rabbie Burns's birthday. And then all you good folk will be coming to continue the celebrations with us.'

They came up one after the other to say their piece. Most of them, needing someone to focus their harangue on, were happy to direct their tribute at their host: James Fergus Ross, seated in the forefront of the crowd, his head tilting back appreciatively, drinking in every word of the tributes and promises. It all sounded so warm and comradely, as it was meant to be. Yet Beth was dismayed to find, after all her commitment to the project, that she was feeling it was all ... well, what? What had gone wrong? It was too contrived. Whatever wonderful nostalgic glow old Mr Ross might be getting, there was a cheap banality about it all.

And already, echoing her own unease, a sour note was coming into the proceedings themselves.

A descendant of the McKenzies was the first speaker not to trot out platitudes about the poetic sadness of their ancestors' cruel dispersal. Instead, he spoke confidently of migrants who had settled in eastern Canada but, bravely battling famine, had ultimately moved yet again and set up prosperous sheep stations in New Zealand. To Beth the irony of it was inescapable. Driven from their homeland by sheep, they had prospered far away by driving off the natives of those other lands to make room for their own ranches.

The speaker for an Australian contingent said boldly: 'You gotta face it, it was maybe a good thing in the end. If you were prepared to work, you got on just fine. Things were a whole lot better than they ever were round here.'

Morwenna was beginning to lose that flush of dedication. The dispossessed claiming that their lot had been improved? This was a blasphemy against the convictions that had brought her so far.

She called on the Cape Breton fiddlers to start their half-hour recital.

Two men strolling aimlessly through the gathering crowd swapped names and backgrounds, began a friendly argument about a past which was still vivid to them because of family tales handed down, and snatches they had gleaned from the movies. Then the conversation grew noisy — boisterously amiable at first, more quarrelsome in a short time.

'Look, we sweated blood to get ourselves settled. Established our own good native tradition in our new land. So why —'

'And what about *their* tradition?'

'Bloody barbarians. I'm telling you, man, our folk didn't go all that way to be scalped by gangs of Stone Age tribesmen.'

Jacques Hunter had been standing to one side for a while, smiling remotely. The smile faded. As the music began, he turned and walked away. It was clear that to him these were just preliminaries. To Beth, it was equally clear that, in spite of her fervent opening flourish, Morwenna was no longer as commanding a presence as she had been on her first appearance in the Ross building; and on the rostrum she was becoming aware of it herself, too blatantly snubbed by her supposed colleague.

The day was growing warmer. A haze began forming above the lochans, with a heavier cloud dancing deep within it — a cloud of midges, swirling like tiny starlings preparing to leave, but in reality seething with the desire to feed on human blood.

At her elbow, Randal said quietly: 'Why the hell did I come back? Too much of this bloody country is still poisoned by its past. Covenanters, Jacobites, Free Kirk men, and Wee Free Kirk men — hordes of conflicting parasites and antibodies forever giving battle in the blood. And my father deciding, a bit late in life, that he's got what it takes to provide an antidote.' He looked across the arena at Hunter's unexplained cohort of Indian braves, assembling close to the fake croft. 'And I've got a feeling it's going to get worse.'

*

Rutherford reshuffled the notes that had been laid on his desk. They made a compelling pattern, if not a pretty one.

'So he held on to that car for a while, then returned it,' he muttered to himself. 'But not until ... just a minute, now ... some time after young Drummond's death. Just a coincidence? On top of Ferguson's murder?'

He reached for the phone. One person he could rely on. Always reliable, DI Gunn — oh, damn it, Lady Torrance — could possibly have been around when Jacques Hunter arrived at the Ross building from the airport. Would she remember the time of that arrival, and could she confirm it was on the very day of the Ferguson killing?

Sir Nicholas Torrance said: 'Sorry, my wife's not here at the moment.'

'Damn. Sorry, I should have remembered. She'll be with the rest of them at the Ross shindig.'

'As it happens, we weren't invited.'

'What, after all the work her ladyship put in for them?'

'Quite so. But I'm wondering ...'

'Yes?'

'Oh, nothing. I've been away in Stirling for a few days, and she wasn't here when I got back.' He sounded angry. And worried. But then he hastened to add: 'Probably gone into town for some shopping.'

It came as an irrelevant echo into Rutherford's mind. Going shopping. Like Mrs Nadine Ferguson?

He said: 'Sorry to have bothered you. I just wanted to check on a date and time she might have been able to help us with.'

'Still picking her brains long after she's been off the payroll?'

AWPC had slipped into the room to drop a sheet of names for his attention. One part of him said briskly, 'I won't bother you again, Sir Nicholas,' while another brought the list into focus. It contained the names of the young men and women rounded up from the trashing of Lockhart House. A couple of them had already appeared too frequently in the gossip columns, and the spoilt bastards would probably be amused rather than dismayed to find their names there again and on MySpace and You Tube bulletin boards. Let it wait. He knew in his bones that there was something more urgent to be attended to. But where did he begin?

He tried the Ross Foundation number.

It seemed that the only executive of any status on the premises was Simon Ogilvie. 'Somebody's got to look after the shop.' Another echo: the same feeble joke as the last time. Rutherford could almost see Ogilvie's petulant expression. In answer to Rutherford's carefully phrased questions about the day of Jacques Hunter's arrival in town, he was more offputting than ever. 'I do not consider myself obliged to make guesses about other people's movements.' But as Rutherford weightily emphasized the duty of upright citizens to assist police in their inquiries, he grudgingly said Mr Hunter must have reached Queen Street quite late on the morning in question. He did at least remember something which displeased him. 'I was not notified immediately of his arrival. If any of that is a matter of some consequence, Chief Inspector, it's something you will have to take up with him when he returns.'

Rutherford had only just rung off when there was a call from Nick Torrance.

'Look, I'm a bit worried. Stupid, maybe. But I've tried to contact my wife on her mobile. It rang a couple of times, and then it was cut off. I've tried again, but no joy.'

'It's not like her? Going off without leaving a message?'

'Not like her at all. Not that we go in for niggly timetables, that sort of thing, but ... Look, it may be crazy, but I don't like the feel of it. I think maybe she got some bee in her bonnet, and she's flitted off to that damn place off her own bat. Chasing some notion of her own.'

'Knowing her,' said Rutherford, 'I'd say she could have had one of her hunches and —'

The Merciless Dead

'Exactly.' Torrance now sounded more worried than angry. 'What the hell might be going on up there?'

'I can't go dashing off on hunches, hers or yours. Or my own. Can't just grab a squad car to go belting off onto somebody else's patch. But I have a nasty feeling that your good lady's hunch could be in line with my own. I'm beginning to see a link between two deaths ... two murders. I can get in touch with our colleagues in Wester Ross, but —'

'I want to get there myself before it's too late. Seems to me it's time I invoked the old pals' act and commandeered some transport. Loyalty of the Lowlanders — Jeddart's here, that sort of thing. If Lesley's been sticking her nose into trouble —'

'I'm with you,' said Rutherford. 'If you've got room.'

'Because she used to be 'One of us'?' said Nick Torrance, trying and failing to keep it light.

'Always will be, as far as I'm concerned.'

*

Lesley's eyes opened gradually. Their lashes seemed to be gummed down, and for a while she thought she must still be at home in bed. She wanted to grope for a handkerchief, but her arms were too sluggish to move. Her whole body wanted to relax back into its comfortable stupor.

Then, dimly, she began to remember where she was, and who had trapped her here. Imprisoned ...? But when she managed to lift a hand, she found that she had not even been tied down. She tried to mutter a question, but it came out as a croak.

The face swimming into her vision was surely the remnant of a dream. Dark, floating in mid-air, surmounted by a huge halo of rainbow colours, it came in and out of focus, blurred and reshaping itself like the left-over of a nightmare monster; and then began slowly to solidify.

'Splendid, Lady Torrance. You've woken in plenty of time for the main display.'

The dark gleaming varnish of a totem pole head with its huge feathered headdress surely ought not to be capable of speech. Lesley ordered her own tongue to obey her. And as her eyes opened wider and took in the whole extent of Jacques Hunter's regalia she heard herself saying: 'The shirt. You're wearing the ghost dance shirt.'

'As it was destined I should.'

She forced herself up into an uncomfortable huddle, propped against a wall.

'You drugged me. How? What sort of crude —'

'Nothing crude, I assure you. No date rape drugs, Lady Torrance. You're aware that you've not been raped, of course.'

'Am I supposed to offer you my most profound thanks?' She was dismayed by the way the words were still coming out slurred.

'You have just had a refreshing doze with the help of one of our most cherished medicine man's prescriptions. You should feel honoured.'

'You're mad,' mumbled Lesley. 'What d'you hope to achieve by this pantomime? You and Morwenna Ross —'

'I grant you that poor Morwenna has been suffering under some pathetic delusions. A few with understandable motives, but so paltry.' He was grinning at her, inviting her to share some twisted joke. 'For instance, your forebears, the Gunn family, behaved somewhat shabbily towards her own pathetic family. She would consider herself having every excuse for eliminating you from this world. But she found it even more rewarding to cling to the Ross fantasies. So much more dramatic.'

Lesley was growing stronger. She couldn't just crouch here and let his words roll imperiously over her. 'You're taking a very high-handed attitude to one of your colleagues.'

'Colleague?' He shrugged. 'For as long as it suited me. Poor woman. She married into the Ross family in order to *become* somebody. Unfortunately the husband proved a disappointment. No sense of history, or romance. It suited her for him to die; and she was eager to believe that she had the gift, the sight, call it what you may, to have willed his death. She has all along wanted to become part of the Ross legend. Only now the silly creature is suspecting that the sentimental cause of the Rosses — all those beliefs she acquired so hungrily from old man Ross — were wrong. 'The wrong Rosses,' indeed. Which I have known all along.'

'So what was *your* motive in working for them?'

'My motive throughout has been to avenge the wrongs done to my ancestors. That woman yearned to belong to the Rosses. I joined their company knowing it was my destiny to rise high in their ranks and then destroy them. What that stupid old man has never grasped is that his forebears were villains, not victims. He was pampered by Morwenna's hysterical devotion. It's been important to me to keep an eye on her, to know just how far she was committed, and to what.'

'To make sure she didn't snarl up your own plans.'

The Merciless Dead

'I knew you would understand. A pity that perhaps you have come close to understanding too much.'

She was still dizzy enough, incautious enough, to let fly. 'Such as the fact that you murdered Sholto Ferguson. In order to get your hands on that ghost dance shirt you're wearing.'

'As I've said, a pity you're so accomplished a guesser.'

'Was it necessary to murder the man? You couldn't simply have made a business proposition and —'

'Do business with scum like that? From the moment I saw it in that blurred picture sent over by Edinburgh office, I knew it was my duty to reclaim the shirt. I drove to his house straight from the airport. Asked him to hand over my inheritance. *Demanded* it. But he was a lout. Yes, he did have the impertinence to ask me to name a price. Haggle over something that rightly belonged to my people in the first place? I could not stand there and hear every aspect of our beliefs sneered at by a blasphemer like that.'

'So you killed him. As simply as that.'

'With the raven head of a totem pole,' said Hunter with relish.

'Surprised you didn't scalp him,' said Lesley recklessly.

His eyes narrowed with cold amusement. She had been on the verge of asking why on earth he was telling her all this; but then realized she didn't need to ask. From past experience she knew the pattern. Real villains always longed to tell their whole story. Thieves, burglars, forgers, financial fiddlers, and above all murderers: not denying their crime, but proud of it in every detail, needing to boast about it to *somebody*. First indignant protestations of innocence; then, when they cracked, it would all come pouring out.

But this one was extreme. He hadn't waited to be cracked. He was boasting shamelessly.

She was fully awake now. Awake to the realization that he had told her so much because he didn't intend her to live.

'You can't possibly think you'll get away with it,' she said.

'I shall get away with all that really matters. I've been in training for a long time.' There was utter conviction in his face. As an arrogant, aggressive businessman he could either have brought about the collapse of the firm he had worked his way into, or built up a reputation of infallibility. Sheer self-assurance had carried him through.

Lesley pushed herself away from the wall and tottered to her feet.

'And Luke Drummond?' she challenged. 'That was you as well?'

'Unfortunate young man. Too inquisitive. 'The wrong Rosses' — I could not risk letting that come out too soon.' Although Lesley was steady on her feet now, he was so haughtily upright that he seemed to grow even taller as she faced him. 'The time for revealing the truth was for *me* to decide.'

'Surely you realize that once this is over and I tell the authorities —'

'When it is over,' said Hunter silkily, 'you will also have reached the end. And for me, it is no matter. Once our dream has come true nothing else matters.'

Trying to look confident, she made a move towards the door. As she reached it, an Indian brave blocked her way.

'Oh, no, you can't leave yet,' said Hunter. 'Things have gone too far.'

He and the newcomer had a brief argument in a tongue Lesley could not understand; but she could guess the brave might be objecting to being ordered to do guard duty indoors rather than joining his fellows in whatever was about to go on outside. But Hunter's lordly disdain was intensifying by the moment. Nobody now would dare gainsay him.

'I have a ceremony to perform. In front of the accursed James Fergus Ross, so that he sees himself shown up as the abomination he is. The older dispossessed have been drawn back here, travelling to their ancient homes within the bodies of their descendants. My people, too, are linked across the centuries and across oceans. What we do symbolically here will echo across the distant plains which we lost but can now restore to life.' In the doorway he looked back at Lesley. 'When we've done what has to be done, I might have considered coming back for you. It could be enjoyable to share confidences with a lady of your calibre. You have obviously worked out a great deal of what has led to this day. But you know just *too* much.' He raised his right hand in a ceremonial farewell. 'It's unfortunate, but I don't think I can set you free. Oh, and if you scream' — he nodded towards the box in the middle of the room — 'it will blend in perfectly with the screams Morwenna has already recorded. And when she presses her remote control, you will come out wreathed in fire and screaming very convincingly. Cheap melodrama, yes. But you will have cause to be proud of having contributed *something*.'

He squared his shoulders and stepped out into the open air.

*

Television cameras reinstated east and west of the arena were covering performances following one another or overlapping. There was ecstatic clapping as a brawny red-haired visitor from Dunedin won a brief caber

The Merciless Dead

tossing bout. At the same time a team from Manitoba finished a lilting strathspey on the platform, leaving some appreciative feet tapping.

Beth glanced round at the different groups and individuals. She had done her bit, summoning and organizing essential guests, and now it was all out of her hands. She felt drained and more and more dissatisfied. Jacques Hunter and Morwenna Ross had assumed command — though Beth was unsure which of them would make the final decisions at any crucial moment.

James Fergus Ross sat in his buggy in a position of honour, his head like a bird's peeking from side to side. But how much detail could he make out: and what did he make of it?

Beth came back again and again to Morwenna's profile, trying to read what lay behind that glaring, almost tragic expression. Morwenna must be forcing herself to believe she could overcome Jacques Hunter's intrusive Indians, the heathen. Could fight off her doubts about the Rosses who for so long had so enchanted her. She could not give up on them, because what would be left? Like the devotee of any hero-worshipping sect, she had to twist the concept of them into the shape to which she had so unquestioningly devoted her love. Whatever falsehoods might have been thrust upon her, she was still blessed with the gift of the stigmata, assuring her that in the end her beliefs could not all be mistaken.

She was holding what looked like a compact remote control for model aeroplanes. Every few minutes she glanced nervously at her watch, and then at the mock-up croft.

Mrs Aird had been standing by the Cairn of Weeping Stones, too diffident to join the heart of the crowd. Then she trod unobtrusively forward, edging closer to Morwenna with a look not so much of contempt as dismissive pity, as if silently boasting that she had all those capabilities, the second sight, the inherited powers, which Morwenna craved to possess.

As two young men from Nova Scotia who had just done a vigorous sword dance vacated the platform, Jacques Hunter strode into the centre of the arena.

Randal Grant said, 'Well, that shirt didn't come from Marks and Sparks,' and took three or four shots as Hunter came to a halt. 'For the next annual report?' he said to Beth.

On the assumption that old James Fergus Ross, thought Beth, will have died by then?

The sight of the headdress feathers and the regal stare which Hunter was offering the audience provoked sniggers from a group of Aussies who had got their hands on some cans of beer and were singing something which bore little resemblance to anything as evocative as the Skye Boat Song.

Morwenna was staring at Hunter as if, Beth shuddered, to *think* him to death.

A deep voice boomed suddenly across the arena. Hunter stood stock still, listening with obvious admiration to his own resonant voice. The pre-recorded commentary would have had to be his responsibility: he would have trusted nobody else.

'We are here to re-create the life once known to our tribe. In the ceremony we have waited so many generations to perform we will rid this country and our lands across the sea of the alien parasites. The time of perpetual bliss is within our grasp. We shall be reunited with our friends in the other world, and there will be no more death or sickness or old age.'

'Like those other Americans waiting for The Rapture,' Randal murmured close to Beth's ear. 'Used to get the shivers from them in the States. Whole communities believing they're due to be transported bodily to heaven any day now, leaving the rest of us behind in misery.'

And ready, Beth wondered, to immolate themselves as other fanatics had done at Waco?

She caught a glimpse of Morwenna, frozen in a trance, still clutching that little device in her hand and still staring obsessively at Hunter.

'The earth will roll up like a blanket.' The voice rolled through the air above the heads of the audience. 'And with it will be taken all that is corrupt and selfish in this contaminated world. Then there will be seen the old-young earth of our ancestors, fresh and young again.'

Six of the motionless Indians came to life and began to form a circle. Jacques Hunter's voice faded, while the man himself strutted forward, an actor launched into his long-awaited star part.

'It was a law of the Cherokee that anyone who sold land without the nation's permission must be executed.' The voice came, this time, not from the amplifiers but reverberating from Hunter's own throat. 'Our lands have been stolen, then sold on and sold yet again. The time has come for restitution.'

He stationed himself in the centre of the group as the ghost dance began.

With hypnotic slowness the men fell into a steady anticlockwise shuffle. An eerie silence fell, so intense that Beth felt she had gone deaf, and yawned to clear her ears. The first sound to penetrate the hush was a rhythmic chant, emanating from Hunter yet without any visible movement of his lips. The men of the circle took up the theme one by one, growing louder and louder, then stopping abruptly while they resumed the silent shuffle with an air of rapt concentration.

They had all gone into a trance. Beth felt the audience around her being lured into just such a hypnotic dream state. The only faint sound now was a mesmeric pulse of breathing, as if the earth itself were breathing in and out. Real life, the rhythms of the contemporary world, had been suspended. The silent, drifting movement of the ghost dancers was more terrifying than any military march played full blast by a phalanx of pipers.

Jacques Hunter stooped, straightened up, stooped again, pacing dreamily around with his hands towards the earth, palms open in an entreaty for it to 'roll back like a blanket'.

Beth tried again to unblock her ears with a yawn; but felt a stab within her head like a sudden migraine, and somehow she was seeing Luke Drummond and he was trying to communicate with her, while in the background white men and Redskin braves were quarrelling along the boundaries of what she somehow knew to be an Indian reservation.

All at once the vision was wiped out and sound was restored. The dancers moved faster, and began to sing more loudly, an incantation that was more a demand than a plea. The circle began to open out. It became a wide arc with Hunter at the centre, leading it towards James Fergus Ross, the ends beginning to curl slightly inwards like arms preparing to embrace the old man — or claws to trap him. Hunter's invocation rose high above them.

'Now is the time for truth to descend on the accursed Rosses.'

Another wild shout clashed with the chanting: a screech that seemed too powerful to be coming from old Ross's shrivelled body. 'What sort of damfool game is *this*? For Christ's sake, somebody, get these clowns off my land.'

'Let the wasichus tremble,' intoned Hunter, his arms appealing now not to the earth but to the heavens.

'Wasichus?' Ross was urging his chair aggressively forward over the lumpy ground, aiming straight at Hunter within the arc.

'Stupid old bugger,' breathed Randal — but admiringly.

'Wasichus?' howled Ross again. 'We were the ones, the white men, who opened up your godforsaken —'

The rest was drowned by the roar of a helicopter circling over the site, looking for a landing space. The old man's fury was nowhere near the intensity of Jacques Hunter's, shaking his fists high in the air and proclaiming in a high monotone imprecations against this blasphemous intrusion.

The spell was broken. The audience fragmented, stumbling about, fending off bewilderment with derision. 'What the shit was all that about?' ... 'Who let that nut case take over?' ... 'Watch him, God knows what he'll ...'

As the helicopter settled on a level stretch in front of the old Rent House, there was a wild roaring and whooping from beyond the Raven Hotel. Randal grabbed Beth's arm and dragged her out of the way as two young men on horseback galloped past, followed by a posse of youngsters laughing wildly and heading their mounts straight into the middle of the crowd as if on a hunt or embarking on their own Riding of the Marches.

'Cowboys and Indians now?' breathed Randal. 'Just what the hell ...'

Beth found herself laughing hysterically. 'It's a rave. Sons and daughters of Mr Ross's old enemies, out for a carve-up. Spoilt brats, out to smash things up. Summoned through the internet to trash the old man's celebrations.' She ought to have been angry at yet another disruption of all her constructive work; but by now it had all become too ludicrous.

'They've left it a bit late.'

As the riders thrust their way recklessly in and out of the crowd, a small coach swung into the car park, discharging a group of uniformed local police who dashed on to the arena. They were met by two men running from the helicopter. DCI Rutherford pointed at Jacques Hunter, who was making no attempt to flee. He stood there in frozen outrage, oblivious to the hoots and insults of the mounted teenagers and to the police converging on him, and disdaining to acknowledge the arrival of Rutherford or the words that he began reciting.

'A caution?' said Randal. 'The man's beyond caution now.'

Nick Torrance stood isolated on a briefly open patch of moss, looking desperately from side to side.

Beth was suddenly aware of Morwenna Ross lifting that device in her hand and levelling it at the makeshift croft which had been her own pet idea. A dramatic finale to the day's programme.

'No.' Beth tried to draw Randal closer. 'What d'you think she's ...'

Mrs Aird was unobtrusively beside Morwenna, a hand on her arm. Her voice was quiet, but carried clearly. 'It's too late. Ye canna bring them back. That red man's spells'll no' bring his land back the way it was. Blow up your silly little bothy, and the spirits of the folk ye've chosen as your own will somehow become flesh? Nae, lassie. Let them rest. Ye were never one o' them. They canna be called up.'

Morwenna hardly seemed to notice when Mrs Aird took the remote control from her.

Two of the invaders rode up to the door of the cottage, looked at one another, grinned and nodded, and leapt from their horses to make a joint attack on the front door. For a few moments they were involved in a fight with someone inside who managed to drag them both out again, twisting the arm of one until the crack could be heard through the turmoil all around.

Nick Torrance sprang forward and went in.

The audience swayed to and fro, breaking up into groups, wanting answers to questions. Some people wanted to rush away, others to stay and find out what dramatic conclusion they might expect to their day. Yet as they drifted away to the edges of the arena, or out to the car park, the ground was unusually clean — a bare, bleak scene, eerily tidy, with none of the usual debris of drink cans and plastic wrappers.

As Jacques Hunter was led away by two uniformed constables, Nick Torrance's arm around his wife led her, stumbling across every tussock and rocky outcrop, to join Rutherford.

The DCI looked her up and down and said: 'If you'd still been on my team, you'd have been up on the carpet for this little bit of nonsense.'

20

Jacques Hunter had been driven away, silent, wrapped in his own unshakeable self-certainties and making no pretence of even listening to the questions Rutherford was asking. There would be plenty of other questions later, in suitably austere surroundings, but Rutherford saw a long, exasperating ordeal ahead.

How could Hunter have gone about things so brazenly? 'He must have known we'd catch up with him,' he said to his Wester Ross opposite number, who was still trying to make head or tail of what had been happening. But for Hunter there had been no uncertainties. The self-belief that had got the man to the top in the business world ruled out any doubts on any other matter. There seemed to be little difference, Rutherford concluded, between a ruthless tycoon and a religious fanatic.

Another police contingent was rounding up the men and women on horseback and herding them into a congested corner of the car park. Confused groups of the overseas visitors were demanding answers to questions about the debacle they had just gone through. There was all the resentment of a cheated football crowd wanting their money back.

To Beth's amazement, Morwenna Ross had come out of her own trance of disappointment and began moving from one group to another, soothing, apologizing; anxious to cling to some authority and to some lingering belief in what she had worked so passionately to achieve. Backing her up, old Ross urged his buggy along in her wake, with his two guards plodding behind.

He came back at last to Beth and Randal, pleased with himself. He was the real James Fergus Ross once more, rejuvenated, coping, reclaiming authority, talking people into agreeing with him, acknowledging the fact that, whatever might go wrong, he was still there, still able to set everything right with a peremptory snap of his fingers.

What, thought Beth, would he make of being told that he was one of 'the wrong Rosses' — all his daydreams poisoned? She glanced at Randal and knew that he was thinking the same thing.

Who was going to tell the old man now?

'Should never have hired that bloody savage,' were his first words. Then he looked from Randal to Beth and back again. 'Come on, you two, let's go where our whole story started.'

The wheels of his chair bumped towards the rebuilt croft. From the reconstructed façade they looked back over the panorama of confusion.

'And now,' said Randal, 'someone has got to tidy up that mess.'

'I was thinking you'd be a great help.'

'You know, sir,' said Beth, 'Morwenna is still on board. She's been committed to you and the whole project from the start. You only have to put your faith in her, and she'll go on believing in the Ross legend.'

'Why shouldn't she? Legend? It's all true, dammit.'

'Depends which way you look at it,' said Randal. 'Or which bits you're looking at.'

'Son.' Old Ross put his bony hands on his knees and stared up pleadingly. 'You know you've got to come back in with me. The group needs you.'

'But do I need the group?'

'Look, David —'

'Randal.'

'Oh, all right, damn you. Randal. You didn't like the way things were going. Okay, make them go differently. Make them go *your* way.'

Randal laughed. 'With you just sitting there and never blowing your top?'

'Oh, I'll raise my voice when I have to. I need someone to argue with. And so will you. Neither of us is the type to want yes-men who are really no-men forever plotting behind our backs.' Then he let out something halfway between a laugh and sigh. 'Oh, come on, let's face it, I won't be arguing with you or anyone else for long. You can see just what state I'm in. The day's not far off when … aw, hell, the day's right here now when I've got to give up. I can appoint a manager to handle routine business, but I want the Foundation to be bigger and better than that. To be in the right hands.' His head turned coaxingly, again as perky as a little bird's, towards Beth. 'Come on, I can see you understand. You've been one of us for ages. You *belong*. You can tell him, can't you? He owes it to us. There was a Ross family here in this croft. The family was driven off to the corners of the world, but we're back again.' He waved his hand like a feeble, fluttering wing at his son. 'You're back again. You can't just walk away again.'

There was a long silence. They watched groups break up and reassemble; saw Morwenna motionless in a cleared space, staring at the mock croft, such a travesty of the solid one at their backs.

Nick Torrance was still holding Lesley's arm, easing her towards a hummock on which she collapsed while he bent over her, talking — reassuring or accusing?

'Well?' asked old Jamie. There was a tinge of defeat in the question. 'I'm asking if you want to be in on it. On your own terms ... Randal.'

'Yes,' said Beth. 'He does.'

Randal protested. 'Hey, now look here —'

'You two,' cried old Jamie gleefully, 'are going to have arguments all the way. And it'll all be worth it. Dammit, you only go on a white-knuckle ride because you want to have the shit scared out of you. And find it's been fun.'

'You,' said Beth, 'are a deplorable, conniving old man.'

'From you, gal, I know a compliment when I hear one.' The old man turned back to Randal. 'With a wife like that, son, you won't go far wrong. Now, make up your goddam mind.'

'He's already made it up,' said Beth.

*

'Right,' said Nick Torrance fiercely. 'Time we went home. Where from now on you'll stay put. Understood?'

Lesley struggled to find something to say.

Her whole being was still wrenched by guilt and terror, and a dreadful anger against herself.

They stood outside the door of the croft which had not, after all, provided the spectacular display to end the proceedings. A few yards away the Indians were huddled by one of the camera rostrums, powerless without their leader.

Nick Torrance was as white with anger as his wife, yet was on his knees beside her, still holding her tightly to him. 'In future' — his voice was shaking uncontrollably — 'you'll stay at home and find something sensible to occupy your time. No more going off on wild goose chases without backup. Your old mate Rutherford could have told you that, right?'

'Right,' she whispered.

'Now let's get out of this pathetic pageant.' He waved in the direction of the helicopter. 'Our chauffeur awaits. And it's going to need a lot of drinks parties to pay him off.'

Lesley was aware of a small, quiet figure beside them. She eased herself out of Nick's arms and smiled awkwardly at Mrs Aird.

The old woman said: 'It was too late.'

'I'm sorry, Mrs Aird. Too late for what?'

'To bring them back. No way any o' them can be summoned back. Nor are these the lands they'd care to return to.' She looked up into Lesley's face, her old eyes startlingly clear and bright. 'And for you, be on your way and carry your son into the future.'

'I haven't got a son.'

'But you have. Ye're carrying him the noo. Be on your way wi' him.'

'Just a minute,' Nick protested. 'I mean, you want us to believe … I mean' — he stared at Lesley — 'are you going to believe this sort of —'

'Yes,' said Lesley joyfully. 'I do believe.'

'Of course.' Mrs Aird's voice was as clear and radiant as her eyes. 'Because you're one of us. Ye have the gift. And 'tis fitting ye should tak' this wi' ye.' From under her shawl she produced a small wooden picture frame. 'This was left wi' us by one o' the true Rosses who'd been helped by my family until banished far away. I've cherished it, but the time has come to hand it on. You're one of us,' she repeated.

Lesley took the frame and peered down on an embroidered sampler, its details blurred by tendrils of damp within the glass. She was able to make out simple but graceful patterns, dominated by a raven in the top right-hand corner. All at once she found herself guessing wildly that this was what they had all been vainly looking for.

This scrap of humble local craft — the rumoured Ross Tapestry?

She laughed at the absurdity of it, then was worried that Mrs Aird might be offended by the laugh. But the lines and blemishes of the old woman's pitted, worn features had become smooth with a sweet tranquillity quite out of keeping with the turmoil which was gradually being sorted out around them.

The red hue of the embroidered words across the bottom of the design had faded, but the text was still legible.

Cha till mi tuille

Through the clamour of voices still seething around her, Lesley heard a thousand echoes across the centuries of the words she found herself whispering:

'We shall return no more.'

If you enjoyed *The Merciless Dead* please share your thoughts on Amazon by leaving a review.

For more free and discounted eBooks every week, sign up to the *Endeavour Press* newsletter.

Follow us on Twitter and Instagram.